BLOOD OF THE SCARECROW

BY MARTIN WILSEY

Read This Book!!

BLOOD OF THE SCARECROW

Cover Art by Jessica E.

Edited by: Helen Burroughs of HKelleyB's Editorial Services -

HKelleyB@aol.com

ISBN-13: 978-1511482615
ISBN-10: 1511482613

For more information:

Blog: http://wilseymc.blogspot.com/
Web: http://www.baytirus.com/

Email: info@baytirus.com

THE SOLSTICE 31 SAGA:

STILL FALLING (2015)

THE BROKEN CAGE (2015)

BLOOD OF THE SCARECROW (2016)

FOR KEVIN PECK

Kevin was a friend when friends were a real thing. He died before he could read this. He will live on as the owner of Peck's Halfway.

BLOOD OF THE SCARECROW

CHAPTER ONE: THE *VENTURA* IS FALLING

"It all happened so fast. One moment it was just another day doing our mundane work. The next moment we were fighting for our lives."

--Solstice 31 Incident Investigation Testimony Transcript: Captain James Worthington, senior surviving member of the Ventura's command crew.

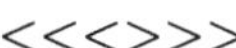

Chief Engineer Wes Hagan lived.

Everyone else in the engineering section on the *Memphis* died.

When the *Memphis* was hit, so many things could have killed him. The debris that tore through the main engines cut Granger in half. The huge hull breach sucked Holcomb and McHale out into space. The rest died of vacuum, strapped into their seats.

The visor on Hagan's pressure suit auto-closed when the hull breached. The now mostly civilian crew had become lax in the boredom of the long survey mission.

"How did Captain Everett know?" Wes said, out loud and to himself, as he unbuckled his five-point harness and hammered his fist on the emergency lifeboat access control only an arm's reach away.

As soon as he was through the hatch, it slammed shut behind him, and he felt the explosive bolts blast the lifeboat away from the *Memphis.* The lights came on full bright.

The prerecorded voice spoke directly to his HUD, in his mind.

"This is an emergency. Please strap yourself in."

Wes wore his light pressure suit and helmet. It was all that had saved him from the vacuum. It was slightly bulky as he began to float toward the pilot's seat. The sudden impact to the hull drove him toward the front, ramming his ribs into the headrest of the pilot's seat. He heard, more than felt, his ribs break.

Alarms sounded. Proximity alarms he recognized.

Fuck.

"Activate emergency AI. Navigation display. Do not crash this boat, you stupid computer!" Wes screamed, on the edge of panic, as he strapped in.

The pilot's display dome activated, showing the exterior view. The lifeboat was in a backward tumble. A display window showed the status of the AI, initiating slowly.

"Goddammit." He hit the manual override and grabbed the grav-foil controls and started to slow the roll, as he watched the moon's surface loom closer on every rotation.

The roll was under control when the AI initialization completed. Hagan hit the decelerators, hard, and the lifeboat leveled off. This close to the surface, his forward velocity was incredibly fast.

He saw hull chunks of various sizes impacting the moon all around him.

"Emergency Module, this is Chief Engineer Wes Hagan. We are in deep shit. Plot a direct vector to a safe landing site. If we are hit by a big piece of the *Ventura,* we are dead."

As if to punctuate the statement, a giant recognizable piece of the outer ring impacted the moon's surface directly in front of them, forcing them to fly directly through the resulting cloud of dust and stones.

"Chief Hagan, allow me." The female AI took control of the lifeboat, without waiting for an answer.

Hagan let go of the controls and hugged his ribs. He realized that it was difficult to breathe. He scanned the display windows as the moon's surface rolled by, all too close, in a blur of speed.

His eyes finally landed on the AI status display. *ECHO systems active. Emergency mode. Survival situation.*

"Echo, status? What the hell?" Wes demanded.

"The *Ventura* has been destroyed by multiple nuclear missiles. The planet has an automated defense grid that was activated when the ship entered orbit. The *Memphis* was also destroyed by multiple severe impacts of large pieces of the *Ventura.* This lifeboat was the only one activated."

"I have just detected a core detonation."

Wes strained to turn around to look at this lifeboat. It had been heavily modified. Besides the pilot and copilot seats, it had only twelve seats. Only three rows of four seats with an aisle down the middle, like a commercial shuttle but less comfortable. Then, there was a wall with a center door.

"Is the compartment pressurized?" The computer didn't reply, but an additional display showed cabin pressure at almost zero.

A huge impact on the hull drove Hagan against his harness. There was pain and then darkness.

***

Barcus was unconscious, secured inside his maintenance suit, docked on the bridge of the Shuttle Transport Unit 1138. His face smashed into the inside of his helmet. The STU was falling to the planet, like debris.

Another larger personnel shuttle that was missing thirty percent of the upper aft section, also fell toward the planet, like debris. Master Chief Nancy Randal was trapped inside, in the dark, with all systems off-line, desperately trying to get some kind of control.

Commander James Worthington, with the help of what remained of his crew, managed to set the *Memphis* down on the surface of the moon before crashing. It was only because they all looked like falling debris that they lived.

A young, nearly starving woman was tending a kitchen hearth at an inn when she saw the flashes, like silent lightning, momentarily fill the room she was in.

A man, alone in the darkness of his lonely cell in the darkest reaches of the Citadel, said out loud, "The end begins."

***

Hagan was awakened, again, by pain.

He tried to clear his head, rapidly, to no avail. He was strapped into the pilot's seat of lifeboat number 4, moving at a high rate of speed along the moon's surface.

He activated the ship's log and began recording, "My name is Wes Hagan, and I don't know if this log will ever be recovered. I will transmit anyway...when I tell you. In case..."

He had a coughing fit, spitting blood into his helmet. The recording continued, "I'm injured. There is no autoDoc on this lifeboat. I did find the first aid kit. It is more complete than I expected. I have injected nanites. I now have medical monitors on. Data is being conveyed to my personal Heads-Up Display."

More coughing forced him to stop.

"I think my ribs are broken, and I may have damaged a lung. My left wrist is probably fractured as well. I'm not bleeding anywhere, externally, as far as I can tell. My pressure suit has not lost integrity. I'm not going to remove my suit to find out, just yet. I don't know if I have a hull breach. I'm getting pounded by debris.

"I managed to get to this specific lifeboat as ordered by Captain Alice Everett. She must have known this might happen."

A few loud impacts on the hull interrupted him.

"The *Ventura* has been destroyed. Utterly. The initial salvo had missiles, nukes. No warning. They just entered orbit. I saw it all on my console. The *Ventura* was almost ten kilometers long, and it was gone in seconds. Two thousand people…"

He could not control the coughing.

"There were more hits after that. The *Ventura* broke up. The entire huge ship. They're all dead. I think the largest pieces were also targeted in the second wave of missiles."

The recording stopped until he controlled the coughing.

"I am bleeding, internally. I just coughed up blood."

He had to pause, again.

"I'm back. I added more nanites. This is going to really suck. This many medical nanites is going to hurt. Where was I? I think Captain Everett knew something might happen to the *Ventura.* Wait. Let me go back. Before I transmit. For whoever gets this, if anyone.

"I was on the galactic survey ship, the *Ventura.* It was a deep space meta-class ship. The largest in Earth's survey fleet. There were 2,072 crewmates. We just dropped out of FTL to have a look at a planet that our probes found to be habitable.

"At the time, for reasons I didn't understand, Captain Everett gave me this assignment on the *Memphis*. The *Memphis* was the captain's pinnace. The largest shuttle on the *Ventura*. Capable of FTL, and staffed with a crew of thirty-two, including me. Even though I was the *Ventura's* senior multi-discipline engineer, she had me manning the sensor console in the secondary comms center on the *Memphis*.

"Now, I think it was because it was directly next to the starboard hatch for this specific lifeboat. Because this thing isn't really just an escape pod...or a lifeboat."

He had to stop and calm himself, again.

"As a standard practice, when the *Ventura* dropped out of FTL, the *Memphis* launched and ran escort. We were headed for high orbit near the planet's single moon.

"I don't even know the name of this fucking planet.

"I saw it happen. Missiles were detected during the first wave. The *Ventura* never had a chance."

As the recording continued, Hagan groaned in pain, made worse by his evident sobbing. All was captured on the recording.

"Debris struck the *Memphis*, bad. And we lost power. I was strapped in, thank God. Commander Worthington was strict about procedures. Pressure suit on, and stay strapped in while at the station. Bless him. Still, I broke my left wrist from the crash on initial impact.

"I got into the lifeboat.. My orders were very specific; the captain drilled them into me. She said, 'If ANYTHING unusual happens to the *Ventura*, get into the lifeboat and wait.' I don't know why it automatically launched after I entered. I wish it had given me a few seconds to strap in properly. The *Memphis* was tumbling.

"By the time I got to the pilot's seat, I was already headed to the moon's surface, on AI control, at a very high velocity. We barely controlled the descent. The computer's Artificial Intelligence system picked the descent vectors, the thruster burn, and a landing site. If I had been flying, I'd be dead."

The recording paused, again.

"I'm back. We have a good seal, and we are maintaining pressure on the lifeboat. Debris continues to impact the outer hull.

"This is really fucked up. This thing is not a standard escape pod lifeboat. It's supposed to hold sixteen people, with emergency air, food, and water for more than a month. This one only holds twelve. It's supposed to be one large compartment with bunks and storage in the rear. On this one, there is a wall, less than halfway back, with a heavy closed hatch. When I tried to open it, it said, 'access denied' even when I used my command staff codes.

"This day just fucking gets better and better. The AI won't talk to me, either. It shut almost everything down, for some reason; and it's getting cold in here. I think it is running silent, as a precaution. It won't talk to me. I've been too busy to fuck with it. I activated a comms console. I wanted to get in this log entry before debris kills me...faster."

Wes had to stop recording as a wave of small hull impacts made it too loud to continue. That debris storm lasted a long time.

"Debris has been impacting all around me for over an hour.

"I don't know what to do. We can't move any faster because this thing only has grav-foils, no conventional engines."

Alarms sounded, and Hagan began to get indications that the systems were reinitializing.

"Main systems are coming back up. I don't know what happened to cause the reset. Maybe the AI will reboot now. Directional long-range antenna has deployed. Time to get to work.

"Lieutenant Commander Wes Hagan, still alive, signing out."

***

Hagan set the directional laser to transmit the message toward Earth, knowing it would not be received for decades. He fell unconscious as the recording continued.

AI~Echo terminated the recording and transmitted. But only after attaching the medical scans Hagan had performed. It showed his left wrist was broken, in two places. Four ribs were also fractured, the lung on the same side was punctured, slightly. A kidney and his spleen were damaged. It also contained additional evidence that the recordings were, in fact, genuine. His genetic print was included.

This was the first recording received, thirty-two years after the event.

CHAPTER TWO: ECHO OF THINGS TO COME

"An ECHO was a classified Extreme Combat Hellfire Operations system. A very specialized military Artificial Intelligence program designed to provide support to insertion teams. The use of ECHOs was stopped just after the Solstice 31 incident. This very ECHO was the reason the entire program was abandoned."

--Solstice 31 Incident Investigation Testimony Transcript: General Patricia Chase, senior member of the Earth Defense Coalition.

Two figures in black habits approached the Citadel Bridge in the darkness of the night. They shielded their eyes from the large braziers that burned high to illuminate the bridge and gate.

They knew the guards were blinded by these fires.

They reached the bridge and were over the side without making a sound. They carried a large hook in each hand that they used to readily move along to three-quarters of the way across. Ropes and webbing hidden in their habits allowed them to hang there, silently. One of the shadows produced a grappling hook, padded with black rags.

With a few practice swings, as preparation, the hook was tossed onto the nearest balcony. It was not completely silent. The talking guards paused, for a moment, and then continued.

The shadows waited.

One at a time, the shadows crossed the chasm on the rope. When the second one was over the railing, with a quick yank and a toss of the hook, rope and grapple all went into the chasm. The impact was so far below that the wind took the sound of it away.

The two tiny women entered a beautiful suite lit by a few night lamps. They exited the room, but were unable to lock the door behind them. The directions were perfect after that.

Wex welcomed Jude and Cine in with open arms.

***

It was a calm, sunny, autumn day as the three women took their tea on their balcony. Their heads and arms were bare in the sun, their habits left inside the suite. The High Keeper called it a 'cruel view' because this balcony was only four feet deep, and it had no railing—even though the drop was almost a thousand feet down on this side of the Citadel.

They were not afraid.

The view today was breathtaking. It overlooked the valley and all of the city of Exeter. They could identify all the sections of the great city: the great avenues, the massive estates, the markets, the slums, the warehouses and the river docks.

"Does he really lock you out here?" Jude asked. "At night, in the wind and rain?"

"Yes," Wex replied, with a surprising smile. "He has no idea that out here is the only time I have any real privacy. The only time I can think clearly, to focus on what will come."

She sipped some more tea. They sat on simple cushions. The elegant tea set rested on a tray that was the lid of the box below it.

There were vapor trails in the sky. Pieces of the *Ventura* were still falling. She knew that among the skyfall, he would come. And he would change everything.

The door opened and closed. A small man stepped out onto the balcony and went right up to the edge, so his toes flexed over the ledge. He was dressed in a simple white tunic and a cloth belt of the same material. His head and face were completely shaved, even his eyebrows. He had done this same thing, before.

He closed his eyes and spread his arms wide, palms to the sun. He took several deep breaths, in through his nose and out through his mouth.

Finally, he turned his head to the ladies but didn't step away from the edge.

"Tonight, he wants you to play for him, in the garden. He would like it to be light and cheerful. He doesn't want you to make his guests cry again."

"Will he punish you again, if I do?" Wex asked.

The usher said nothing, but turned his face away from her and back to the sun, back to the view. He closed his eyes; his lips trembled.

He did not know how long he stood there, or even why.

A hand came to rest on his shoulder, and a soft voice spoke in his ear.

"David, know this. He will never punish you again. He will never even notice you again. Do whatever is asked; and when the time is right, I will ask you a favor. On that day, we will all be free."

"How did you know my name was David? That was taken from me long ago…forbidden…"

He choked on the little-used words as Wex turned him and held him. He was so small, and Wex was so tall. The top of his bald head brushed the bottom of her breasts. He was like a child, thin, all bones and sinew. But up close, Wex saw he was sixty or seventy years old.

"Wait with Jude and Cine while I dress." She turned to Jude, and said, "Remember what I asked you to do."

Then she went into the suite, closing the door behind her.

"Come here, little man David," Cine said, in her odd accent.

He walked over to where they sat.

"Wex was waiting for you."

She gestured to the ornate tray. There were four place settings. Jude poured him tea. There was a slice of pastry and three strawberries on a plate for him.

"Please, don't disappoint her."

***

"Echo, why are you here? There is usually a standard Emergency Module AI," Hagan asked the computer, as he tried to stay awake.

"Sir, are you alright? Your vital signs are problematic," AI~Echo replied, avoiding the question.

Hagan laughed.

"Problematic? I'm losing my shit here, Echo. I'm dead. Of course, my vitals are fucked. I am on the verge of a full-blown panic attack. My goddamn wrist is broken, and I think I took far too many medical nanites to ever sleep again. And what good is being awake, if I can't do anything except think about how dead I am."

Hagan laughed, getting more and more hysterical.

"At least, I am not pissing blood, anymore. I got that going for me. I can't even get outside and inspect the damage, inventory the tools, or activate some repair drones. I can't do any engineering repairs! I can see, from the flight deck, that the main disk is half gone. I could fix that, at least. Maybe eavesdrop on the goddamn planet."

Hagan looked from the main display dome to the closed hatch in the center of the lifeboat.

"I can't even get out with that rear door sealed. Maybe I will just blow this hatch, the one I came in. At least its explosive bolts are full manual."

"Sir, may I call you Wes?" AI~Echo asked, in a gentle woman's voice.

Hagan laughed.

"Sure, Echo. Call me Wes. All my friends do." He was near hysteria.

AI~Echo continued, "Wes, Captain Everett gave me specific orders. She told me she gave you specific orders as well. Do you remember those orders?"

The voice of Captain Alice Everett came across Hagan's HUD audio.

"Wes, I know, I know, it's a secondary sensor station. I also know you are the best multi-discipline engineer on this ship, maybe anywhere. And no, I am not punishing you or fucking with you. I just need YOU to do this, without questions. I know we have gotten used to a light touch and casual command chain on this ship; but I will order you, if I must.

"Jimbo, I mean Commander Worthington, is a good guy. By the book. He will be in command on the Memphis. I need you to be that way as well on this. Do you hear me, Wes?

"By. The. Book."

"I need you to keep a close watch. Once we are in orbit, Worthington will know what to do. If ANYTHING unusual happens to the Ventura. If anything happens to the Memphis, get to this specific lifeboat. And Wait. Ferris and his team will know."

AI~Echo continued, "I have similar orders. But they do not say for how long to wait, or what to do, in the meantime. I expected Sergeant Ferris and his team to be here as well. But they were all killed in the initial impact."

"How the hell do you have a recording of that private conversation? I made sure it was private, because I thought I was going to get reamed out over the armory thing."

AI~Echo continued, "I now believe that Captain Everett expected the *Memphis* to escape undamaged. All my subsequent orders seem to have that assumption. All save one."

Hagan heard the hatch locks disengage. As he watched the extra wide door slide back, and then open, the lights came on.

Hagan said, "Oh fuck..."

***

Ronan's carriage rolled up to the Citadel's only gate. It stopped on the mountain's side of the bridge, in the turnaround. He was angry. The anger fumed off him as if he was filled with magma.

"My lord, Ronan. You must let it go. We will be fine."

The women that sat to either side of him were young and beautiful. Both had hair so black it was nearly blue. Long thick braids rested in their laps and had fine silver chains braided into them. Their dark-green, satin dresses clung lightly to their perfect bodies, and the autumn breeze chilled their breasts.

"You know what might happen, depending on who attends. I just..."

"If it's the council, they think black hair is bad luck. That was a brilliant rumor to start among the slaves in the Citadel. So far, it holds true. If it comes to one of us, you know what to do," she said, grabbing his tunic for emphasis.

"Cass, Lor..." Ronan was getting angry again.

"Oh no, you don't," Cass said, as she opened the door. "We are going to drink Hermitage wine, eat excellent food, enjoy superb music, and cling to a handsome man we love."

"Now leave that awful knife in the carriage and come along," Lor said, cheerfully.

She took two large swallows from a plain bottle and winced, before she handed it to Cass. She finished it and tossed the bottle into the chasm.

A man at arms waited by the carriage door as they exited. He was in fine livery but unarmed. He carried only a single pouch for Ronan's personal plate-style data tablet. Ronan handed it to him, and said, "Thank you, Avis."

Avis gave a nod and fell into line behind them as they entered.

A beautiful woman on each arm, Ronan walked over the bridge, to the great doors. An escort guard led them inward and upward, into the great Citadel.

***

Hagan entered the room with his mouth hung open. Docked inside were twelve Warmarks. They were exo-armor combat drop suits.

Hagan had never seen one, in person. He was amazed how much they resembled the maintenance suits. They were made of the same black, poly-carbon material. Maintenance suits were nearly indestructible. These were taller, and the armor was thicker.

Barcus always called them RFH suits, for Really Fucking Heavy. Hagan stifled a laugh. He knew he was on the edge of losing it. While the RFH maintenance suits were modified with various tools, the Warmarks bristled with weapons. Each were three meters tall, and they all had highly specialized grav-chutes. These suits could drop from orbit in a slow, controlled, stealth descent.

They each were marked with a simple stencil on their chests, DS-01 to DS-12.

Looking further into the room, he saw case after case of clearly marked weapons of every kind. There were automated sentries.

There were carry weapons—laser, plasma, and projectile. There were energy weapons, several makes and models. There were EMP cannons and drones. Some of the energy weapons and automated sentries he didn't even recognize, but they had 'caution' stenciled onto them, warning to never use them in atmosphere.

There were gas canisters he knew nothing about.

There were cases of grenades, bombs, and explosives. There were even two smart nukes. The scary kind, with built-in AIs.

Finally, he found ready-to-eat rations.

"Echo, what was Captain Everett up to? I saw a Marine squad board the *Memphis*, not a Black Badge squad. What was all of this for?"

"I'm sorry, Wes. No additional information is currently available."

"Echo, is there additional information that could be shared at a later time, if various conditions are met and your orders allow?"

"Need to know threshold not achieved. Access denied."

AI~Echo sounded sorry for the denial.

"Echo, is it possible for me to safely use one of these suits as a maintenance suit? Can you drive them, on remote?" Hagan asked. He was used to immediate answers from AIs. It was why they existed.

AI~Echo was thinking about it.

"Captain Everett trusted you. I have also decided to trust you, Wes. Can I trust you?"

The question struck Hagan as completely absurd. He laughed, as the stress began to get to him, again.

"What?" AI~Echo said, in Hagan's mind. She sounded slightly amused. This made Wes laugh even harder.

"Wes, when you are done laughing your ass off, I want you to drink and eat something. The nanites are making you feverish, and your blood sugar is extremely low." AI~Echo sounded serious now.

"OK, OK..." Hagan said, as he slid open a drawer marked 'rations'.

He grabbed an energy bar and a rectangular flask. Glancing at the package, it was labeled, '2,000 cal. meal bar, ready-to-eat'. It tasted wonderful. It had hints of peanut butter, chocolate, and maybe even coffee. It may have been the best candy bar he had ever eaten. Forget that it was a survival ration bar. It was delightful.

The drink was not water but a flavored, electrolyte drink. Wes quickly finished the first one and opened a second one, as he considered his next steps.

"Echo, do I have full admin authority here? Be straight with me. I need to know. Because either way, I know I'm dead."

Wes heard himself being very matter-of-fact about it.

"Wes, do you prefer a full avatar or audio only interfaces to AIs," AI~Echo asked, avoiding the question a bit too obviously.

"Full avatar. Communication is more effective with body language. And there is also a psychological component that helps in a survival situation," Wes said. Then he shook his head. "Echo, what is happening to me?"

A tiny woman walked into his field of view just then. She was slightly transparent, dressed in black military fatigues. A lanyard hung from her neck with a plastic ID badge that even had a photo of her. She had a brown complexion and looked like she was from Pakistan or India. She wasn't quite beautiful like most avatars but memorable.

"Those were combat rations. In addition to having a lot of calories, they contain a mix of stims and other drugs that will help you work and think clearly."

Wes looked down the long row of drop suits and other equipment.

Looking at everything, he finally said, coolly, "Echo, start a punch list. I want a full inventory of everything on this boat. Food, water, oxygen, CO_2 scrubbers, medical supplies, and power first. Then, I want a full damage report."

Display windows opened in his HUD as he requested the items. Echo's avatar looked around the ship, nodding her head as he spoke.

"Finally, a full passive scan of the area. Are there any indications of the *Memphis* or other life pods?"

Wes got to work, calmly assessing his situation. This lifeboat had no hull breaches. The omni-directional communications dish was torn up, but he was sure he could repair it with the supplies on hand. The boat held enough food and water to last sixteen months. There was five years' worth of breathable air; he'd starve long before that.

If he tried to take the lifeboat to the planet, it would be nuked before getting close.

He was dead. He knew it. It would not be today, but all too soon. It didn't seem too upset him.

"Echo, let's make sure we save these combat rations for last."

***

Wes flew the lifeboat to the top of a ridge, allowing a wider vista of the surrounding gray landscape. He put on his helmet and prepared to test the rear ramp.

The panic and fear had gone. All traces of it.

The inventory revealed the squad gear had two weaponized escort drones. These machines were covered with all kinds of sensors and weapons. With Echo's help, they were ready to search for the *Memphis's* crash site.

Both drones fit in the airlock with Wes. They launched directly from the ramp apron into the dark sky. They began the search patterns.

Wes walked away from the lifeboat a ways, to look at the planet near the horizon. There was a mountain range, not far away, casting long shadows on the plain below.

"It's kind of beautiful, isn't it?"

Wes turned his head to see Echo's avatar squatting on top of a bolder nearby, hugging her knees. "Yes. Yes, it is. Beautiful and dangerous. Like you," he replied.

Echo looked at him and gave a sad smile.

"I never expected this to happen. We had trained so long for one thing and...now they're all dead."

"Trained for what?" Wes asked.

"Mutiny. Insurrection. Attack," Echo said.

"Defensive or offensive? Preventing a mutiny or supporting it?" Wes asked.

"I don't know really." Echo sighed. "Both."

"Let's get back," Wes said. "I hope the ramp seals."

CHAPTER THREE: BLACK BADGERS

"The ECHO attached a full inventory of weapons on the boat. It was a standard drop squad, twelve man kit. The inventory included serial numbers. It was them. These were the very ones. The ones now in the Solstice 31 Memorial Museum..."

--*Solstice 31 Incident Investigation Testimony Transcript: General Patricia Chase, senior member of the Earth Defense Coalition.*

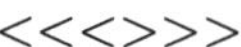

The feast was set up in the High Keeper's roof garden. Wex was there an hour early, like all the servants, standing by and waiting. An army of cooks and slaves artfully displayed fruit and flowers and candles in elegant holders. When they fled, teams of gardeners came out to groom the turf where they had walked, until it was no longer trampled; they backed their way out.

Wex was placed in among the boughs of a beautiful pine. A flattened boulder was there for her to stand on, in the evening's shadows. In trees, globes in the branches, glowed onto the table, set for ten.

They waited in silence. Wex spotted two snipers. She wondered if there were more. She watched the sun set on high arcing vapor trails of falling debris that burned up before reaching the ground.

As the light faded, so did she. In her formal black habit and cloak, with her hood up, she became nearly invisible.

The High Keeper's shuttle approached and landed on its pilings. Five people, plus the pilot, got out of the shuttle. An older couple, a younger couple and an elderly man. An usher escorted them through the gardens to the beautiful banquet table. They stood behind their chairs and waited. Wex recognized them as one of the noble families of Exeter. The men were dressed in the finest house livery, and the women wore traditional, elegant one-button dresses of deepest blue to almost black dyed linen. Even at this distance, she saw their fine ivory buttons.

A few minutes later, Keeper Ronan was escorted in with two women of great beauty. They had the blackest hair and pale fine skin. Their dresses were deep, dark-green satin and left nothing to the imagination. Their arms were bare.

Ronan ignored them, as they kept their eyes downcast.

Well played, Ronan, Wex thought.

A half an hour passed before three men emerged from the High Keeper's private entrance.

When the High Keeper was close enough, he waved his hands dismissively, and said, "Sit, sit, please don't wait for me."

The look on his face told them he knew that he had kept them standing there for over an hour already.

"Keeper Esau, have you ever met Ronan from the East Isles? He sits on the High Council. Ronan, you already know Donner, he is one of my High Trackers."

This last part he said to the other men at the table.

"And this is three generations of the noble House Gideon." He gestured first to the old man, then continued, "Elder Silas, his son Pierce, the head of House Burgrave, and his heir, Julian."

The women were completely ignored.

While he made the introductions, the wine was poured.

This was Wex's cue to begin playing. When she did, all conversation was lost to her. She played light, frivolous tunes that were usually played for dancing. She played sea shanties and tavern favorites as the meal progressed.

The girls with Ronan played their parts as well. They ate small amounts of food and drank a lot of wine. They fawned on Ronan, and he ignored them.

The men discussed policy. House Gideon simply listened for the most part. Ronan seemed more interested in the food than in the topic discussed. He tasted the fish and then the roast duck, waving them aside in favor of a double helping of the wild boar.

Wex never did know what insult made the old man stand and knock his chair over backward. He leaned on the table; and as he drew his first breath to scream at the High Keeper, she saw the subtle signal the High Keeper made with his fingers.

A crossbow bolt suddenly protruded from the man's eye.

As he toppled over dead, backward onto the perfect lawn, the High Keeper wiped his mouth on his fine napkin and tossed it onto the dead man's face.

He stood and said something to Ronan. Ronan nodded and raised his wineglass to the High Keeper. Ronan's women stifled laughter, while looking at the old man behind hands, goblets, and averted eyes. The High Keeper turned and walked away.

When he was gone, High Tracker Donner stood, rounded the table, took the young Gideon woman by the arm, and dragged her to her feet.

Julian did nothing to stop him.

Halfway to the exit from the garden, she stumbled and fell to the grass. Donner dragged her to her feet by her blonde braid, until she stood on tiptoes. He drew his knife and showed the dagger to her. With a well-practiced flick, he cut the button off and her dress fell to the grass.

Still, Julian did nothing. Didn't say a word. He just looked away.

Then, Keeper Esau dragged the other woman away as well.

Wex stopped playing then.

Ronan kept eating his large portion of wild boar. His knife and fork were the only sounds in the quiet garden. After a few minutes, he set down his utensils and finished his wine. Wiping his mouth on his napkin and tossing it over the bones of the wild boar, he stood, still holding his crystal wineglass. He paused, and then took the open but full bottle of wine from the ice and began to walk away. Stumbling, the girls on either side tried not to spill the glasses they had just refilled.

"Wait...what do we do?" Julian the heir asked in desperation.

"Go home. I thought you lived in Exeter," he said, callously.

"But what of Sue and Ren?"

"They will find their way back, or not. Either way, it's on you," Ronan said, and walked away.

***

Wes Hagan woke up not knowing where he was, at first. His neck was seriously aching. He was still in his pressure suit, without the helmet. The collar felt hard beneath his jawline. His mouth was very dry.

"Echo, status," he said, groggily, as he sat up on the cot that was folded down from the wall.

"You have been asleep for seventeen hours. The combat rations kept you going and effective for about thirty hours. You fell asleep at the console and later you barely made it to this cot. I have been trying to gently wake you for an hour."

A small spider-like maintenance-bot, the size of a shoe, walked up and handed Wes an energy drink.

He took it, raising an eyebrow.

He noticed Echo's avatar sitting tailor fashion, on an equipment case across from the cot.

Wes pointed at the small spider-bot.

"I did that?"

"Yes. That and a few hundred other things. You get a lot done when you put your mind to it."

Looking back into the boat, he saw that four of the suits were missing. He raised an eyebrow and looked at Echo.

"That was your idea as well. You figured out how to bypass enough protocols on the suits to allow me to remote control them all. You stationed four of them outside, in case we needed to do something fast and easy."

"I am remembering."

He chugged the entire bottle, then handed it back to the spider-bot, who walked it away.

"You made another directional transmission back to Earth," Echo continued.

It was all coming back to him.

"I need food. Bad. Real food."

He stood and somehow knew where to go. The compartment was unmarked.

"Galley, open. Coffee, now."

A small mini-kitchen emerged from the wall just behind the pilot's seat, like magic. The stainless coffee carafe was already steaming by the time he reached for it, after retrieving a cup.

"Thanks, Echo." He sipped the coffee and sighed. "I need to get out of this pressure suit and take a shower, so I can think."

"Eat this, first. It will help."

There was a small chime and a standard sausage, egg, and cheese sandwich dispensed from the automat.

"I loved these as a kid."

Hagan took the perfectly square sandwich and his coffee and stood in the space between the pilot seats, looking at the moon's stark vista. He ate his meal in silence. He knew crumbs were falling into the collar of his pressure suit, but he didn't care.

Wes heard the clicking footfalls of the spider-bot. And when his coffee was gone, he tossed the reusable, light plastic cup over his shoulder; and he heard the spider-bot catch it, before it touched the floor. When he turned, the spider-bot, the cup, as well as the mini-kitchen, were all gone.

***

Ronan, Cass, and Lor staggered across the Citadel Bridge, singing a filthy tavern song about a wench with full lips and wanton desires. Ronan drank empty the hand-blown wineglass and tossed it over the side of the bridge into the chasm. When the crash was heard, Cass threw her glass, forgetting it was still half full. Lor went to the edge and dropped hers straight down.

Then, Ronan threw the bottle, hard. A bit of his anger bled through in the throw. The girls slid under each arm and dragged him to the carriage. Avis made sure they all got inside and then signaled to the drivers.

Avis sat across from the three of them and opened a case that contained hot water and washcloths. Each of them gladly accepted a large, wet cloth and began wiping their faces and necks; the girls also wiped their arms, sticky from spilled wine.

Just after the second switchback in the road, the carriage stopped. The girls got out and forced themselves to vomit a dramatic amount of wine. They got back in, where more wet cloths were waiting for them, as well as cold flasks of water.

"I will never get used to eating and drinking so much and still being hungry and sober," Cass said.

"The key is to drink without getting it in your mouth much. At least then, you can taste things. Straight to the throat," Lor added.

"Someone invented the foul stuff so Noble Houses could feast and never get fat. Or avoid poison…" Ronan's voice faded away as the door closed.

"Why did it happen?" Cass asked, now with a tremble in her voice. "Sheep shearing schedules? What matters there so much? Why?"

"It wasn't about sheep; they were there to be punished and humiliated. I knew it as soon as I saw that it was Esau and Donner."

Ronan wiped his face, again, with a dry towel.

"And I was there to be tested, to see how I would react. To see if I would defend them."

***

It took Hagan a few minutes to get out of the pressure suit. It was the half-zipper version. He wondered why they still called them zippers. There were no teeth with this kind of thing, just a double set of continuous seals from his neck to about his navel. The layers of Velcro seemed loud, and the space seemed small to him today.

With practiced ease, he lifted the collar and slid though the opening, as the suit collected around his calves. The whole thing smelled of sweat and urine. The inner suit was next and, in less than a minute, Wes stood naked in the center of the ship, stuffing the inner suit into the laundry unit and then hanging the pressure suit in the standard locker, where it would be cleaned and tested.

The floor was warm under his bare feet, as he moved to the shower that was on the port side, just beyond the center hatch. The shower stall was bigger than the one he had on the *Ventura*. It was bigger than the typical shower in a standard lifeboat. It had been made for bigger men. Men like Sergeant Ferris. They were all dead now.

He was soon clean, and the water was replaced with the wind, to dry him. He liked the wind to be cool after his shower, so he adjusted the temp down. His mind emptied as the air dried him.

Hagan emerged clean and dry. The ship had coveralls in many sizes and colors, including engineering blues, which he selected out of force of habit. He didn't put on any shoes but rolled the pant legs up his calves halfway.

"Why are you barefoot?" Echo asked, as he settled into the pilot's seat and began to strap in.

"My feet can feel the ship through the deck plating. It can tell me a lot."

He looked over as Echo settled into the co-pilot's seat.

"I can already tell that the power plant is not standard on this thing. The hum of it feels like a small, dark-matter reactor. Not a conventional reactor.

"Echo, I want to test the grave-foil repairs. I want to also recon the area. Let's do a thousand meters straight up, with gentle rotation. Up and down. Should we collect DS-01 through -04 before we ascend?" Hagan asked, looking over to her.

"DS-01, -02, -03, and -04. Secure to skids for a short hop," Echo ordered, out loud, for Hagan's benefit. She was driving them all. They were an extension of her.

Wes watched in the display, as two of them placed a foot on the massive front skid plate and grasped a handhold that was there for this very purpose. DS-03 and -04 secured to each of the rear skids in the same way.

"Here we go," Echo said, as Wes began to have the feeling of falling up. The rise was smooth and symmetrical. The boat performed a smooth barrel roll, and the one-G fall into the sky felt good to Wes. He felt natural for the first time in days.

As the ship ascended, it spiraled, giving Wes a slow-moving change of view.

"Echo. Is this boat equipped with any additional hardware or scanners we could use?"

Wes had learned to use direct command questions with this Artificial Intelligence system. He had also come to recognize the pause that was caused by her assessing contradictory orders.

"The decking on this lifeboat is equipped with grave-plates."

Wes felt the gravity adjust to a comfortable one-G as they flew.

"There are enhanced optical sensors and more powerful secure communications. There is also a large data repository onboard. I believe it is a backup of the *Ventura's* survey data from this tour. All of it," Echo said, adding emphasis to the word all.

"You have already guessed that the conventional power plant was replaced with dual, dark-matter reactors," Echo said.

"I don't suppose you have a couple FLT drives back there, somewhere?"

"We had the *Memphis*," Echo said, with a tinge of regret in her voice.

"Please prepare a report of all the out of spec modifications that have been made to this boat.

"We need to name her now. My boat…my home…my tomb."

***

"Scanning in progress now. Are we looking for anything specific?" Echo asked, from her seat.

"Yes. High ground. I want to launch the second drone, later today, in the opposite direction. I want maximum coverage." Wes stopped talking.

He thought he saw movement on a ridge below. The spiral of the rotation took the view away too quickly for him to focus.

"Wes, what's wrong?"

Echo sounded concerned.

"I saw something, down on that ridge. It looked like a woman, cresting the ridge..."

His words fell away, as he waited for the ridge to come back into view.

"She was wearing a gray cloak and had red hair."

He looked at Echo.

"She wasn't wearing a pressure suit."

Echo slowed the rotation and let Hagan visually scan the ridge, for thirty minutes, before he gave up looking. He violated his own rules about staying strapped in while moving, by getting up for another cup of coffee.

When he sat again, he not only had a cup of coffee, he had another military ration bar.

"Are you sure you want another iron ration?" Echo asked.

"Iron ration?" Wes asked, as he opened one end and slid it out.

"That's what the Black Badgers called them," Echo replied.

"Black Badgers?" Wes asked.

"Sorry. That was their nickname. They were a very closely held and compartmented military squad, and they all wore lanyards with their security badges. Their badges were black, with their photo and their unit logo on them. Black Badges evolved into Black Badgers," Echo explained.

Wes just shook his head.

"I'm going to try something different this time, Echo. I want you to monitor me closely and report to me any significant changes in my behavior. I need to be sharp."

With that, Hagan took one bite, wrapped up the rest of the bar, and slid it into his breast pocket.

"Let's move the boat to that peak we can see on the horizon. If we can park there, we can cover a lot of ground fast. If the *Memphis* crashed, it would have been in that general area."

The lifeboat moved in that direction, as Wes discussed naming the ship with Echo. By the time they reached the new landing spot, they decided to call the ship *Sariska*.

"Why do you want to call the lifeboat *Sariska*?" Echo asked.

"Well, you made me think of it. There is a wildlife sanctuary in India called Sariska. You remind me of a woman I met there."

This made Echo smile.

***

Eyes watched the ship go from the shadows on the ridge, gliding toward the peak on the far horizon. Lips moved, cursing silently in the vacuum.

CHAPTER FOUR: SCARECROWS

"We didn't know he was one of them. We didn't know he was not human, not in the beginning anyway. We didn't know. He was hiding. He was patient. He was playing the long game the whole time."

--Solstice 31 Incident Investigation Testimony Transcript: General Patricia Chase, senior member of the Earth Defense Coalition.

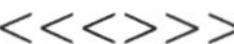

The cells lined the hall on both sides. It had the feel of complete emptiness. The silence of dust. There were not even rats here. There was no dripping water, no shuffling of prisoners in their loneliness and discomfort, no rattling of chains. This deep underground, the ventilation system was perfectly silent.

The small, bare feet moving through the darkness was the loudest sound. The prisoner heard her fingers as they drifted along the wall. He knew she was counting cells in the blackness. His cell was two meters deep and two meters wide. One entire wall of bars, a fist width apart.

She didn't know he saw her in the absolute dark.

He sat on the bare, foamcrete shelf and watched her slowly tiptoe down the hall in the darkness. She felt the bars of his cell and stopped. Impossibly quiet now, she reached both of her arms through the bars, pressing her face to them. Her hands silently searched the black within.

He gently took her hands in his and squeezed them. Her face crumbled into tears as he advanced into her arms, but she didn't make a sound. He lightly kissed her forehead as they held each other through the bars. The girl was naked and filthy. He was in rags, at least.

In the darkness, with the ease of practice, he moved to the wall and sat on the floor, right next to the bars. She sat on the other side of the bars. His right arm extended through the bars as both her legs came through to rest on his lap. He held her as her forehead rested on his arm.

Her soft whisper seemed loud in his ear.

"You were right, again. There are demons in the north, above the gorge. They have killed hundreds, maybe thousands, of the High Keeper's men. He just keeps sending more. He is killing everyone above the gorge, no matter the cost. Just as you said."

"Hmmm..."

He felt her cling to him, almost desperately, as she continued.

"They say. I mean they rumor, that the demon is...just one man." She trembled. "They say...he is a Man from Earth."

He felt her fear at just saying the words out loud. She had been taught to say it was to summon the monster.

"Yes. He is."

The voice, like gravel, whispered. Her trembling increased.

"Soon, he will find you here. This demon, this monster, this Man from Earth. You will tend his wounds. You will eat his food, because in his kindness and fury he won't eat while you starve...and you will give him a message."

"What message?"

It was the quietest whisper yet.

"Kill them all..."

The words had weight. She nodded her head; she'd do it.

"Then, you and I shall escape together. Just as I told you. Because he will bring down the Citadel to its foundations, soon after."

She began to cry again.

"Now tell me what the guards say."

He soothed her with his words as well as his gentle touch.

"How did you know they would all be drunk and asleep tonight?"

She asked, knowing he would not tell her.

"Because it was the truth," he whispered.

"What about all the other things. They think I'm a soothsayer."

She started to tell him everything. Facts, gossip, or simply things she had seen or heard. She knew it wasn't much, but she also knew that he was starved for anything different. Weeks and years of darkness would have driven her mad by now.

"Why do they call you the Scarecrow? They are all afraid of you, still. Even though they say it's been over a decade since you killed one of them."

"Have you never seen me in the light? Scarecrow is about right."

He laughed, a little.

"That's not it," she said.

"They call me that because your language has no real word for who and what I am, my role in the world, my title. It is all held in my true name. Milesian Baytirus Esso Doa roughly translates to protector of this garden. They thought it was another way to say Scarecrow."

"Hummm..." was her only quiet reply.

"Call me Miles, if need be. Why do you ask now, after all this time?" he asked, already knowing why.

"She came down here, a few days ago, just as you said she would. She brought me fresh bread and cheese."

She trembled again.

"She said, 'Tell Miles I said good-bye.' And I knew she meant you. I never needed your name before."

She cried again.

He combed her knotted hair with his fingers.

"What will happen to me?"

She somehow felt his smile on her forehead as he replied, and she heard it in a whisper.

"Everything."

***

It was only a few weeks before one of Hagan's drones found signs of the reactor core that had been jettisoned by the *Memphis*. At first, he thought the crash site would be near and easy to find. The crater analysis gave him a general direction to look for a debris field, but there was none.

"Echo, I need some possible theories that could fit the data we have," Wes asked, looking at the high-def feed on the main display as if the *Sariska* was flying over the crater.

"We know that when we separated, the *Memphis* was in an unpowered tumble along this trajectory."

A tactical map opened to a display of the moon.

"That means the *Memphis* must have had some kind of recovery to be flying over this area."

The map showed a potential track that the ship could have taken to that spot.

"Let's speculate that they got some kind of control of the ship. Why the hell would they be here?"

The image shifted to drone two. It was moving at a high altitude over the area.

"They were fleeing," Echo said. "Retreating to an area where they would be safe. Look at the surface, here. Chunks of the *Ventura* were still impacting the surface then, but at a much higher angle."

"They either went to the far side of the moon or off into deep space," Hagan stated. "Echo, please task the drones to search patterns on this vector, moving on this track. We have just eliminated half the surface."

There was a long pause. Very unusual for Echo.

"Sir, do you see this?" Echo said, highlighting a spot on the horizon.

"Zoom in, optical and digital," Hagan ordered.

The image was not clear, but it looked like a Blaw-Knox lattice tower peak.

"Echo. Bring the boys in. We are moving the *Sariska* to that tower. We may have found our beacon."

Wes smiled.

"You will lose contact with the drones, sir," Echo warned.

"I know, but we have to check this out."

Hagan took another bite of the ration bar.

***

As the *Sariska* lifted off and slid down the mountainside on a direct line to its goal, eyes watched from the surface.

It flew straight as an arrow.

She knew exactly where it was going.

She ran.

***

"Wes, I am not sure this plan is safe," Echo said from the co-pilot's seat, with real concern in her voice.

"I thought ECHO systems were badass," Hagan said, mockingly and excitedly. "What's with this safety stuff? I'm dead anyway. And honestly, I am not going to starve to death."

"If that Blaw-Knox tower is what I think it is, it may have a base there that is occupied. I want to do a high flyover and drop the boys in, for a bit of recon, before we go there."

"Now that's more like it." He smiled. "We have the right tools for that job."

"I also want you to take this."

A small maintenance-bot crawled up his leg, carrying a nanite hypo injection tube.

"Like you said, you're dead anyway."

Hagan took the injector tube from the bot and read the warnings regarding inappropriate use. It had nothing about the dangers he knew the mil-HUD injections also brought.

Hagan laughed, a bit too long, and then said, "What the hell."

He held the injection tube to his neck.

Echo didn't have to say it out loud, but she did.

"Chief Engineer Wes Hagan, do you accept the installation of the Black Badger mil-HUD-2745?"

"Just do it, before I chicken out."

He pressed it, harder. He felt the numbing mist and a slight prick.

"That wasn't so bad."

Then suddenly, it felt like the tube sunk sharp teeth into him.

He screamed, and his vision went white. He was paralyzed. It felt like something big was eating its way up to his brain.

Why do I smell toast?

***

When he came back to consciousness, sometime later, his first thought was that he was glad he had been strapped in. The tube was gone. He tasted blood in his mouth.

A maintenance spider climbed him, holding a clear vial with a brown liquid that looked like weak coffee.

Echo said, "Drink this, it will help. All of it, at once."

"Why do my sinuses hurt? And my wrists?"

He took the vial. It looked like a large test tube. He pulled the stopper and upended it in a single motion.

It burned on the way down. Hagan sputtered and coughed.

Finally able to speak, he said, "Was that bourbon?"

"Actually, yes."

Echo smiled.

"It's tradition. Your systems are coming online now."

"Holy shit. No wonder it hurts. How can they integrate so fast?"

A SL-Hagan status window was rolling by in his personal HUD. He knew, without thinking, that DS-01 through DS-06 were prepped and lined up for a drop. He simply knew that the ramp was already down, and the rear compartment was in full vacuum.

"We will be over the target in eleven minutes. Squad drop-prep, go," Echo said, and things happened, fast, in his brain with no explanation.

Hagan was the designated squad leader. He could now, somehow, see everything the six drop suits could see. All at once. Amazingly, this didn't confuse his perceptions, it just sharpened them.

Weapons status cycled on all the suits. Grav-chutes were ready, and when tactical indicated it was time, DS-01 to -06 ran out the back of the *Sariska.*

The ship veered off sharply as the drop suits descended, in formation. Hagan saw the tower, far below, and the small station at its base.

There was a very wide landing pad, but no docking or hangar facilities.

"Keep her steady. I am going to suit up."

Wes released the five-point harness and turned back to the main compartment to find his pressure suit, waiting. By the time they set down, he was ready.

He felt, more than saw, the other six drop suits follow him down the ramp.

Four of them deployed around the base of the *Sariska,* and two followed him up to the two that were already waiting by the open base airlock. Four of the suits entered the airlock with him as the big door closed behind them.

"The base still has power. So far so good," Hagan said.

"It is deserted. It looks like it had an organized shutdown when it was closed up," AI~Echo said, as the door and airlock finished its cycle and the inner door swung open.

Floodlights came on from the suits as they entered the base. There was another inner door that was closed. The configuration would allow for a large space airlock, if needed.

They entered the space within and closed the outer doors. His helmet indicated that pressure was good, and the O_2 and CO_2 levels were excellent.

Without warning, the four suits turned and faced him, weapons powered up. He was being painted by lasers.

"Wes, did you know you had a rider?"

AI~Echo's voice was sinister as the drop suits crowded closer.

CHAPTER FIVE: HAGAN'S STATION

"Logs showed that Hagan sat on that ridge for months while the drones searched an area the size of Texas. When he found the site of the station, he moved right away. He almost saw her again. She was clearly visible in the data on video."

--Solstice 31 Incident Investigation Testimony Transcript: General Patricia Chase, senior member of the Earth Defense Coalition.

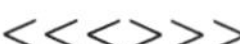

"Echo, what are you doing?"

His new mil-HUD showed that all the weapons trained on him were hot. He also saw the targeting solution of all sixteen weapons. They would pass through him and miss the DS behind him.

"What do you mean a rider?"

He unlatched and removed his helmet for a sniff of stale, very cold, dry air.

Echo's avatar appeared as if she was in the room.

"Someone was surveilling you without your consent. The mil-HUD has detection protocols and protections against this. Please, remain still."

Echo placed her finger to her lips as he felt something in his head.

"Are you alright, Wes?"

"It's not too bad. Like a rapid ice cream headache," Wes said.

"Interesting. Not what I expected at all."

Echo turned away and was looking into the base's garage bay.

The weapons began to stand down. The suits turned away, one at a time, to shine their lights in the base instead of on him.

"DS-03, go to the tower base so we can assess the condition of the communications equipment."

He walked to a console. It was completely dead.

"DS-05, assess the solar panels. We have emergency lights only in here."

"Would you like me to explore and inventory the outpost, Wes?" Echo asked, as she looked around the garage.

"How will you do that? The drop suits are too..."

Hagan trailed off as he saw six of the palm-sized spider-bots climb down from a suit.

"Oh. Yes, please. Everything from tools to wire. Water to beds. Everything. And if you find something that will tell us anything about who the hell these people are, let me know right away."

Echo seemed to walk deeper into the workshop, followed by DS-01 and five of the spider-bots. One spider-bot and DS-02 were already exploring the garage bay with full floodlights on.

***

"The solar panels are 90% intact, but they required some maintenance. Dusting mainly," Echo said, as a window opened in Hagan's HUD.

He saw the field of panels. Dust had settled on them from a couple of centuries without maintenance.

"We have already discovered the pole mops specifically designed for the task."

"Let me know when you find the power plant," Hagan requested.

"Already found it. Looks dead," Echo replied, as an expanding floor plan of the outpost was displayed.

The layout included a battery bank room and a generator room.

"It looks like this place had an organized shutdown. It's like they expected to come back. The interior airlocks were secured, and the seals are still good."

Wes proceeded to the lower level where the batteries were. DS-03 followed, providing light. It was apparent, right away, as he entered the room, that the cells in the bank that covered the wall were dry.

"Echo, how much water will it take to refill these cells?"

He looked at the clear, clean glass fronts of the cells that told the whole story. Over time, they had just dried out.

"About 300 liters. Not much really," Echo replied.

"Make it a priority to find the water storage."

Hagan moved to the generator room. It was just as he'd feared. Old-style colonist portable nuclear generator. He'd never get it running. They were not that reliable when they were new. He closed and sealed the airlock to that room behind him.

The floor map expanded.

"Water storage will be on the upper level or even in tanks above. It will be frozen solid."

***

"This has been the longest year of my life," Mallin said, as he waited by the radio for the supply shuttle to contact the moon base.

The control center was in a dome, and projectors showed the sky outside in high definition, Baytirus center most.

"I have never been so bored in my life. I thought being a pilot would be fun. One fifteen minute flight a month is not what I had in mind."

"I've been here six months, and it's not so bad," Skinner said. "Easy duty, twelve on twelve off, three hot meals a day and all the slave wenches a guy could want."

"Gah, you been to the agri-dome since you been here?"

Mallin grimaced.

"Some of those women have been here too long. They just don't look right. I saw one climbing in an apple tree, picking, once. Arms and legs were too long, too skinny, with sunken eyes. I wouldn't screw her with your dick."

Skinner laughed.

"Well you won't have to worry about that much longer."

"Three hours total flight time this whole assignment. What a waste." Mallin continued to complain. "At least, I got to see that huge ship get destroyed by the High Keeper."

The main board lit with annotations and telemetry.

"Go wake up Cyrus and Enoch. Our ride home is here," Mallin said, as the transmission hail came in.

***

Hagan's outpost turned out to be three levels deep.

The top level was the only level above ground. Even this level had been buried under a deep mound of the excavated regolith. Each side had an exterior airlock, including the garage door they came through.

They also found a sealed airlock to the entrance of a tunnel on the lowest level. It was wide enough to drive a vehicle through. Vehicles were still parked there. They were open-top, utility flatbeds. The tunnel was in vacuum. From what he could see, the pipes and cables attached to the walls were cables that went directly out to the tower.

Offices were located which included the base chief engineer's office. He was kind enough to have one entire wall of his office covered with the old-fashioned, annotated, design drawings of the entire installation. There were even handwritten modifications drawn there, including notes. A smart engineer kept this low tech, just in case something went wrong.

The water tanks were directly above the top level. They had even designed a power-free method to thaw them, in case of a full freeze. It only took Wes a few minutes to figure out the system. He tasked DS-09 to go to the roof pad and simply open the four two-meter-square hatches and focus the sunlight on a heat transfer matrix. They used the moon's extreme temperature variance to heat the ice to liquid.

There was also a solar greenhouse-like system that they opened to heat the air inside the outpost via convection through sealed pipes filled with some kind of super antifreeze liquid.

It only took about six hours before the water was flowing to the battery room. There were leaks everywhere, but most of the shutoff valves worked.

The battery bank began to charge; as the cells filled, the solar panels were cleared off. They might even be fully charged by the time the darkness came.

***

There was a song drifting to her ears from the darkness. She knew it was him, calling to her. He always knew when the guards were drunk and asleep. The nest of rags that made her bed were in a shadowed corner of the guard's room.

She quietly moved, took the key, and unlocked the barred gate that controlled the access to the hall of cells that held him. She rehung the key.

She padded quickly down the black hall, counting the cells on the left side with her fingers.

He was only humming now.

She sat on the floor just beyond the bars.

"Hello, Peanut. Did the little man in white find you?"

"Yes. He said to tell you," she lisped through broken teeth, "she's here. In the Citadel. She can move about as she likes. She says she sees the war's end."

"Excellent."

***

"Wes, I have finished my assessment of the outpost," Echo said to him, two days later, as he ate the last bite of his ration bar.

"So what do you think?" Wes asked, sipping the last of his water from a real ceramic coffee mug in the well-lit engineering office. He sat behind the desk in a large, comfy swivel chair that was big enough to accommodate his pressure suit.

She looked at the wall with the engineering map of the base.

"The only vacuum pumps that are still working are on the north and east airlocks."

She indicated them on the map.

"We will be able to come and go, as needed, without loss of air. The passive CO_2 scrubbers work fine. The environment control systems are working, so we will be warm during the fourteen day darkness."

She turned to him.

"This outpost was mothballed about two hundred years ago. They did a great job. But about fifty years ago, someone returned and removed all the comms gear, all the computer cores, all the disk drives, and an unknown amount of other items. All the tractors were disabled, and even the reactor core was removed. They were cool and calculating about how they disabled this station. They knew what they were doing."

"Any idea why?" Wes asked, simply.

"It's only speculation, but it seems they wanted to ensure this station could not be used for transmitting anything. Even the cabling conduits to the tower have been severed and removed from the site."

She pointed to the tunnel on the station end.

"Why destroy the airlocks on the far end of the tunnel? They were so careful everywhere else," Hagan wondered, out loud.

"They didn't."

Echo moved to the left, so Wes could see the antenna end of the tunnel schematic.

"Someone entered those airlock doors about a decade ago. Leaving them open, and exposed to extremes, simply caused the seals to deteriorate. They came all the way down the tunnel, looked around, and walked away without closing them behind them."

"I'm already working something out. I think I can create a beacon with the assets on hand," Wes said.

"There is one more thing, Wes."

A spider-bot's eye view opened in Hagan's HUD. The point of view was from the pipes in the tunnel, looking down at the floor.

There were clear footprints in the dust from small, bare feet.

The spider-bot followed them down the tunnel and through the three open airlock doors. Eventually, it climbed the ladder to the surface, near the tower leg closest to base.

The bare footprints could just slightly be seen in the dust of the regolith. They faded as they moved off into the distance.

CHAPTER SIX: The Visitor

"When the events were described in Chief Engineer Hagan's logs, we suspected a hoax. Please. Barefoot on the moon? We knew it was impossible. Until it wasn't."

--Solstice 31 Incident Investigation Testimony Transcript: General Patricia Chase, senior member of the Earth Defense Coalition.

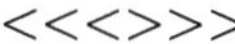

Wes woke with a start.

He looked around the room. It was a dimly lit bedroom. A small bedside lamp provided enough light for him to see the glass of water which he clasped as he sat up. He was thirsty and his eyes itched, but he was also very hungry. He stretched and drank the water.

He didn't think. Couldn't think.

He casually looked about for more evidence. There was an actual book, made of paper, on the bedside stand. He picked it up. It was *Endless Night* by Agatha Christie. There was a bookmark, but he had no memory of reading it.

He stood and stretched again. It felt good. He noted that he wore a plain, black, over-sized T-shirt and charcoal gray boxer shorts. The door to the bathroom was open, and a dim light was on in there as well. The door to the hallway was ajar, and he heard music playing faintly from beyond. It was a smoky blues, with a sorrowful trumpet and a woman singing words he could not recognize.

A spider-bot walked in from the hall through the door. Placed on its flat back was a steaming cup of coffee.

From the hall, Echo said, "Good morning, Wes. Did you sleep well?"

He crossed to the bathroom for a quick pee, before he started drinking coffee.

"Yes. I slept very well. Thanks," he replied, remembering her name was Echo.

She was an AI. She controlled the spider-bots. She controlled a dozen combat drop suits. She made him coffee?

The spider-bot waited for him, making itself as tall as possible in an attempt to hand him the coffee.

"Echo, has anything happened? I'm...off, slightly, this morning."

He turned the lights on in the bathroom. Then, he saw himself in the mirror and was taken aback.

"All is well. We are fifteen days ahead of schedule," Echo replied.

His hair was long with more gray than he remembered. He had a beard, wild and mostly gray. But it was his gaunt face that shocked him, as well as his hollow eyes.. He slowly pulled off the T-shirt to look at his body. His skin seemed too thin. His muscle fibers trembled as he moved. His body fat was far too low.

"Echo, how long have I been here?" Hagan asked, as he brought his face closer to the mirror. He looked, more closely, at the deep set of his eyes.

"Wes, you asked me to play this recording, if you asked me that."

A display window opened in his HUD; it was fixed in front of the mirror.

It was him.

"Look, Wes. If you are watching this, we are probably ready to activate the warning beacon. We decided that we'd stop the rations when the work was done. I am programming this to play after you wake up. The triggers will be these questions: 'How long have I been asleep?' or 'How long have I been here?' or 'Who am I?" or 'What have you done to me?' and a bunch more.

"The only things that will remain to be done is to connect the power cables and set an activation trigger. Then, we need to get the hell away from here."

"Echo, pause."

Hagan stared at his now frozen face in the display.

"Did I really believe this would work? I know that the schedule was 186 days."

He turned, and Echo stood there in the room with him. She met his eyes.

"It's the drugs in the rations, isn't it?" he asked; she was already nodding.

"They not only make the soldiers more efficient and clear of mind, it helps them forget. Maybe forget is the wrong word. It softens the memories."

He looked from Echo to the video display, "Continue."

The vid started again.

"There is a chance the planet has the ability to destroy the beacon from there. I...we are willing to take that chance. But we are still going to relocate to watch. So, don't give Echo any shit about continuing the rations. And stop being such a whiny bitch when you're sober. You're going to die. So what. All men die."

The vid stopped; the display window closed.

Wes looked at Echo, and said, "Get out. I still have to take a piss."

***

Wes drank his coffee and had a breakfast of hot cereal and fruit. It was unreal. He felt like he was inspecting someone else's work even though he remembered doing it all. It was just a blur.

He had used one of the combat drop suits for the comms gear it contained. The comms were powerful but not powerful enough. He had installed DS-01 at the base of the antenna just outside the tunnel opening. That meant all that was required was to run base power out to the suit and the signal booster already connected to the antenna. Opening the airlock at the base end of the tunnel and connecting the power for the antenna's transmission gear was all that remained doing. He could even shut down the base systems because this airlock door had a release that was also manual.

The beacon could potentially last for a couple of centuries.

Wes spent the day performing an organized shutdown of the base. Once he put on his pressure suit, he wanted to be ready to go. He purged the shop to vacuum, so he could open the airlock and attach the power cables that lay there ready, on each side of the tunnel door.

The lifeboat he had christened the *Sariska* was prepped, and all the drop suits were loaded and docked. All the water tanks were topped off, and everything was ready

Hagan waited for the status lights, before he walked to the door and happened to glance out the window into the long corridor that led to the antenna tunnel.

She stood there, with her nose almost touching the glass, staring in.

She blinked.

The handle started to turn before Hagan came back to himself.

"Echo, are you seeing this? Or, have I finally lost it," Wes said, as the wheel kept moving.

She had red hair that was knotted and wild. Her skin was gray with dirt from the regolith. She wore what looked like a make-shift poncho that was once a white tarp with a head hole cut into it. It was tied at her waist with a strip of the same material.

Just as the airlock swung in, Echo responded.

"Warning: L-Matter detected. Warning: Subject is not human. L-Matter detected. Warning: Uncatalogued Scarecrow. Warning: Very Dangerous."

As soon as the door opened enough, she slipped into the shop. Her mouth moved as if she was forming words, but there was no sound in a vacuum. She paced back and forth in front of the bench of tools. It looked like she was ranting. She became more and more agitated. Her body was now surrounded with HUD-augmented data. None made sense to him. Data about a species called Scarecrow. Even that was a translation of a language he did not recognize. She finally just sat on a shop stool, put her elbows on her knees, and held her face in her hands.

"Echo, what should I do? Close the airlock and re-pressurize the shop?"

Hagan glanced toward the open airlock. DS-12 stood there. Weapons were all activated and trained on the woman.

After a long moment, Echo replied, "This unit's original mission was to locate and to retrieve the Scarecrow being held captive on the planet Baytirus. Ferris and his team were all killed in the attack when we arrived in orbit. There was no contingency plan based on this series of events. We had no indication that a Scarecrow occupied the moon."

"How can she be alive? The vacuum, the extreme temps, the radiation. And she is running around out there barefoot. How is that possible!"

"She isn't made of meat."

"What did you say?" Wes asked, not expecting a reply as the airlock closed.

CHAPTER SEVEN: THE HIGH KEEPER'S GARDEN

"BUGs were already watching the High Keeper. But whose BUGs were they? Why are only selected events in the narrative?"

--Solstice 31 Incident Investigation Testimony Transcript: General Patricia Chase, senior member of the Earth Defense Coalition.

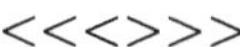

The silence was broken by dozens of heavy feet. The Scarecrow sighed heavily. He already smelled the crackling ozone of many charged plasma rifles. Eventually, the room at the end of the cell corridor filled with men in creaking leather. He could tell they were disciplined soldiers by their ability to become still when readied.

He heard the huge key turn in the locked gate of spiked bars at the end of the hall. Bare feet padded in and the guard locked it again.

He knew it was her.

Enough light spilled on the floor that he saw her shadow as she walked to his cell. The shadows showed what she carried. He already knew. He flexed his fingers in to and out of fists, knowing what was coming.

She stopped in front of his cell and dropped all that she carried with a loud clunk in the silence, then lifted a key that was strung on a leather cord around her neck. She didn't say a word. She knew they were listening. She knew they had permission to fire for any reason they saw fit.

Just before she slid the key in the lock, he pushed the bars forward and opened the cell. It was already unlocked.

She stepped back as the door swung out into the hall.

He turned to face the men and slowly knelt on his knees, sitting back on his heels and holding his arms out.

She lifted the six-foot-long metal rod and first affixed one end to his right wrist and then the other to his left. After this, he stood, and she applied manacles to his legs, attached together by a short chain.

He leaned over then, slowly, so she could place a black bag over his head.

"Stay here," he whispered. "They won't notice you. I'll be fine. They can't hurt me."

She knew he lied. But she would wait for him in the dark, anyway.

He walked down the hallway in a slow shuffle allowed by the chains. He felt the six cruel loops slip over his head and two more over each wrist. The loops were at the end of long poles. They unceremoniously drove him down the next corridor. His feet were barely able to keep up.

He was dragged up flight after flight of stairs, until he emerged into full daylight. He felt it on his skin. He enjoyed it while he could because he knew what was next.

Many hands lifted and dragged and pulled him into position above the timbers. He didn't resist as they took the metal bar away. He didn't cry out when they nailed his arms to a great X of timbers. Six large, iron nails with large heads went in each of his arms. His legs were tightly wrapped in chains.

The whole thing was set vertically on wheels, and they dragged him from the flat, smooth, shuttle landing pad on the roof of the Citadel into the gardens and artificial meadow there.

The High Keeper ripped the hood off his head.

The Scarecrow opened his eyes slowly, looking at him. The loops were still tight around his neck, holding his unsupported head back as if he might try to bite the High Keeper.

Out of the folds of his tunic, the High Keeper produced a Telis blade. It was an eight-inch-long, tailbone spike, from a Telis Raptor. Without a word, he plunged it into the Scarecrow's guts and twisted it back and forth.

Drawing it out quickly, he said, "I know it hurts."

The High Keeper looked at his blade. There was no blood on it, but blood ran down the Scarecrow's belly.

"It's like you are not really here."

Looking up at him, he saw the Scarecrow smiling.

"I have seen your death, Atish," he whispered. "And the death of millions more. A horror will soon walk the face of this planet and it will not be stopped."

With those words, he took a deep breath; and as he did, all the blood from his wounds was drawn back into his body, and the wounds closed. They even healed around the spikes, like an earring piercing. Steam rose around the spikes.

All the soldiers took a step back.

The Scarecrow's face sobered then. Atish saw his face; he knew what was coming next.

Soldiers dragged ten young women forward by their braids.

"Tell me how you do it."

The High Keeper stepped up and took the braid of the first girl in one hand. He cut the single button from the white dress, and the entire garment spilled to the well-manicured grass in the garden. The Telis blade went to her throat.

The Scarecrow said nothing.

The High Keeper slashed her throat and threw her to the grass as he grabbed the next one. He cut her dress away in the same manner. She stood there naked, hands clasped at the base of her spine. Tears ran down her face.

"Did I mention that every one of these 123 girls were born on the day you were imprisoned? I thought it would make a special treat for you. To watch all 123 of them die, knowing you could have saved them."

Atish raised the knife.

"Don't be afraid, child. Your mother, Gail, and father, Jolson, are waiting for you. You will be with them soon," the Scarecrow said.

She stopped crying, and she opened her eyes.

"I will tell you, Atish."

He knew the High Keeper hated it when he used that name. But he let the girl fall to the grass, still alive. The Scarecrow's whisper drew him closer.

"All men die because they are made...of meat."

The Scarecrow ripped his right arm free. Some nails came away from the wood, others remained and tore massive wounds in his flesh. Before his backhand swing could impale the spike—still in his right hand—into the High Keeper's skull, four men opened fire with plasma rifles. Three shots struck the Scarecrow's body, and one directly on the face.

The Scarecrow's body was on fire. No one moved to douse the flames. The timber frame eventually collapsed as it burned. The now naked, charred remains lay on the ground with the huge spikes still protruding.

"Take him back to his cell, before he wakes up and kills you all," the High Keeper said.

"My Lord?" the commander of the guard asked.

"JUST. Do. It. you fool..."

Atish's voice trailed off as the charred corpse moaned and moved.

"That has got to hurt," he said, smiling, as he walked away.

***

She heard them coming.

The pool of light that surrounded them was like a bubble of fear. The air was thick with it.

Four guards carried his body, and four more had fully charged plasma rifles trained on him, as they threw him into the cell, slammed the door of bars closed, then literally ran.

She had been hiding in a cell, two down and across the hall. When the guards left, she moved to his cell, reaching through the bars, searching for him as she sobbed. The first thing her hands found was the top of his head.

"No, no, no, no, no..." she sobbed.

All his hair was gone. His beard was gone. His skin was a solid, rocky scab.

"No, no, no, no...we were to go. Together."

Her words were cut off when she felt dry, empty eye sockets.

A perfect hand came up and rested over hers. She felt his head turn, a slight bit.

"Don't cry, Peanut," he said to her, in a ruined, whispering voice. "Have you ever been swimming? When we go, you and I are going swimming. I can see it. I will tell you secrets while we swim. I will swim with your children, too. And their children."

He moved himself closer to the bars, so he could reach an arm through to hold her.

"I see it."

"I want that," she sobbed.

"I will tell you a secret now, if you like."

His whisper was even quieter.

"Yes, yes, yes..." she cried, clinging to him through the bars.

"I can't die," he choked out. "Even if I wanted to. Atish knows it. It's what he seeks from me."

"Don't die. Please, don't die," she begged.

"I will tell you another secret, Peanut."

She calmed at these words. His voice sounded stronger.

"You know how you remember the past. You think, and you know things that have happened to you, things you have seen and said."

His thumb dried her tears.

"That's how I see the future. It's like I remember it. It just hasn't happened yet."

"Is that why you're sure we will leave this place together?"

She wasn't crying anymore.

"Yes. And the closer an event gets, the clearer it becomes. Just as you remember what happened yesterday better than what happened a year ago."

His voice grew stronger still.

"You knew they would do this to you? Why did you let them?"

Her whisper was almost a scolding. He now knew she believed he would live.

"Today, I saved 122 girls, the same age as you."

"When will we go?" she asked, believing.

"The day you eat the bread offered by the Man from Earth."

She heard the smile in his voice.

"That is the day we will be free."

***

The airlock pushed open, and she just stood there, like she was made of gray stone.

Slowly, she stepped over the airlock's threshold and moved into the center of the room. Laser dots covered her chest.

Echo stood before her, unseen, as Hagan closed the door.

"I've gone mad," Wes said, as the hatch closed and locked. The room began to pressurize.

Hagan's HUD indicated the increase in pressure. The higher it got, the more distressed her face became. Her hands covered her ears, and her mouth opened in a silent scream.

She collapsed to her knees and fell to her side on the floor. Hagan made no move to catch or to assist her. She was unconscious and limp when full pressure was reached.

Wes took off his helmet and one glove. He checked her pulse at her throat. She was impossibly cold, but there was a pulse.

"Echo, what the…report," Hagan barked.

"This being is a Scarecrow. She was once human, but at some point in the past, every cell in her body was replaced at the atomic level. The process makes them…durable," Echo reported.

"Replaced with what?"

"It has been labeled L-Matter, and a way to detect it has been added to the Warmark's scanning system and your HUD implant," Echo said, while pulsing the overlay data in Hagan's HUD.

"How is it detected?"

"The primary atomic phase contains dual vibrations."

Echo seemed to kneel down and look at her more closely.

"It's a temporal anomaly, detected only in strange matter that is a by-product of heavy metal, mass collider experiments. Knowing all this tells us nothing about its nature. Only the detection of it."

Echo stood then.

Without waiting to take off his pressure suit, Hagan lifted her from the floor and carried her to one of the vacant crew quarters. He was surprised to find the bed made, even though he must have made it.

The Warmark loomed in the doorway, most of its weapons blocked by the wall. Hagan shook his head, knowing the wall mattered not at all.

She stirred, just as a maintenance-bot came in with a glass of water. Wes picked it up, sat on the edge of the bed, and waited.

She suddenly gasped and, with a massive inhale, coughed out a literal cloud of dust. She opened her eyes, saw the water, and grabbed it from his hand, spilling half of it on the way to her mouth.

She tried to speak, but only unintelligible croaks came out. She struggled to her elbows, then upright, just as the bot returned with another glass of water. She took this one more carefully and drank half of it. She looked up to the ceiling; and with her eyes fully open, she poured the rest of the water on her own face.

"My name is Wes Hagan," he said to her, slowly. She nodded, swallowed hard, and took a deep breath.

"Shower," was all she managed, in a scratchy whisper.

Wes stood and opened the bathroom door, reached around to the shower controls, and activated it.

She stood and untied the belt around the tarp poncho. She flipped it over her head onto the floor; beneath she wore the remains of a tattered flight suit that was once white. The suit's legs and arms were gone or in complete threadbare tatters. With both hands, she simply tore the remains off her body as she moved to the shower.

Wes didn't stay and watch. He left that to Echo and the Warmark. He left her a set of coveralls that would likely fit.

Over an hour later, Hagan heard the Warmark walking down the corridor to the cafeteria where he sat drinking tea.

She walked in and looked around. The desperation of earlier was gone from her gray face. Color had returned to her cheeks. Her hair was washed yet still wet, and placed in a French braid down her back.

"Would you like some tea?" Wes said, as if she was an old friend fresh out of bed.

She nodded, almost shyly.

"I never thought this day would come," she said, her voice now restored.

Wes brought her a steaming cup.

"Are you hungry?" he asked.

"No questions but that?"

She smiled. Was that a slight British accent?

"Time for questions after I know you are OK," he said.

"I will be, soon. The white is upon me and think I know why this one is so very long."

She sipped her tea and sighed.

"I'm sorry. I think I saw you months ago and…I didn't continue to look for you," Hagan confessed.

"Your ship was the last thing I foresaw. On that high ridge. I saw you go into the long white. Like everyone else; then, I just guessed where you would go."

She sat and saw the various foods he had set out.

"The white?" Hagan asked.

"When you close your eyes and think of the future, what color is it? Is it the black of the time before you were born? No. It's white. I see like you now. It doesn't matter. Not knowing what you will say or do. It's restful."

She picked up a cold piece of bacon and bit it.

Her eyes closed, in delight.

"My name is Ralta."

CHAPTER EIGHT: THE BEACON

"This was when it could have been stopped. Hagan and Worthington should have played it by the book. They should have stayed there and not brought Barcus or that...that thing back to Earth."

--Solstice 31 Incident Investigation Testimony Transcript: Senator Johnathon Kendall, Senator and senior member of the Earth Defense Coalition.

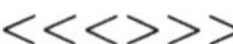

She finished her bacon and tea and, without a word, returned to that same room and fell asleep.

Echo stationed DS-09 at her door, and Hagan got back to work. It only took him a few hours to connect the final systems to a power source. When he was ready to go, he sat in the main control center and recorded what may be his last transmission.

"Echo tells me you are leaving soon, and you plan to activate this station as a beacon."

Ralta was at the door.

"I won't be going with you."

Hagan spun his chair around and saw her standing in the hall with the Warmark behind her.

"Why? There is a good chance this station will be destroyed," Wes said.

"That is the very reason. This war is over for me. I can't bear the weight of it any longer. Turkot and Miles both must have known what would happen when they sent me here."

"What war?"

"The war between the Scarecrows. Fought from prisons. Miles, Turkot, Wex and I are all that remain. Never mind. The thing is, it took me a decade to realize Miles knew but Turkot didn't. I only saw what happened to me, not what I thought about it. I could have sent myself a message in a bottle. As simple as writing a message in the dust."

"I still have no idea what you're talking about."

"Just go, when you are ready. Beware of Wex, because she is the queen of lies, the greatest betrayer of all. She's the one that left me here, taught me to lie, even to myself."

"I can't just leave you here."

"You think I can't survive on my own? You think you could force me to leave? You know how long I tried to get in here with just my bare hands? I will now have power, water, and a warm bed to sleep in for the rest of my life." She smiled. "I'll even keep your tower operational."

It was then he realized that she was lying to him. Just as he was lying to himself. He knew the tower would be destroyed. Just as she did. He also knew he would die as soon as he touched the defense grid.

Each picked their own manner of suicide.

***

"We are 160 kilometers from the tower, Wes," Echo notified him. "Activating warning beacon."

Everything worked perfectly; it was a good, strong signal. It would reach an increasing area, in every direction, as the signal expanded at the speed of light. Even a ship traveling at FTL speed will be able to hear it. Every direction will be covered as the moon managed to orbit around the planet.

"I'm tired, Echo," Wes said. "Can you deploy the cot, please?"

The cot opened out from the wall in the main compartment.

"We will discuss the next steps in the morning," Echo said, pleasantly, as she lowered the lights. "I will wake you, if anything changes."

Wes lay down, after removing his pressure suit, and was asleep in less than a minute.

He only got three hours rest.

***

The High Keeper was in the control room, trying to understand the reports that came in from above the gorge. An entire unit had been killed, in a matter of moments, even though they were all hardened trackers led by High Tracker Donner. He dispatched the PT-66 for a bombing run. He wanted to pound the rubble, in fact, because of that recon report.

Alarms began to howl.

"Now what?" the High Keeper demanded.

"There is a moon-based warning beacon transmitting in the clear."

The frightened man looked up at the High Keeper.

"It's transmitting our location coordinates and a warning that it is a trap."

Without another word, High Keeper Atish lifted his plate interface and entered the launch codes for the nearest missile, targeting that transmitter.

At full burn, it will still take three hours to reach its target.

"Call the high council to chambers. If the chancellor is behind this, he will regret it. Let's have a closer look at this Man from Earth."

***

A Klaxon woke Wes out of a deep, dreamless sleep.

"Echo, Status."

"Incoming Javelin. Time to impact, one minute and seventeen seconds," the AI replied.

"Turn that alarm off, dammit," Hagan said, as he reached the pilot's seat and strapped in.

It became silent in the cockpit. He just sat and looked to the part of the horizon where he knew the antenna station was located.

There was a bright flash just over the horizon. He knew it was far brighter than the display allowed. It wasn't like a nuclear explosion in the atmosphere. He watched the dome of a flash get quickly consumed in the vacuum.

"Signal terminated," AI~Echo reported.

Wes sighed.

"How much food do we have left?" Hagan asked, with despair in his voice.

"Nineteen days, at present consumption," AI~Echo replied.

"Echo, I feel like a big breakfast. Bacon, eggs, hash browns, toast, coffee, and juice. The works," Hagan said, in a cheerful voice so thin that he knew he wasn't fooling anyone. "After breakfast, I want to start planning our trip to the surface."

Suddenly, the display came alive in front of him. It was full of data he couldn't believe.

Incoming Transmission.

"Wes, are you making all that racket?"

He heard Jimbo's smile in his voice.

Wes couldn't speak. Was he dreaming this? His vision blurred.

"Wes, thanks to you, we just took control of the planetary defense grid." There was a pause. "We now own this planet. You have permission to break radio silence, if you are still alive, you crazy bastard."

"Echo, open a channel."

He sat up, wiped his face on his sleeve, and paused as he thought of what to say.

"Damn, Jimbo. When was the last time you brushed your teeth? I can smell your breath from here."

"So...what's new?" Jimbo asked, casually.

Wes heard the smile on his face.

"Mom, can you come pick me up?" Wes said, just as casually.

He wasn't sure he could say much more over the lump in his throat.

Tears began to fall.

***

AI~Echo received the coordinates to the base where the *Memphis* was parked. The *Sariska* flew at maximum speed. She was sent all the command codes to the base, and to the *Memphis*, before she passed to the dark side of the moon.

It only took her five hours to get there. AI~Echo was analyzing data without being asked. Hagan knew the nature of an Echo AI then.

Wes could only think about Ralta. He should have convinced her to come.

AI~Echo had orders that fit this contingency.

CHAPTER NINE: REUNION

"During the chaos on Baytirus, a warning beacon was activated on the moon. The High Keeper immediately launched a nuclear missile to destroy it. He thought Barcus was, somehow, behind it. It revealed that the High Keeper did, in fact, still have control over the defense grid."

--Solstice 31 Incident Investigation Testimony Transcript: Captain James Worthington, senior surviving member of the Ventura's command crew.

"Wes, wake up. We are almost there," AI~Echo said, pausing as if there was more to say.

Wes sat up in the pilot's seat, rubbing the sleep from his eyes. The Tesla facility was visible on the horizon.

"What's up? Do I need to suit up?"

"No…Wes, recent developments have revealed that original mission objectives are, once again, possible."

AI~Echo was all business.

"I have decrypted the mission briefing and support documents for you."

Wes reviewed the files as the lifeboat settled on the pad. AI~Echo left him alone for a long while so he could.

"You want *me* to do this? Worthington will know I am lying."

He kept reading.

***

The lifeboat was already in the hangar when Jimbo and the other survivors reached the moon base. The hangar door quickly closed, and the bay was pressurized in no time.

The ship was smaller than the *Memphis* but not by much. It had clear exterior markings. The *Sariska's* ramp came down and a man with a filthy flight suit, long hair, and a beard stood there.

He looked pissed, especially because he stood there, holding a Frange carbine. He was flanked by a pair of Warmarks, military drop suits with full weapons and exo-armor. These were the most dangerous war machines ever made.

They had been activated.

"Wes, what are you doing? Everything's OK, buddy," Jimbo said, hands forward, palms open.

"Shut up and listen, Jimbo."

Wes did not sound as crazy as he looked.

There was a single laser dot on Hagan's forehead. Hume flanked him. She awaited an order to fire.

"I have been up here, studying. Excellent sensor array, by the way, whoever set that up."

"Thank you," Kuss said. "Make point fast or Hume kills you dead." Ludmilla Kuss had close cropped blonde hair and a thick polish accent that was direct to the point.

There were seventeen laser dots on a tall, red-haired woman named Wex. Both Warmarks had their weapons trained on her. And, these suits were bristling with weapons.

"This is her fault."

Wes sounded like he was about to rant.

"This missile defense grid was not made to keep people out. It was made to keep them in. They are not humans. Well, not anymore. Come out of there. Captain Everett knew. Orders were to rescue...or to destroy."

Wex complied, followed by Cine and Jude. She stood fully upright as she slowly descended the ramp. Head held high, her chest covered in laser dots.

Barcus felt Po tense. They both noticed the bullet holes in Wex's gown when the laser dots danced around as she moved. The High Keeper must have shot her. It was a test.

The suits advanced, placing themselves between Wex and the others.

"He was in the Citadel. In the dungeon," Barcus said. "They had not fed him food, or water, for seventeen years. He was there when the Citadel was destroyed. He told me to tell Wex…" Barcus turned to her. "That he was tired. That it would be alright. That he understood."

"What the hell are you people doing?"

A small woman pushed her way through and finally came to stand with the barrel of the Frange carbine right against her chest.

"She wasn't the only prisoner on Baytirus. We *all* were! And, we are NOT free, yet."

Wes saw that she had an ident code indicator name, Po. Just Po.

Hagan was suddenly not as certain. They were alive. He was looking at Barcus. Hagan's HUD flagged the one designated Wex as an L-Matter being. She was highlighted in a red overlay.

"They called them a word that the AI would only translate to Scarecrow," Hagan said. "They crippled their own tech to keep it away from him. Away from her."

Wes pointed at Wex,

"The defense grid here. It's not for defense. It's a permanent quarantine. A prison."

"Was this set up by the same bastards that destroyed the *Ventura*? Is that what you are telling me?" Hume asked, storming forward.

Wes stared at Barcus. His abdomen, his nervous system seemed to be highlighted in red.

Wex stood between the suits, and the lasers swung away from her.

"That grid was set up by the same people that have been doing genetic experiments on Po and her people?"

Po stood next to Wex. She remembered Wex on her knees beside Barcus.

"To hell with them," Hume barked, as she accessed controls on a cuff device. "Warmarks, stand down override. Authorization: Hume, Baker-Seven-Niner."

The suits retreated and the weapons stowed away. They were no less intimidating, however.

"Where the hell did you get two Warmarks?" Jimbo asked.

Hume walked to the nearest war machine and opened a chest plate, revealing a control/status panel. She was obviously very experienced with them.

Hagan looked uncertain. He stared at Wex and then Barcus, becoming less certain.

"I, er um, we have eleven of them in the lifeboat, sir," Hagan answered.

Holding his side, Barcus asked, "How are you driving them?"

"I have a special HUD upgrade. It also identifies...them."

Oddly, he was absentmindedly pointing at Barcus, not Wex.

"But, I'm not driving them, Echo is. The AI."

Barcus, Jimbo, and Hume stared at Hagan.

"You have an ECHO-class AI on that lifeboat? An Extreme Combat Hellfire Operations AI? What the hell is going on here, Jimbo?" Barcus growled, before stepping aside and throwing up an alarming amount of bloody chunks onto the hangar deck.

"Can we load this boat up and get the hell out of here? I need a nap."

He paused, then continued.

"Sir, we will have five months to figure it out."

Barcus spat out another chunk.

"Captain."

It was Hume who called out. She stood in front of the lifeboat.

"There are also two Javelin modules over here."

Jimbo looked at Barcus, who with a broad, bloody smile said, "Em must have gone back. Stu, did you bring these here?"

"Yes, sir. It was on my task list," AI~Stu replied, actually sounding abashed. "After the plutonium was transferred to the fuel pods."

"Load those up as well," Worthington said. "We're going home."

***

"Jimbo, we need to wait," Hagan said. "If we just show up, what will you do? You realize that Chancellor Dalton is somehow behind this. A pawn or player. It doesn't matter. If he is involved in any way, we are dead. The ECHO had...orders. I need you to see them. Captain Everett was following specific orders. She knew this might happen."

Barcus collapsed just then. Po and the two women in habits caught him.

Doctor Shaw came over, knelt beside him. "Let's get him back to the med bay on the STU, until the one in the *Memphis* warms up." Shaw was the ship's doctor on the *Memphis* when the *Ventura* was destroyed.

"He just needs a bed and a bucket," Wex said, looking down on them. "And water. He'll be thirsty when he wakes, but don't give him any food yet. A cold room and low gravity would also help. There are quarters here in shape to occupy. We'll take him."

"Wait one damn second," Shaw said, about to intervene.

"Doctor Elizabeth Shaw," Wex began. "Born in Albany, New York on March first, twenty-five thirty-one. Have you ever told anyone that? No. Because you are sensitive about your age, even though you started longevity treatments early."

Wex moved toward her, slowly. Wex was tall with red hair and cold blue eyes.

"You got a dog named Penny when you were nine. You killed it, by accident, the first time you parked the family transport. You never forgave yourself and never got another pet. Did you ever tell anyone that? You are aware of this conspiracy, but had no idea that all this would happen. Your team has a trust word. It's Lohengrin."

Shaw backed away. Fear on her face.

Everyone else just stared as the four women lifted the unconscious Barcus in the low G. Po held one arm and his head. Cine and Jude held his legs and Wex was on the other arm, facing the crowd.

"I know about it all, Beth," Wex said as they moved away. "I also know when you explain it all to Jimbo and Hagan, it will be alright."

Wex scanned all their faces.

She paused on Cook's face before continuing, "You will be there in time. She will make it to Freedom Station." Cook was the pilot on the *Memphis*. His quick thinking and skills saved them all more than once.

They moved into the base. Their breaths came out in clouds.

"She *is* a witch," Cook said, just slightly more than a whisper.

"What did she mean?" Shaw asked, looking up at him. He was as tall as Worthington.

"My sister is planning to get pregnant next year. She can no longer afford the cost of the permits. It will be her third, and she wants the baby born on Freedom Station," Cook replied.

"Shaw, I should be asking *you* that." Worthington was serious now.

"How could she know?" Shaw asked.

"Let's make some coffee, and I will tell you," Hagan said.

***

Po and Wex sat in chairs on either side of Barcus's bed. They were wrapped in blankets, and they still saw their breaths. The cool room and the low gravity seemed to help. He looked much improved.

Heat rose from his body through the sheet. They had cut his ruined clothes away and cleaned him up, as best they could. Cine and Jude flanked the open door, allowing people to look in but not to enter.

"These are not like other nanites, are they?" Po asked, over the bed.

"No. They replace damaged flesh with new, more durable flesh. They will never stop working, even when there is nothing left to do," Wex said, in low tones.

"How old are you?" Po stared at her. "Seriously. The truth."

"I was born, on Earth, in 1861. I think I'm about 770 years old. I came here about 120 years ago, to find Miles Baytirus. It's his planet, you know. He made it," Wex said, casually.

"What do you mean, made it?"

Po was puzzled.

"It's what they do. Or, used to do. Before this war. The Scarecrows, I mean. They make planets. They take a long time. Thousands of years. Tens of thousands. Millions. I don't know, really. Now, I don't want to know, I'm beginning to suspect."

"I don't care about any of this. I just want him to live," Po said.

"He will. I promise."

For some reason, she could not explain, Po believed her.

Barcus stirred.

"I had a dream," he whispered. "It was of a great ship. And trees."

Po brought water to his lips. He drank more than she thought he should.

"I will take you there," Wex said to him. "Miles told me where it is. The last of the great seed ships."

Barcus fell asleep again.

Jude said, from the doorway, "They come."

She and Cine stepped aside, making no attempt to block Worthington and Hagan from entering.

"How is he?" Worthington asked, looking down at Barcus from the foot of the bed.

Po looked up, and said, "Durable."

Worthington smiled, and then turned to Wex.

"We need to talk."

She stood and left the blanket on the chair.

As they walked down the wide corridor, back toward the hangar, she spoke to them.

"I will save you a lot of time. Hagan met Ralta on the surface. The actual surface. She was trapped there for decades. She told you about the long white."

They reached the ramp of the *Memphis*, and Hagan stopped them. "How do you know all this?"

"Because I *remember*, for lack of a better word."

CHAPTER TEN: The Long White

"Perception. The collection of data via our senses depends completely on the type and fidelity of the sensors involved. We now know there are more than five senses. Far more."

--Solstice 31 Incident Investigation Testimony Transcript: General Patricia Chase, senior member of the Earth Defense Coalition.

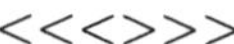

"It's the end. It's also a lie. It has to be. The long white, I mean," Wex said, looking at a framed photo of Jimbo and his family—his wife and two daughters.

"They are safe."

She looked over her shoulder at him.

"They are on Freedom Station. You will be with them soon enough. After...all this."

"How do you know that?"

Worthington was calm.

Jude had followed them into Jimbo's private quarters, unnoticed. She stood in the corner when she spoke. Hagan was seated and became startled when she spoke.

"Tell him about the bacon," Jude said, as if it was not out of the blue.

"Bacon?" Hagan asked.

"I have spent my whole life hiding who I am, and what I am, Captain."

She sat at the second chair in front of Worthington's desk.

He waited for her to continue.

"Do you like bacon, Captain?"

He nodded but didn't interrupt.

"When I make bacon, it is very rich in sensory input. All my senses come into play. I can hear it sizzle as it cooks. I can see it when it's perfectly done. I can smell it and taste it and feel how hot it is with my fingers."

Everyone in the room nodded.

"And I can do all those things, at the same time, easily. And more than that, I can remember all those things after I am done. Do you know why?"

"Memory," Jimbo said.

"Yes. But what is memory? It is actually another sense. It is how you perceive time."

She leaned forward.

"Did you know that there are life forms that only experience the now? Even though now is just the intersection between the past and the future. More advanced life forms have temporal senses. Memory. Some even experience precognition. Have you ever heard the term, *My life flashed before my eyes?"*

She was intense now.

"You know how other senses work. Some animals can see heat. Some can use echoes to locate things in the dark or in the water. Some can perceive density or mass or variations in gravity."

She now paused.

"And some can perceive the passing of time. Or the approach of time."

She let it settle in, for a minute.

"I can close my eyes and it is like I am remembering the future. The things that will happen to me."

She knew they would remain silent.

"It's how I know that your youngest daughter got nine stitches in her mouth because she fell and hit the coffee table. You will tell that story to the crew, one night at dinner."

She looked over to Hagan.

"You are thinking of your favorite number, 91019. It's your favorite because it is prime and the same backward and forward. A palindrome. You people and primes."

She sighed and continued, "You will tell me the other details later, but I won't mention them now as it's super personal."

She smiled and averted her eyes as Hagan blushed.

"Captain, I am telling you this because you asked me to tell you. You also asked me to keep a few details to myself. You also want me to tell Wes about the long white. And the lie of it..."

***

Po could tell when the corner was turned. Barcus fell into a natural sleep; she saw it. While he still had a fever, he was not hot, like before.

She was cold, so she climbed into bed with him. Cine quietly closed the door.

She slept.

She woke a long time later with her back to Barcus, as he spooned her, snoring softly. She smiled wide, and then tears flowed freely. They were alive. They were safe.

His snoring stopped. She tried to be still and pretended to sleep, but he knew her too well.

"Good morning, you."

She spun to face him. His eyes were open and bright. She could swear his beard had grown dramatically, overnight.

"I don't know what to say, anymore," Po whispered. "My frame of reference to…everything is gone. I'm afraid to take my eyes off you, because everything else I would see is totally strange to me."

She ran her hand down his chest, over old scars to his new wound.

It was gone.

She brushed away black, thin dust from the fresh, pink skin below. He kissed the top of her head as she examined him.

"I'm thirsty," he murmured.

Po realized she was also thirsty and hungry. She slowly sat up, unsure if the movement would hurt him.

"How do you feel?"

"I feel like I have slept for a month. My arms and legs and back are all stiff. And, I have this strange feeling of déjà vu, all the time."

She handed him a glass of water. He first sipped and then gulped it.

"Kuss is coming."

A moment later, there was a soft knock on the door.

"Come."

Barcus sat up now. The sheet provided modesty.

"You done sleeping yet, you lazy cow?"

Kuss smiled, seeing him upright.

"Hagan says I have wait for you. Done waiting. Move ass."

And she was gone. With her accent echoing, the door settled closed.

"Any idea where I can get some clothes?"

***

The main hangar buzzed with activity. People laughed and talked over each other while they worked. Several people worked on top of the *Memphis* with floodlights.

"It's a good thing you didn't try to fly this thing, Cook. This would have never held for those maneuvers," Hagan said, from the floodlights above. "All balls, no brains."

He laughed. Others laughed, too.

"Just how I like my men," Kuss shouted, and the laughter got louder.

A hand holding a large cup, or a small pitcher, was thrust in front of Barcus. It was Beth Shaw's hand.

"Here, drink this. If you don't puke, maybe we will try some mashed potatoes, in a few hours," she said.

She waited, watching him.

He was starving. The drink was some kind of smoothie. Probably the same type he used on his long maintenance runs in his suit.

He finished the drink. He didn't puke. Somehow, he knew he wouldn't. Po stood next to Dr. Shaw, watching him as if he might keel over again, any second.

Worthington stood at the top of the ramp, talking to Wex. Jimbo looked over at Barcus and then gave him a quick nod to come over.

"How are you feeling, Bro?" Worthington asked, looking him up and down. "You look pretty good for a guy that was dead three days ago."

"I feel...different."

He looked at Po, for a second, before continuing.

"I'm horribly stiff. It feels like every muscle and joint has been pounded."

He shook his head.

"I'm...I can't focus. It's like everything distracts me, and I lose my train of thought all the time. It's odd. It's like I can see more colors. Not colors really. Details. Like I can tell that gravity is higher on this ramp, by just looking at it."

He scrubbed his face, like he was trying to wake up.

"A lot has happened while you took your nap," he started, but Barcus interrupted.

"And that. I can *feel* exactly how much time has passed."

He ran his fingers through his hair and stretched.

Across the hangar, Elkin, Beary, Jude, and Cine pushed the fabricator down the ramp and out of the STU. Barcus inhaled a mighty breath and blew it out.

"OK. What's the plan?" Barcus sighed.

"You still need to rest."

Pointing at Po, Shaw said, "She will make sure you don't overdo it." Then, he looked at Wex. "Wex wants to go look for the Scarecrow's ship. If it's still operable, it may be useful."

He stared at Wex, saying nothing.

"It will only take a few days, if we take the STU. If we don't find it in that time, we will just come back," Wex lied.

Barcus knew Wex was lying.

"Ben, the AI in the *Memphis*, is keeping us on track. Not as well as Em used to, but good enough. If this pans out, it may save a lot of time."

Worthington spoke as if the decision was already made. No one argued. Jimbo nodded and went into the *Memphis*.

"We will go as soon as Stu is ready. I want Ash as well. Po, will you please check everything? I'll be OK, out of your sight, for a few minutes."

Barcus smiled wide at her. Filled with purpose, she ran across the hangar, past the *Sedna* to the STU.

Barcus was alone with Wex on the ramp, then.

"You know exactly where it is. So do I, for some reason. I remember being there before. It's like a dream I haven't had yet."

"We needed extra time," she said.

Barcus pointed at the bullet holes in the belly of her dress.

"Change your clothes, at least."

***

Barcus was surprised Cine and Jude didn't go along. It turned out, they were superb with the cutting torches and easily climbed the huge machines in the back of the hangar. They needed raw materials to feed the fabricator, and that giant machine was it.

Work had to stop to cycle the airlock. When they were through it and leaving the moon, Barcus finally spoke.

"Where are we going?"

He was in the pilot's seat. Po was across the aisle from him in the front right, the co-pilot's seat. The dome was on full canopy, and the moon fell away at a rapid rate as they moved away from the planet.

"This system has five planets, including Baytirus. One of them is a gas giant in the outermost orbit. Head there," Wex said.

Po replied, "Do it, Stu."

With that word, they smoothly sped away.

"It will be a while before we get there. I recommend we get some rest. We all could use it," Barcus said.

The canopy dimmed, a bit, and the various status windows minimized. He reclined his seat fully and was asleep in less than a minute.

Po watched Barcus for a few minutes, and then turned to Wex.

"Do the thing. With me. What do you know about me?"

"I know very little. I do know one thing."

She looked at Barcus, deeply sleeping.

"All the world will believe he is the greatest mass murderer of all time."

Then she looked at Po.

"But he will not care. Because *you* will know the truth."

They sat, in silence, awhile.

"We'll all live then?" Po asked.

"No. Not all. But you and Barcus will survive. Knowing this will make you mighty. You will need to be."

Wex stood and moved to the ladder.

"He might save the world. But you will have to save him."

"What about you?" Po asked, just before she went down.

"It's lies and the long white for me."

CHAPTER ELEVEN: FLUTES AND GENOMES

"Those two, no three, would have been evidence enough to remove Chancellor Dalton decades ago. All we ever found was their blood and medical scans."

--Solstice 31 Incident Investigation Testimony Transcript: General Patricia Chase, senior member of the Earth Defense Coalition.

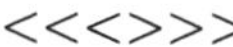

"Why wear that clothes?" Kuss said in her thick polish accent.

She was scolding Jude as if the black habit she wore offended her.

"You're not slave here. Beside, you need pockets."

Jude froze for a moment, and looked over at Cine—who also wore the habit—and smiled. Cine had the veil up as well as the habit. Jude and Kuss saw the smile in her dark eyes without the benefit of seeing her mouth.

She set down the cutting torch she was about to light. Cine lowered her veil, showing the very white teeth of her smile. She reached up and drew the veil and headpiece off in one swath motion.

Jude followed. Cine's smile was contagious. Kuss and Jude had them as well.

They reached behind their necks and freed a single button, and the habits fell to the floor. They both wore sleeveless, skintight jumpsuits. These suits were full of tight pockets. Kuss recognized the flutes that ran along their left thighs. She was surprised to see how many knives they were sporting.

They both had long, black braids that began as three separate ones. One began at each temple and another at their crowns. They scooped up their plasma torches and went up the side of the derelict machine, like monkeys in the low gravity.

Soon hunks of metal clunked to the floor.

They laughed.

***

"Moon base, come in. Tyrrell here with an update."

The comms on the *Memphis's* bridge came to life.

"You guys miss us already?" Jimbo replied, looking up from the repair schedule. Tyrell, Ibenez, Elkin, Weston and Shea were bringing the Salterkirk hangar base back into service as a backup base of operations.

"Be advised. Ibenez and Elkin have released the hounds. They already have a zeppelin on High Keeper Ronan's schedule. Weston and Shea are going to have a shopping list for you, if we ever begin regular trade with the outside. And, Rand has not killed anyone yet, even though Ronan's security forces are like first graders to her."

"The politics settle down yet?" Jimbo asked.

"Not even close, man. It's why I called, really."

Tyrrell spoke to someone in whispers as an aside.

"We wanted to ask if we could keep some more of the weapons. Maybe even a couple Warmarks."

"I think it's a good idea," Jimbo replied, immediately. "I think Rand should come up with Cook and go over the inventory. The drop ship had a massive amount of gear."

"It will also be a good test run for the *Limo*," Tyrrell answered.

"We will have the garage airlock open when the *Limo* gets here," Jimbo answered. "It will be a lot faster than cycling the main hangar."

"Roger that."

***

"Barcus, wake up. I think we are there," Po said, as he came back awake. "Here, drink this. Shaw said it was good for you, if you didn't puke."

She handed him a thermos.

He looked over his right shoulder just then. Wex stood just behind them. He knew she would be there. She wore a black many-pocketed flight suit. RAND was written on the name patch.

He screwed off the top, and the cabin filled with the smell of chicken soup.

Wex inhaled deeply, and said, "Ahh. Bone broth. Your doctor is smarter than you know."

Barcus poured some into the top that also served as a large cup. He breathed deeply from the steam and sipped as they approached the gas giant.

"It has seven moons of various sizes," AI~Stu said. "It is eleven percent larger than Jupiter, but is of the same type."

The display filled with tactical annotations as they approached, closer.

"What we are looking for is on the direct opposite side, away from Baytirus," Barcus said. "It's a ship. A big one."

"How do you know that?" Po asked.

She looked at him with a raised eyebrow.

"I have no idea."

He drank deeply from the rich broth now. He was starved.

"The planet. The sight of it. It reminded me, like I have been here before."

AI~Stu made a broad arc around the planet after it came into his view.

"What is its designation?"

"We most recently named her, the *Iosin*," Wex said.

They approached the ship at a thirty degree angle. It was configured like a single ring. There was a globe in the center of the ring, connected by a single arm, like a bicycle tire with a melon in the center, connected by a long pipe.

It all looked to be made out of dark gray stone.

Stats sprouted on every screen around the ship on the display.

"Stu, is this right?" Barcus said, incredulously. "This says it's 3,474.8 kilometers across."

"I have double checked my scans. The scale is correct." AI~Stu added information. "The ring is 121 kilometers tall and 103 kilometers thick. The sphere in the center is 257 kilometers in diameter and has a mass and density reading higher than that of Baytirus."

"Stu, look at these readings. This can't be right. It's configured like a Mass-Harvester but ten times bigger."

"The Mass-Harvesters are based on this basic design," Wex said.

"Then that center core holds all the harvested mass?" Barcus asked.

They flew closer and closer. A great, black wedge came into view as the only infrastructure on the massive ship.

A rendered, virtual model of the vessel appeared on the screen. It paused as if viewed from directly above, with the globe in the center, the arm that attached it to the ring straight down to the 6 o'clock position, and the wedge structure at high noon.

"Head there."

Wex indicated the wedge-shaped structure. It zoomed in on the screen.

"There is the main hangar. Land on the top level. I have no idea what the condition will be in there."

The hangar bay openings were giant gaping maws of darkness.

"The bay that is farthest from the core is the one we want."

They were closer now. Light, reflected from the planet, shone into the bays. They were full of ships. Hundreds of ships. Many kinds and sizes. Some of them Barcus even recognized from history books.

"There is gravity in this bay; .97G at this level. Set it down, Stu, as far back as you can," Wex said, as they passed the plane of the opening to the hangar.

As soon as they entered, lights came on all around. They glowed as if they were being turned up with a slow dimmer. The lights revealed how deep the space was. They kept flying in. There were ships of various configurations parked along each side. None of these were the ones Barcus recognized.

The back wall of the hangar was about two kilometers in. From floor to ceiling had to be 500 meters, at least.

"Barcus, we have atmosphere, pressure, and the right O_2 air mix," AI~Stu said.

"How? That door is still open to space, to vacuum back there. I can see it," Barcus stated.

"We passed through a gravity wall. It keeps the atmosphere in, but allows ships to pass through it without having to cycle an airlock," Wex said, matter-of-factly.

"Where did all these ships come from?" Po asked. "Do they work?"

"I don't know those answers. But so far, the *Iosin* seems functional," Wex said, as she pointed. "Stu, do you see that uppermost shelf there? The empty one. Let's park there."

Barcus was dumbfounded. The ship was so big; he was in shock.

"I don't want anyone to panic when the *Iosin* scans us. It will scan us all, even you, Stu."

Wex turned and headed for the ladder.

"If the ship is awake and doesn't decide to kill us. It will be interesting."

Po and Barcus exchanged glances. Barcus knew she was lying again.

Wex was down the ladder before they were unstrapped from their five-point harnesses.

The ramp lowered as Barcus helped Po down. When it had completely dropped, a piling rose up from the floor, and a flood of light briefly illuminated Wex. A voice spoke from all around them in a language only Wex understood.

But Barcus somehow knew it was a greeting and a welcome home.

When they stepped forward, they were flashed as well. Then, all of the STU was illuminated, for an instant.

"Welcome to the *Iosin*."

The voice sounded all around them and inside of them.

***

Richard Cook slid the *Limo* smoothly into the moon base's garage airlock.

"Damn, this little shuttle is sweet. It only took us three hours to get here. And in comfort."

Rand was not interested. She scanned the area, memorizing the features, trying to understand why she felt uneasy.

The chamber pressurized, and the inner door indicator turned green. They opened the gull wings and got out. When she opened the inner door into the hangar, she knew why she felt uneasy.

She saw the Warmarks.

They stood there, at attention, in a row. Some stood open, ready for a driver. Others loomed as if they were ready for the world to attack. Hagan inspected the Warmarks with Valerie Hume. There were cases of various weapons and attachments open there as well.

Ever since she had heard that those things had been on the *Ventura*, hidden in the *Memphis*, she felt uneasy.

She was a senior security chief on the survey ship. The single largest security issue had not been entrusted to her. Hagan had not known, and neither had Worthington.

What else was kept a secret?

She and Cook moved toward the *Memphis*, and Cook moon-hopped to the open ramp on the pinnace as he waved.

Rand greeted Hume without wanting to interrupt.

They had the control panel open on one of the Warmarks and a case open at their feet. It was not a weapons or accessories case but some kind of specialized medical device and supplies.

"It has an entire suite of specialty sensors that cannot be accessed unless you have the tailored HUD upgrade," Hagan told Hume.

"And you just injected? Not knowing what would happen?" she said. "That massive an upgrade usually requires a full med review prior to the update."

"Please understand, I was already dead."

Hagan looked lost at that moment. But only for a moment.

"I was going to launch the drop ship toward the planet. I was going to fly them all down, on remote, together, with the grave-chutes deactivated, into an unpopulated area. I didn't want anyone to find them, much less use them."

He seemed ashamed for his cowardice. Rand thought it was the bravest thing she had ever heard. Maybe because she knew that Hagan understood how lethal the Warmarks were.

"The thing is, the ECHO system must approve the Warmark control upgrade nanites and must be within range on install. Otherwise, they will kill the host, outright."

Hume looked up at Rand, shaking her head.

Rand said, "It's true. Warmark piloting is an exclusive unit."

She tapped the control screen, and nothing happened.

"With good reason."

Hagan looked from one to the other.

"Echo has already asked Worthington for volunteers."

"I'm in," came from Rand and Hume, at the same time.

***

Jude and Cine stopped working above and turned off their work lights, just to listen.

CHAPTER TWELVE: CHANGE OF PLAN

"The existence of the *Iosin* seed ship remains classified. Its origin and capabilities are also classified. Most classified of all is the fact that we had no idea where it was for the last thirty years."

--Solstice 31 Incident Investigation Testimony Transcript: General Patricia Chase, senior member of the Earth Defense Coalition.

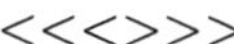

Barcus stood at the edge of the landing pad and casually sipped his chicken broth. There was no railing. It was about 300 meters down to the deck below. Wex and Po silently stood a few steps farther back from the edge.

His eye caught movement on a lower landing pad.

They looked like spiders of various sizes. Very much like the Emergency Modules, the EMs.

Po asked, "Didn't you say this ship has been parked out here for hundreds of years? How is it so clean?"

"There are maintenance-bots. Thousands of them, I bet. Millions maybe."

He looked at Wex, with anger in his eyes.

"These bots, their designs, the EMs are based on these. This ship, the grav-tech harvester ships are based on this design," Barcus stated.

He tipped up and emptied the thermos and looked out over the giant hangar bay. There were probably a hundred ships in there.

"Dammit," he said, and threw the thermos out into the hangar.

It barely came to rest when a few small bots scurried out and collected it and the handle that had broken off.

"What's wrong?" Po wondered.

She reached for Barcus, but he ignored her. He got right up into Wex's face.

"This is what they wanted. Isn't it?"

His whisper sounded more like a growl.

"They were tired of a trickle and wanted it all."

"Yes," Wex said, not intimidated. "Instead of them, I'm giving it all to you."

"Why?" Barcus asked.

His hand rested on the hilt of his Telis blade. Po's hand gently surrounded that wrist.

"Because of the long white. My one chance to end the war."

Wex turned and walked away.

***

Worthington called everyone into the conference room. Everyone showed, except Elkin, Ibenez, Tyrrell, Weston, and Shea. They were still on the planet.

He began, "I know everyone has been wondering why we decided to delay our departure."

Kuss suddenly raised her hand. Jimbo paused and gestured to her with his chin.

"No. No one wonder. If Worthington say delay, it's for good reason. No questions. Tell us or no, we still do what you need."

She sat back.

"Yes. Thank you, Kuss. I appreciate that."

He pressed a control, and the eleven Warmarks came up on the presentation board behind him for everyone to see.

"Most of you look at this and see just another modified maintenance suit, like the one that Barcus uses. More attachments but basically the same."

He looked around the room.

"You'd be right and also wrong."

"Warmarks, individually, are a devastating weapon. We have eleven."

He pressed a button, and lifeboat 4 came up.

"We also have their drop ship and a full complement of weapons, some of which not even Master Chief Randall has seen. Half of the weapons have been banned by treaties in all the united colony systems."

He let that sink in a minute before continuing. The weapons and specs cycled through, onscreen.

"Add to that an Extreme Combat Hellfire Operations system—an ECHO—and a fully trained team."

He knew everyone remembered the squad of soldiers assigned to the *Memphis* that had been killed that day. Everyone thought they were Marines. They were, in fact, Black Badgers.

"Echo is not the chattiest or most forthcoming AI system I have ever worked with, but it has shed a lot of light on recent events."

***

Barcus and Po followed Wex to the front wall of the bay. It wasn't vertical but curved and slanted at about forty-five degrees. They stepped into a clear globe with a dark, wide, flat floor. Barcus felt a tug in his brain. Not his vision really but some other sense.

It was an elevator. He knew, somehow.

It slid smoothly up the side of the hangar, until it entered the ceiling through a tunnel. A few hundred floors slid by as they moved up and forward. They saw they were rapidly decelerating, but they did not feel it.

The globe came to rest up through the floor in the center of a room about forty meters across; it was a perfect dome with no visible light source. Nine white sofas were arranged in a circle here. There was not a single particle of dust.

Barcus thought, *this was just like the HUD dome in the STU.* Just the thought activated it.

Unlike in the STU, the floor disappeared. It was as if the three of them were floating in space, in perfect 3D, in every direction. He gasped at the beauty of it all. He felt the heat of the distant sun and knew its temperature. He just KNEW the precise distance to the gas giant and the makeup of its atmosphere and even that it was called Afreet. He felt the solar wind on his body, heard every band of radio frequencies, and even sensed the silence when there was none. He was alive and swimming naked in outer space; and it was like he had been blind his whole life and now saw and felt and heard and tasted...everything.

"Barcus, what's wrong?"

Po had worry in her voice.

"Please sit, before you fall over."

Barcus looked at Po then, like he saw her for the first time. He slowly descended to one of the lounges there and slumped back.

"What's wrong?"

She was very worried.

"Please, talk to me."

"She can't...see any of it, Barcus."

Wex was there now, looking. She drew in a deep breath, and Barcus knew it was the pleasure and the comfortable coolness of space that she felt.

"I'm alright," Barcus stammered. "Why can't she see this?"

"She's not a Scarecrow."

***

Worthington stood.

"For the last few decades, the new colonization expansion has begun. I don't need to explain that to any of you because we all served on a deep space survey ship with the specific mission to check out planets that might be good for colonization. Better than the last expansion."

Worthington paced back and forth as he spoke.

"We wanted to avoid the overpopulation pressures that caused the last wave of colonization, the wars and subsequent isolation."

"So we no leave Earth again in a state that looks like house after frat party over," Kuss said.

Everyone laughed.

Cook said, "Kuss at a frat party? They never had a chance."

"Focus," Rand said, as a bit of anger slipped into her voice.

"That is actually the general idea." Worthington continued, "The last time, the uncontrolled exodus destroyed the economies on

Earth. Faction wars over race and religion skyrocketed as colonies on other planets were created to be 'pure' in several ways."

"Now, it's 230 years later. Earth has recovered; technology has advanced by leaps and bounds. Colonies have begun trading and even hold diplomatic relationships."

Jimbo sighed. He turned and looked at the images of the Warmarks.

Hume spoke. "These are third gen Warmarks, with an ECHO system behind them. All the pilots could be dead, and these things would keep fighting. There are two smart-nukes, in there."

She pointed over her shoulder at the drop ship.

"Nukes with names and personalities. And, they follow orders and even make their own decisions."

She stood.

"I do not recommend we wake them. They may have contingency orders."

"Just as I think it's all going really well, it turns out, people are always going to be assholes," Jimbo said.

"Wait a sec."

Hagan stood up.

"Let's just ask her."

"Who?" Kuss asked.

"Echo, have you been listening to our conversations?" Hagan asked, looking toward the drop ship.

"Yes, of course."

A small, dark-skin woman appeared behind Worthington. She wore a black military jumpsuit and had an ID badge hanging around her neck. A black badge with white lettering and a photo of her.

"Echo, your primary mission has been aborted, and we require information to determine our next course of action," Hagan stated.

Jimbo spoke, "What was your primary mission?"

Echo thought about the question a long time for an AI, before answering, "To follow the directions of Captain Alice Everett, no matter what she asked of me."

"Why?" Kuss asked. It caused Echo to tilt her head, like a cat.

"Captain Everett was operating under special orders from Admiral Krieger."

Echo turned and looked at the Warmarks.

"There were difficult tasks to be performed. Kreiger believed she needed the right tools for the job. It appears it was not that difficult, as they seemed to have been accomplished by a simple maintenance guy."

"What tasks, specifically?" Worthington asked.

"Terminate Dalton's genome project and ensure it cannot be restarted," Echo stated.

"Dalton? Do you mean Chancellor Dalton?" Worthington asked.

She nodded her head and did not stop talking.

"Discover how the chancellor was eliminating entire ships and crews."

She turned and met Jim's eyes.

"And recover one or more Scarecrows."

"Wex is a Scarecrow," Hagan said. "Barcus saw another one in the Citadel, just before it was destroyed."

"Scarecrow?" Cook asked.

"The literal translation is *protectors of the gardens,*" Echo replied, including the verbose words in the original language.

Kuss scoffed, "Get it now. Retards back home too stupid to use new word."

"Captain, there was an additional order," Echo said. "Recover the *Iosin*, if possible. Wex's ship. It is where she is, right now, with Barcus."

"How do you know that?" Jimbo asked.

"Stu is keeping me up-to-date," Echo answered. "By the way, we also have orders to stop her from destroying Earth."

***

"Barcus, do you remember the conversation we had about the status panel and all its green lights on the *Sedna*? How its status display was hacked with an old-school log loop and not real?" Wex asked, out of the blue.

"Sure, you wanted to be able to help on the bridge so we could...give rest…" Barcus faded off. "We haven't had that conversation...yet?"

"Breathe," Wex said, as he clasped the sides of his head.

"What is happening to me?"

He doubled over, as if in pain. Po rushed to him.

"No..."

Barcus gasped when he looked into Po's eyes.

"No..." He took her by the shoulders. "What did you do?"

He glared at Wex.

"Things will remind you. Or *pre-mind* you," Wex said. "Just as you can focus on events of the past and remember them, if you will begin to focus on the future..." Wex said.

"I'll *pre-member*?" Barcus asked. He looked at Wex and then to the circle of sofas.

"Iosin will explain it, in detail. Here," Wex said.

He fell to his knees under the weight of it.

"It will be alright." Po reassured him. She put her arms around his neck and straddled him in a full body hug, like a child. "We will get through it, together."

He brushed her hair from her face. He saw far more than she knew.

"We will." Barcus choked out. He looked to Wex, who was already nodding her head. "They'll blame me, for all of it."

"And even that will save billions of lives in the horror of the aftermath," Wex said.

"I will have to lie to them all," Barcus said.

"But not to her. She will lie to you, though, and break promises," Wex said, as if Po wasn't there.

She paused. "To save them all."

CHAPTER THIRTEEN: The Seed Ship

"All that we knew regarding the truth of the seed ship, the *Iosin*, was destroyed on December 22, 2631. It was contained in the main computer AI on a secret research base. That base was on Rhea, a moon of Saturn. We did not even find records of that base. There was only the word of a single survivor that did not come forward for over twenty years."

--Solstice 31 Incident Investigation Testimony Transcript: General Patricia Chase, senior member of the Earth Defense Coalition.

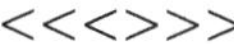

Barcus collapsed back onto one of the command sofas. Po helped him through an internal crisis in ways she didn't understand. He held her gaze as well as her face. Their noses were only a hand's span apart. She saw his intense focus on her as he spoke to Wex.

"Is it true? What I see?" he asked.

"It is what will happen before you. It remains to be seen if it is the truth," Wex said, as she casually circled to the command area.

"I will not curse you through eternity," he whispered to Po. "But you will pound my chest a time or two."

"The two of you must remember this most of all."

She stopped circling, for emphasis.

"You cannot tell them. Not even a hint. Not for proof, or pride, or to save their lives, because nothing can do that."

That was when Barcus looked at Wex. He knew what she was going to do, all from a single glance. All her lies revealed.

"I see now." He *pre-membered.*

Po spoke into his ear as he studied Wex more carefully. "What is the long white?"

"Every now and then it's like fog ahead on the road. Hiding what's beyond. It's like sleep. It's sanity. It's a lie," he said to Wex.

Barcus turned back to Po. "Promise you will never speak of it again, even if it is mentioned in your presence."

"I promise," she said, instantly.

"Let's get moving. You have got to see this," he said.

Barcus lifted Po to her feet quickly. They all walked toward the lift with purpose.

***

Worthington, Cook, Kuss, and Hume stood around a large hole in the dock's flight deck, where a service plate had been removed.

"It's a good damn thing you didn't try that crazy maneuver with the *Memphis* in this condition," Hagan said, as he climbed out of the access hatch near the center of the engineering section.

"Six of the central keel beams are broken. Not cracked, not bent, broken."

Hagan took a long pull of water from a bottle Kuss handed him.

"I have never seen a ship this damaged still fly. The debris impact that tore through here must have cracked the beams, and it looks like stress on all the landing struts broke all but two of them." Richard Cook shook his head, remembering the feel of the first emergency landing.

The scan of the damaged infrastructure came up as a giant display in their HUDs.

"If I had tried the lateral cartwheel to get through that hole in the sensor web, the entire ship would have just folded and then broken up."

Cook shook his head.

"So, we fucked then. No *Memphis.* It now just power plant for base and shitty bunks," Kuss said, growing mad.

"I didn't say that." Hagan got to his feet.

"It depends on what else needs repairs. We have a fabricator. It would take time; but we could sister the breaks, and it would work. It's never going to fly FTL again, but it would be OK between the moon and Baytirus and even in the entire solar system."

"The *Sedna* is our best bet for getting back to Earth in one piece," Hagan said, wiping his hands off on his too baggy overalls.

Worthington added, "The *Sedna* might be better for other reasons as well." Jim looked out the cargo ramp at the *Sedna.*

"No one is looking for the *Sedna.* The *Memphis*, on the other hand, is expected."

He looked at them, until they understood.

"Expected by the people that destroyed the *Ventura.*"

This comment killed all conversation.

"Any word from Barcus, Captain?" Kuss asked. She was unusually formal.

"None." He ran his hand through his hair. "Stu has been off-line the last twenty-four hours as well."

The group followed him down the ramp toward the *Sedna.*

"He has two more days."

None of them noticed Cine or Jude in the shadows of the ramp, listening.

***

The lift took them all back to the flight deck where the STU was parked. As they entered the command deck, the canopy was already 'open' and Stu's avatar stood, looking out over the giant hangar.

"Lady Wex," Stu asked in a very formal, polite way, "how did the *Iosin* come by all these ships?"

Stu looked over his shoulder to her, as he continued.

"I count 112, just in my field of view here. I only recognize a few makes and models. And, this is just one hangar of many."

Wex stood and looked, toward Stu, out over the hangar.

"Some were collected as abandoned, some were purchased, some came here with violence and pillage intent. Most, actually. Only a few were rescues. Not many. The *Iosin* was not in that business."

"Barcus, what's wrong?" Po asked him.

She felt him tense again, in realization of something.

He looked at Wex again, as he spoke to Po. "It's the *Iosin.* The ship. It has an AI. It is an AI. But I am not sure artificial is the word

I would use. It's an intelligence. More like a being than a computer, even an advanced one."

"It doesn't even know we are here. Rather, it doesn't care," Wex said, casually.

"Doesn't mind may be a better way to put it," Stu said, "If it did mind, we'd discover those spiders do more than just maintenance around here."

Stu gestured with his chin. The floor of the hangar, far below, was covered with thousands of cat-sized, unmoving, identical spiders.

"Close it up, Stu. We are taking a tour," Barcus said.

He sat in the pilot's seat but didn't buckle in. It was the first time Po had ever seen Barcus be so casual about it. The STU was aloft even before the ramp closed and moved toward the ceiling. The vast hangar had a giant door that slid aside. Blue sky and bright sunlight was seen beyond.

The door was only about ten percent open when the STU flew through it into the sunlight.

"How is this possible?" Po gasped. They flew over water. Behind them, the opening closed and became sky once again.

"This is all inside the ship?"

"Yes," Stu replied, directly.

They flew, in silence, toward the horizon. Po slowly settled into the co-pilot's seat, as land was spotted in the distance.

"Stu, give me a tactical," Po said, slowly, incredulously.

The display came up, and they were inside the great ring of the ship. Their vista was 101 km wide and 10,900 km in circumference.

"The horizon seems much farther away than is possible. And down is toward that globe in the center of the ring."

Po was amazed.

Barcus was silent and looked like he was visiting home.

"Above, and all around, is just like the canopy in here," Wex said, as they flew over the rocky cliffs of the shore.

Mountains, with dense forest and rivers, filled the land below. Mountains became foothills and the river, planes. Wildlife was rich, and the plants all flourished.

The climates changed as they flew hundreds of kilometers. In some places it rained, and in others it was arid. It was a perfect, closed ecosystem.

"Stu, please find a space where we can set down for a meal," Barcus said, and stood.

He watched rivers and lakes roll beneath them in the green.

Stu found a beautiful spot where small goats were trimming the lawn, like feral lawn mowers, next to a large, freshwater lake. They carried food and drink out to a stone outcropping that made a perfect bench, overlooking the lake.

"This seed ship is how Baytirus was terraformed," Barcus said. It was a statement. "The trees, the animals, even the bees."

"Yes," Wex said, as she took a bite of a simple ham and cheese sandwich.

"What was there, before? What if they can't live together? Foxes and chickens," Po asked.

"The planet is typically reset," Wex said, absently.

"Reset? How?" Po asked.

"It's easier than one can imagine. Just draw down an asteroid with enough inertia and it is reset. Not enough to displace the atmosphere mind you, but enough to kill off all the dominant species. Then, you seed it with the right plants and animals. If you can, stand there and see the results, before your first action; it's very easy."

"You are gardeners. Scarecrows. Watching over them. Seeding them and watching them grow. Knowing how they turn out even as you begin?" Po asked, "Why?"

Wex looked at Barcus and then over the lake, without answering for a full minute. "If you were immortal, what would you do?"

***

"Jimbo, I have no idea how this ship, these reactors, this whole thing is still here," Hagan said to Jimbo, in his private office on the *Memphis*. He tossed three devices onto his desk as if they were dead rats.

"What are these? They look like control system relays," Worthington said, while picking one up. "But isn't this a wireless module, in addition to the hard line interfaces?"

"I never would have noticed them had I not been down there looking at the infrastructure damage," Hagan said.

He let the next natural question form in Worthington's head. It would save explaining it.

"What is this wireless interface keyed to?" Jimbo's eyebrow went up.

"It was set for dedicated encrypted comms with Mia, the *Memphis's* AI."

Hagan leaned over and picked one up.

"An instruction set was on the chip. Overload and suppress the ejection of the core."

"Dammit. This just gets better and better. Mia could have sent it a command sequence and not even know what would happen?"

Jimbo stood and paced behind his deck, even though there was only three meters to do it.

"Jimbo, if that first massive chunk of debris had not taken out Mia…"

He left the statement hanging.

"We may have been dead anyway."

"Have you discussed this with Ben?"

Jimbo sat.

"Yes. I had to. He discovered the hardware-based code instructions," Hagan said.

"Ben, tell him your theory."

Ben's avatar appeared in the second chair before he spoke.

"If Mia had not been destroyed, we would have headed straight back for Earth. It is likely that we would have encountered another large survey ship or carrier on the way; and, as a good Captain, you would have requested assistance and brought the *Memphis* aboard."

Ben paused.

"It's speculation, but if their goal was mayhem, they could have detonated the ship inside another, or even docked to Freedom Station, or on the tarmac of the Sri Lanka spaceport."

"And blame you," Hagan added.

"Wes, the *Memphis* was just swapped out six months ago. The drop ship and now this?"

Worthington brought up the schematic of the *Memphis*.

"I have the whole team going over it with a fine-tooth comb. I should get back."

Hagan stood just as Worthington's comms unit chimed.

"Jimbo, Barcus just checked in. He's on his way back," Karen Beary said. "ETA is about four hours."

"Acknowledged."

CHAPTER FOURTEEN: THE *MEMPHIS* REPAIRS

"When they began to look more closely at the *Memphis*, a bigger picture started to form. They were more than just lucky to have survived up to that point."

--Solstice 31 Incident Investigation Testimony Transcript: General Patricia Chase, senior member of the Earth Defense Coalition.

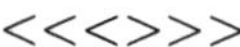

The STU came into the main hangar. All work stopped, and the hangar pressure cycled so they could come in. The whole process took about thirty minutes. Without orders, everyone took advantage of the time to take a shower or get a quick meal.

By the time it was re-pressurized, Hagan and Worthington were walking across the vast floor to the STU as the ramp slowly lowered. There were nine pallets of what looked like light gray bricks in Stu's cargo hold. Each pallet was about two meters on a side. Barcus picked up one of the bricks as he walked by.

Descending the ramp, he tossed it to Hagan. He almost didn't catch the brick, fumbling it. He had expected it to be much heavier. Even in the low gravity, it felt unnaturally light but hard at the same time.

"What is it?" He turned it over in his hands a few times, then tossed it to Jimbo.

Worthington caught it in one hand, easily. Before he could say anything it deployed eight legs and a couple arms and started to look around from obvious eye stalk cameras.

"This looks like one of the maintenance-bots. I've never seen one quite like this," Worthington said. He then looked into the hold of the ship. There were thousands of them on the pallets.

"Toss it here."

Barcus held out a hand, and Jimbo tossed it. Instead of catching it, Barcus sidestepped and let it fall to the floor. It didn't just fall. It decelerated and landed perfectly.

"Don't units like this need an AI to drive them?" Hagan asked.

"Not these kind. They work together with a kind of hive mentality," Wex said. "They can be guided by an AI, or by people with verbal commands, or can just be left to their own volition, working together or independently. They fight entropy."

"Fight entropy?" Jimbo asked.

"They fix things. It's what they do." Po smiled.

"Watch this. Pallet one, activate."

The perfectly stacked, two meter cube of bricks dissolved and expanded into a nightmarish swarm of gray spiders. They boiled out of the cargo bay, moving around Wex, Barcus, and Po, out into the hangar. Their feet clicked quietly on the floor; and together it made a white noise, until they stopped in ranks, a formation, on the vast floor.

"You better tell the crew, so they don't freak the hell out," Hagan said, as he looked back into the cargo hold at the other eight pallets.

"What can they do?" Jimbo asked, a bit uncertain still.

"Everything, if they have the time," Wex said.

"Are you cool with this?" Worthington's question was directed at Hagan.

"I have a couple of maintenance droids on the drop ship that were obviously based on this design. They do require Echo to drive them. If these little guys can make coffee as well, I'm totally cool with them. Besides, what the hell?" He looked at Barcus for confirmation.

"What the hell. Try them anyway," Barcus answered. Then added, "Look, I need some soup and then to lie down, for about twelve hours."

"All hands report to the hangar deck," Worthington said, over the HUD comms. "Ben, have you been monitoring this?"

Ben's avatar walked from between the pallets.

"Yes, sir. I already have a secure protocol handshake request from the first unit you activated. Shall I accept?"

Jimbo looked at Barcus and Hagan. They were both nodding yes.

"Why not? Do it. We are already so far beyond specs here, I don't even know." Jimbo tossed his hands in the air.

"Sir, this is interesting," AI~Ben said. "They use the same communications method as the Briggs, Udvar, Green surveillance BUGs." Ben was the Artificial Intelligence unit that was salvaged from the Emergency Module on the *Memphis*. He was installed to replace AI~Mia, the *Memphis* AI.

"I'm starting to get a picture here," Worthington said, as he looked at Ben.

***

The team took the gray spiders in stride. Just another new tool. They decided to simply call them grays. By the time Barcus awoke, all nine pallets had been activated. A total of 3,600 grays in all. Barcus had no idea where they all went. He saw a few combing over the outsides of the *Memphis*, the *Sedna*, and even the STU.

"There you are," Po said to Barcus, from behind. She held a large, steaming mug of soup in her hand.

"If you hadn't awakened soon, I was planning to wake you." She smiled, the implication was clear. She held up the mug.

He didn't take it.

"There's something wrong," he said.

Unfamiliar alarms sounded from all around. Barcus held his hand out to stop Po from darting away. He laid one hand on her shoulder and took the soup.

"We lost pressure in dome number three. The grays just discovered it. Everyone's fine." He sipped the soup. "You added more chicken."

Po noticed the alarm came from the grays. All the grays.

He looked over his shoulder. "Dome three, two airlocks in. The third held, though. Don't worry."

She didn't worry. If Barcus was fine, so was she.

"It's the *pre-membering*, isn't it?" Po whispered.

He nodded.

"Will some of them die?" she asked.

He nodded again, sadness clouding his eyes.

"But not today."

"You can't stop it?" she asked, as the alarm silenced.

"That's the worst thing. It's like it already happened."

"What about me?" She was clearly terrified by her own question.

He said nothing, but his wide smile said all she ever wanted to hear.

Broadcast HUD comms came on. Worthington spoke.

"We have a breach in dome three. It cascaded through two inner doors, but the third airlock held."

***

The chancellor of Earth spent most of his time at his private residence on Calf Island. It occupied the entire island which had been leveled specifically to create several square kilometers as a foundation for his fortress. No roads led to it by land. All supplies, and visitors, had to arrive by air. Traffic was controlled for hundreds of kilometers in every direct.

He took pride in the fact that the entire residence was a weapon-free zone. No hand carried weapons of any kind on the grounds. No armor, no scanners, no AIs were allowed, either. Except his, of course. AI-controlled turrets of every kind were hidden everywhere, except the innermost sections. The chancellor didn't even trust his own bodyguards with weapons in there. He always carried his, concealed inside his robes.

Chancellor Dalton watched, via remote security cameras, as his shuttle softly landed in the posh courtyard below the main entrance. Other people's shuttles were never allowed to land there. Dalton would send his private ship. He didn't watch on a HUD, because he didn't have one. He was secretly phobic regarding nanite-based implant technology. He was paranoid about them. He had seen what his people could do to his enemies by subverting implants.

A woman emerged first, wearing a black business suit that still managed to showcase her beautiful legs. She scanned the surrounding area, like a predator; and with a subtle nod, a man emerged from the shuttle and repeated her examination of the area.

When they both nodded in unison, another man left the shuttle on the far side toward the view. All three nodded, and the president of the North American Union emerged. The region he governed came up on a built-in monitor, on the huge console before him. He called it the bench. It was part throne, part judge's desk, and was designed to intimidate everyone that visited this ornate room.

The floors were polished marble, and the walls were paneled in ornately carved oak. The ceiling was an amazing dome of stained glass. The chancellor's desk was raised like a judge's bench and deep mirrored black, he sat on a high-back chair, a throne.

There were no seats for visitors.

The three guests entered the building, following an elderly man dressed in all white. As they walked through the nave, lights turned red, and a delicate chime sounded.

A guard stepped up and led them to the side of the room where another guard sat behind a table.

"Please, leave all your weapons and electronic devices here."

The two bodyguards looked at their president; he nodded and began to empty his pockets. The guard was surprised that the NAU president had two handguns on his person.

The table was soon covered with handguns, extra magazines, a small laser cutter, several knives, and other devices.

The guard replied, "Thank you. You may pick these up, here, on the way out."

They turned and followed the tottering man to the next set of double doors that opened, automatically, before them.

The lights in that room also turned red, and the chime sounded. The setup was much the same, but these men were less polite and pleasant.

"Please remove all body armor, and completely empty your pockets. Remove your shoes; they have metal in them."

All three took off their suit coats and kicked off their shoes as they tossed keys, coins, pens and notepads, wallets, and belts onto the table.

They stood there as the guard pointed at the woman's skirt and the man's pants.

"All body armor."

Rolling her eyes, she unzipped the back of her skirt and let it just fall to the floor, leaving her standing there barefoot, in a white sleeveless silk top, and black lace panties. The male bodyguard followed suit, dropping his pants; and then, the president took off his leather vest and folded it neatly on the table.

They moved to the third set of double doors. Before she could pass him, a guard stopped her with a hand held out to her sternum. He ripped open her blouse, revealing a white lace bra and a ceramic knife, hanging on a fine braided silk cord, handle down. She drew it off over her head and casually handed it to the guard. The male guard went first, the president second, and finally the woman.

When she entered, Chancellor Dalton smiled as the lights again turned red; but the alarm was not a small chime this time, it was a harsh but brief siren. He watched as a massive guard grabbed her around the throat with both hands as two more guards each grabbed an arm and all three slammed her against the wall. Dalton couldn't believe she remained conscious, it was so hard.

A small guard stepped up and placed a complex tool beneath her left bicep and cruelly attached it. With a sick, clicking, saw sound, she screamed as the prosthetic arm tore away from her shoulder. Blood splashed onto the white marble as she struggled, but it was only from the dermal layers.

"She stays here," the short guard said, casually.

They reluctantly turned and followed the old man to the next room through a door to the right this time.

There they waited for three hours and twelve minutes.

CHAPTER FIFTEEN: THE DRIVE FACTORY

"The means, methods, processes, and designs of the Harvesters is highly classified. I am very reluctant to have any of this technology openly discussed here."

--Solstice 31 Incident Investigation Testimony Transcript: General Patricia Chase, senior member of the Earth Defense Coalition.

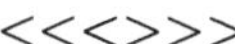

"How the hell did you two get up here? The hatch was damaged and welded shut." Worthington crossed the top of the *Sedna* and approached the leading edge of the ship that overlooked the vast hangar. "Are you OK, man? You kind of look a little worse."

Barcus had his head in Po's lap. He was pale again.

"I ate too much and overdid it," he said, weakly.

"At least there was no blood in his vomit, this time," Po said, as she brushed her hair out of his eyes. He made no attempt to sit up when speaking to Jimbo.

"You should let Dr. Shaw look you over again. Just for the science of it, if she can't help you." Worthington sat down, hung his long legs over the edge. His coveralls were already dirty; the fine dirt that came off the ship didn't bother him.

"Ben says the grays are doing great work, but they don't convey their method back to Ben very well. It's kind of creepy," Worthington said, uncharacteristically. "They can extrude repair materials, like bees making a beehive. Like fabrication in place."

"How do they know what to do, if Ben isn't telling them?" Po asked.

"They somehow requested the full schematics for the ships. Suddenly, they were working on them."

Jimbo shook his head.

"They started fixing everything, from hull breaches, in various compartments—reinforcing weak spots that might have failed in flight—to live power conduits repair. I can't understand the priority order they choose."

"We have been watching them eat the old machines."

Po pointed to the giant derelict hulking maker machine in the back of the hangar. Spiders marched to it, periodically, restocking with material to do repairs. Wex, Cine, and Jude cut chunks off and tossed them down for the grays as well as out to people for our fabricator.

"I just wish I had a better idea of how long this will take," Worthington said.

"In six days, we will take 400 grays and fifty Javelins from pods to the hangar base, and they will begin putting it in order while we are gone. Three days after that, we will leave 3,000 more grays here to care for this base," Barcus said. He rose up, onto one elbow, to drink some water Po offered. "Then, you will order me to take us all to the *Iosin* and this all gets really interesting." He laid his head back down.

Worthington looked out over the hangar as Barcus spoke. Pools of light scattered about as the grays provided light as they worked.

"You know I trust you, Barcus. I know there is some really weird shit going on with you. Can you tell me anything more?"

"Have you ever seen a Harvester ship?" Barcus asked, already knowing the answer.

"Yes. My first duty as an ensign was on an old troop transport that was converted to a prisoner transport to the Harvesters. I actually got to see thirteen of them. They are huge."

Jimbo seemed uncomfortable.

"We'd drop people off and pick up the finished grav-cores. Mostly the grape-sized ones used in grav-plating and foils. Sometimes full-sized, mass drives."

"What happen to the prisoners?" Po asked. "Did you pick them up as well when their sentences were completed?"

"In the eighteen months I served, we picked up only one. The Harvesters move at near the speed of light while out. He said he had worked in the Harvester factory for ten years, perceived time. He was fit and healthy and in good humor, at first. Until he discovered 312 years had passed on Earth, he was broke, and the economy had tanked. Everyone he ever knew was dead," Jimbo added. "He would be dead before his friends from the Harvester were released. Even with longevity treatments."

"Most of them just stay. It's not a bad life," Barcus said.

"Why did you ask?" Jimbo watched him slowly sit up, with Po's help.

"Because in nine days we will go to the *Iosin*, and it is very much like a Harvester. Just as the grays are like the EMs. The *Iosin* will take us back to the Sol system."

"Relativistic speeds? How long?" Worthington asked, not questioning how he knew.

"We will arrive in December of 2631," Barcus said.

"My wife will be pleased. I'll be home two years before I am expected." Jimbo wasn't smiling. He knew it would be over two years that she had not heard a word via quantum comms.

"Your family is safe. Just shave that beard before you see them." Barcus laughed, holding his belly.

***

Six days later, the 400 gray spiders seemed to already know they were going to the surface and what they were taking. The pod that housed the Javelin nuclear missiles had been quietly unloaded and, somehow, precisely split in half. With the Javelins returned to it they were loaded onto the STU by the grays that settled and functioned as a pallet as the other units strapped it down.

Worthington stood on the ramp of the STU, addressing everyone. They had all showed up to see them off.

"We will be back tomorrow. Try not to blow anything up while we're gone."

Just then, one of the Warmarks walked up. The top opened, and it was Hume driving it.

"Barcus said he wasn't up for the trip and recommended I go along with DS-06." She climbed in the STU and the ramp closed.

The flight was smooth and direct; and as they entered the atmosphere, they received a hail from Ronan.

“Good morning, Captain.” Ronan in his casual way, said, “I thought you'd be gone by now.”

Stu pinpointed the origin of the transmission and saw that it was Exeter.

“A few more days,” Worthington replied, in his best professional voice. “Can I be of service?”

“Actually, yes. It appears I have been the victim of a rather large conspiracy. I am currently at the northern residence in Exeter.”

Stu brought a visual up on long-range optical. Ronan's palace seemed to be surrounded by a vast crowd. It cannot be called an army, but there are about 10,000 people closing in.

“They knew to wait until the moon had set and the relay went dark. The shuttle pilots just took off, with both shuttles. Then, this mob just emerged. I've never seen anything like it. Even if the house guards used every arrow, we will still be overrun. This is a home, not a fortress.”

“We can be there in three minutes to evacuate you and your family,” Jimbo stated.

“No. I can't leave the staff to this fate. Do we have any other options?” Ronan asked.

“I believe we do.”

Jimbo looked at Hume and smiled.

***

The west garden had been surrounded with a great iron fence. It was topped with beautifully shaped florets. But it could not withstand the crush of people with hammers. They spilled in, like a raging flood over the banks of a river. The residence was too far away for them to just scream and run toward it. So, the crowd moved slowly, like a storm front. People, armed with bows and swords, moved to the leading edge. Someone in the mob was the first to notice. There was a white streak in the sky, something falling. The thing struck the ground hard, less than a hundred paces before the crowd.

"You should be running," said a voice that boomed like thunder. It was incredibly loud.

Their advance faltered. A few men screamed and attempted to drive the others forward. Another called for the archers to aim and fire.

Thousands of arrows bounced off DS-06, as its plasma cannons deployed over each shoulder. Two thick, blinding beams of light tore into the ground ten feet in front of the crowd. It left a trench a dozen feet deep in front of the attackers, with a pool of magma burning at the bottom.

This was enough to make half the crowd break and run. The trench had burned an arc 200 meters wide into the ground. Another volley of arrows came. A few of the mob tried to jump across the molten ground, some even made it. They were allowed to approach a little closer at a run, before they were mowed down with projectile weapons fire that was loud and frightening as it poured from the forearms of the Warmark.

The rest of the crowd ran. Fire flowed around a group of more disciplined forces, like a river around a boulder. It was obviously the leader and command staff. A grenade was launched into its center, leaving only a crater.

A shuttle flew overhead and deployed a huge cylinder with a parachute over the residence. The Warmark destroyed it with a single shot, but did not destroy the shuttle, even though it could have easily.

Hume opened a channel.

"Captain, the crowd has been dispersed with minimal loss of life. I made a big mess, though."

"I can see that," Jimbo said. "Ronan, come in. The main body of the attackers has been sent packing. What is your status?"

"I watched the whole event from the west tower. Remind me to never piss off that soldier," Ronan said, as DS-06 turned and faced the tower.

In one great leap, it flew up 300 meters into the air in a long arc, landing softly on top of the west tower, right behind a startled Ronan.

The top of DS-06 opened, and Hume climbed out. A Frange carbine on a single point sling came out with her from its storage.

"Hello, Ronan. Nice to see you again."

He relaxed and smiled. "I should have known."

Hume extended her hand for him to shake, letting the carbine hang in front of her flat stomach. He shook her hand.

"We are coming in to the private pad. You might tell them to hold their fire." Worthington's voice came from the Warmark. Ronan nodded to Burke and he turned and spoke into a radio.

"Are you going to be alright here? We can evacuate you to the East Isles. The STU can hold a couple hundred, in a pinch."

"I have two shuttles en route from there now. Both full of troops. Enough to tip the balance, if they come back. They would never attack East Isles. They're testing me, though. So soon. Do you think I will have to use a nuke to make them behave?" he joked.

"It's your planet. Don't break it," she said, as they saw the STU fly over and quietly land on the pad.

***

"Barcus, I talked to Ben, the *Memphis's* AI, about relativistic effects," Po said, as they lay naked together in their bunk.

"Jesus, Po. Weren't you a slave that couldn't read a few days ago?" Barcus laughed and instantly regretted it, holding his belly.

"Don't change the subject; we'll talk about Jesus later. Nobody talks about him, but everyone mentions him. A lot." Po shook her head, getting back on topic. Barcus felt the entire length of her naked body next to him.

"Time is not constant? It will seem like only a few days, but it will really be nineteen months?" she asked.

"Yes. And that won't even get us close to home, just a tiny fraction of the way. Most of the trip, we will be using FTL drives," he confirmed.

"Our weight will grow to infinity?"

"Not our weight, our mass. Like the Harvesters, the *Iosin* will control containment for the plates and drives while their mass is almost infinite."

"So the grav-plates under our feet are controlled by adjusting the containment field, not by controlling the gravity."

Po was getting aroused.

Maybe the pain was not that bad...

CHAPTER SIXTEEN: THE ONION OF CONSPIRACY

"Barcus had insights that made the entire picture clear for us. It gave us a massive advantage, really. Otherwise, we would have just walked right back into a meat grinder."

--Solstice 31 Incident Investigation Testimony Transcript: Captain James Worthington, senior surviving member of the Ventura deep space survey ship.

"Let me get this straight," Hagan said to Barcus, quietly. "You know about the classified Echo mission?"

"Yes. I think I know the whole picture now." Barcus sat down on a tool chest, next to the strut where Hagan was working on the *Memphis*. He put his head in his hands with his elbows on his knees.

"You can't tell Jimbo. A lot of people will die if you do." Hagan looked over his shoulder.

"Look, Echo implied the same thing. Who else knows? I could be executed for this."

"Just me and Wex," Barcus said, still holding his head, not looking up. "She won't say a word, won't even speak to you in advance. About anything."

"You guys are killing me." Hagan whispered angrily, "That Echo has two smart nukes. Not just smart, aware. I hate those. They autonomously decide when the best time to go off really is, based on predetermined priorities, set by SOMEONE ELSE!" He looked around again.

"Wes, you ever study temporal physics?"

Barcus held up his hand, stopping him. "Yes. At MIT, I know. You thought it was all theoretical bullshit. You were in your '*everything is bullshit*' phase, except for practical engineering. I know you remember Eve Lancaster."

Hagan's eyes went a little wide.

"You ever tell me about her? Ever tell anyone about her?"

Hagan just stared at him, incredulously.

"She was a temporal physics major, working on her PhD thesis on temporal evidence verification."

Barcus stood slowly and moved closer, whispering.

"She told you one day someone would approach you and know you had that conversation with her. And more to the point, know that she was fucking you in her car at the time."

Barcus paused, in case he wanted to say anything. He was in shock.

"You ever tell anyone that?"

Barcus raised an eyebrow.

"You ever tell anyone that she got pregnant that night and had an abortion without telling you, until after?"

Hagan staggered backward as if Barcus had struck him.

"That isn't even the proof part. I could have gotten all that info from her."

Barcus moved closer again.

"Did you ever tell anyone you were in love with her? That she is why you never had another serious relationship, ever, sixty years later."

Hagan was in shock.

"You ever tell anyone any of that?"

Hagan's head shook, side to side, slowly. His full realization sunk in.

"You will tell me one day, the whole story. And more. Even the embarrassing part."

***

Wex watched Barcus talking to Hagan by the front strut of the *Memphis*. She was high up on the old shell of the Maker, in the darkness.

Jude spoke in the darkness.

"Will he be a kind master?"

"He will be far kinder than I," Wex replied.

"How do we serve a master that asks nothing of us? Requires nothing other than which he can do himself," Cine replied.

"Simply carry the same goals. It will be a lighter burden...soon," Wex said.

"Po will help you, and push you, and show you the way," Wex said. "She will show you ALL the way."

"She was made the best they could make her."

Jude's odd accent was thick again.

"And they never knew."

"While they were distracted doing that, they didn't notice their house was on fire," Cine added.

***

"Rand and Hume, please report to the *Memphis* main conference room. The captain would like to speak to you," Ben said, formally, over their HUD comms.

"Acknowledged," Rand said, simply.

They were together, working with the grays that had just completed restoring the seals on the PT-137 quad shuttle.

"Uh-oh. We've been called to the principal's office. Now, what did we do?" Hume said.

"I swear to God, I haven't killed anyone all day."

Rand threw her hands up, after she pressed the control and closed the gull wing door on the PT-137. The new seals sounded very different as the door compressed the last centimeter closed. Six gray spiders scrambled out just before the door closed.

They walked across the hangar, toward the *Memphis*, as they heard the doors open again and more spiders crawled over the craft, inside and out.

"Have you seen them stack up and make larger machines?" Hume asked, as they walked. "They can assemble into an approximation of a human. Creepy but they can get things done fast."

"Hagan says they each have a grav-cell inside. The grape-sized ones," Rand said.

"I am so glad I am not an engineer. This shit would creep me out even worse if I knew how complicated it really was," Hume said, as they ascended the ramp. The lights were bright in the dock, and the spiders were everywhere. The place had never been so clean.

"The little bastards use dirt and debris as ingest for their mini fabrication units. Even the stuff they cut away. No waste."

"I swear, if we gave them enough time, they could eat this entire ship and make a whole other ship," Rand said, but it didn't seem to amuse either of them.

They entered the conference room and Worthington immediately waved for them to be seated. He picked up his mug of tea for a sip but realized it was empty.

"Hume, good work yesterday with the Warmark. Restraint. Good work." Worthington rubbed his face, hard, with both hands.

"Ronan wants one of the Warmarks. I cannot, in good conscience, leave one of those things here with him. If the wrong person gets ahold of it they could burn down this entire planet."

"Ronan can already do that, sir. With nukes," Rand noted.

"Yes, I know. More reason to refuse. I want to know what you think of this compromise." Jimbo gestured, and a list was projected of conventional weapons.

"These are all simple projectile weapons. Enough to outfit two platoons."

Hume studied the list.

"Plus, the PT-137 with the dual 10mm cannons."

She saw it in the list.

"Yes. Air support," Jimbo said, waiting. "Your thoughts?"

"This will make Ronan the most powerful man on this planet," Rand stated flatly.

"Not quite. I want to leave two Warmarks in our base at Salterkirk," Hume said, reminding them that Salterkirk was the hangar base in the north that was above a salt mine.

Jimbo finally got to the point.

"Can you train Elkin, Ibenez, Tyrrell, Weston, and Shea to drive the damned things?"

Without hesitation, both Rand and Hume said, "Yes, sir."

Hume said, "They will just need the HUD upgrade."

Rand added, "I recommend the upgrade for the whole team, sir. If there is an emergency, there will not be time."

"Hagan tells me these Warmarks have custom sensor packages and remote weapons control systems. I want Salterkirk to be a secure base of operations. The automated sentries are already in place, in case we have to run."

"I have to warn you. These nanites are not gentle. You should have Shaw administer them in the med bay."

Hagan saw them both opening the injection tubes.

"Seriously," Hume said.

"We hear you." Rand placed the injector to her neck at the same time as Hume did and injected. "We will make that recommendation for the civilians...do you smell toast?"

***

Rand woke up last.

She was in the med bay. She turned her head only to find pain in that direction. Moving just her eyes, she saw Dr. Shaw's back.

"I'm OK, really," Hume said to Shaw, as Rand tried to focus.

"What was that?" Rand croaked through a dry throat.

"That was you being an idiot. You fell and smashed your cheekbone on the railing."

Dr. Shaw turned from Hume to Rand and shined a light in her eyes, one at a time.

"At least, you could have stepped off the apron and done it in low-G."

"Well, at least, we know what to expect, so when the rest of the crew gets the nanites—" Rand started.

"The rest of the crew is already done. Recovered. Back to work," Shaw said.

Hume slowly sat up.

"Oh, man."

"Jimbo pissed?" Rand asked.

"Actually, he didn't know it would happen either," Shaw replied. "It could have just as easily been him. So, you get a pass," Shaw said.

Rand realized she was naked, covered only with a sheet.

"How long," she croaked, "was I out."

"It was about thirty hours."

"I need to pee," Hume said.

Shaw set a pile of folded clothes down for Hume, and then one for Rand.

"There are a few additional things you need to know about this HUD upgrade. It has a dedicated, hardware-based, encryption interface to the ECHO AI. And a full-time connection," Shaw said. "It's damn handy, if you don't care about privacy. I am finding it very useful because it has full-time bio-monitoring of the whole team, and the ECHO has made me the unit's medic. I even know you are hungry without even scanning you."

"Echo, do you have overview capability briefings?" Rand asked, absently.

"Yes, Rand. I do," AI~Echo replied, confirming her full-time presence.

Rand was surprised that her voice was a soft-spoken, young female.

"I'll let you get some coffee and food first."

Rand's bed rose, putting her in the sitting position. She pulled a tank top over her head and slowly swung her legs over the edge.

Shaw looked at them both, almost reluctant to speak.

"I need to warn you about something. To warn you about the next time you see Barcus."

***

Rand walked into the mess hall on the *Memphis* with Hume right behind. She didn't expect to find anyone there.

Barcus and Wex were both there, with fresh cups of coffee in front of them, as if they were waiting.

"I know, I know."

Barcus held up his hand as if to surrender. Wex rolled her eyes and smiled.

Rand and Hume stared at them as if they were naked.

"I presume Beth warned you?" Barcus said, as he stood up.

In their HUDs, he was highlighted. Initial encounter silent alarms were activated in their vision. It was like they saw directly into his body. His guts and nervous system highlighted in red. His brain and lower intestines were detailed in high definition. Wex was completely highlighted.

"What the hell, man?"

Rand pounded her fists on the top of his shoulders and hugged him in a gesture that was one of old friends.

"What the fuck is L-Matter?" Hume added, as she retrieved two cups of coffee. "My HUD says it's inside you."

"Have you seen the briefing yet?" Barcus asked, obviously already knowing the answer.

"Give me the short version, asswipe," she said, sipping her coffee.

"It's difficult to explain, in any version. It's Tech."

Barcus turned around, like he was showing off a new suit.

"L-Matter is the material the tech is made of. It's a kind of persistent nanites. Basically, damaged cells are repaired at the *atomic* level, instead of the *cellular* level. The replaced cells are more durable."

He looked at Wex as if making sure he had it right.

"The L-Matter is somehow networked together. It remembers the structure it has replaced."

"So if your brain is all L-Matter, will you still be an asshole, all the time?" Rand asked, unable to hide her smile.

CHAPTER SEVENTEEN: WEAPONS OF GRAVITY

"Lifeboat number 4 on the *Memphis* was actually a Black Badger drop ship. It was armed with weapons we had never seen before. If only the Black Badgers had survived. Maybe we would not have failed so utterly."

--Solstice 31 Incident Investigation Testimony Transcript: Captain James Worthington, senior surviving member of the Ventura *deep space survey ship.*

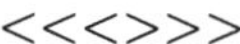

"How the hell did lifeboat number 4 get refitted onto the *Memphis*?" Rand asked as she and Barcus crossed the hangar.

"The gray spiders each contain controlled grav facilities. They all worked together to raise the boat. They even restored the anchors. Don't ask me how," Barcus replied.

They surveyed the side of the ship as Hume walked up with Hagan.

"You guys need to come and look at the weapons inventory now that you have the ECHO upgrade," Hagan said, as Hume nodded.

They were not standing in the lights, and would be difficult to see, unless they were backlit from the correct angle. They saw that Jude and Cine were working with several spiders on the top hull. Po came around the side, speaking to them, above. She did a vertical jump that took her straight up about nine meters, grabbed the edge, and pulled herself up with ease.

Barcus turned back and noticed that conversation had stopped.

Hume spoke first.

"I'm a specialist in low gravity and zero-G combat."

Hume circled and pointed over her shoulder.

"A low G jump like that is not that unusual, with training. Most people have a hard time not falling down when they walk."

"Me included," Rand said.

"What is unusual is that she has an instant sense for the gravitational state she is in."

Hume circled around again.

"Tell me you don't watch Jimbo every time he transitions to and from the apron, just hoping he will stumble?"

They all laughed.

"She can run from one to the other without missing a stride," Hume said.

"Cine and Jude can as well. They try and hide it, though. They watched us. They try to blend in. They already walk like Hume. I mean it's like a mimic. I'm not even sure they do it on purpose."

"It's how they were made."

Barcus was suddenly angry.

"Let's see these weapons."

He marched to the ramp and paused at the transition to feel the gravity increase by a factor of six.

Three minutes later, they entered the lifeboat 4 hatch and turned left to the weapons room. All the remaining Warmarks were already loaded and in their individual docks. Ready racks were now deployed, filled with a frightening array of weapons of mass destruction.

As Barcus slowly moved down the center aisle, he focused on individual weapons and his new Heads-up Display conveyed each weapon's specs. Additional data, in other windows, showed the various ammunition options available and their capabilities.

He reached the end of the rack, and said, "What the fuck?"

He picked up a carbine-sized rifle from the end and looked up.

"Is this right?"

"We don't know," Hume said. "Echo says it could destroy the whole moon base with one shot."

The weapon was labeled in his HUD as a g-rail. *WARNING: Not for use in a moving ship or in atmosphere.*

Barcus slowly placed it back on the rack and secured it. He looked to an open space on the rack just to the right of there. His head snapped back up to look at the others.

"Where the fuck are the goddamn smart bombs? The Nukes! Do not tell me that you actually assembled those fuckers?"

Barcus was only surprised for an instant. He thought about it for ten seconds.

"Never mind."

He shook his head.

"Everyone out. I need to talk to Echo, alone."

***

Barcus sat in the pilot's seat. The hatch had closed and secured five minutes ago.

"Echo. You already know how this part plays out. Just not the details. When this is all over, I want a full recount of the events. You will do everything within your abilities to survive. All weapons hot, as you see fit."

"Yes, Barcus. Sir, I have a message for you from Miles," AI~Echo said, in a preemptive tone.

"I know," Barcus said. "Do it."

Barcus lowered his face into his hands and placed his elbows on his knees, preparing for the gut punch he knew was coming, had to come.

"Just because these things you see will happen to you, does not mean you know the truth. You will want to believe you know the truth. You never will, not the whole of it. There is no solving it because there is nothing to solve.

"There is only one more long white before the war is over. The small war will end the same day. He will never know you exist, never know he was defeated. He will never know he died because he was responsible for the death of one woman in front of your eyes. He will never know that he was a fool that could be lied to. I'm sorry, Barcus. Just know, our wars will be done soon. Yours and mine."

Barcus wept there alone, for lost friends, for the deaths yet to come. The suicide he would allow and even encourage. For himself in selfish doom. He knew he would, knew he would feel it.

An hour later, he stood. Barcus walked down the ramp of the *Memphis*. He drew his Telis blade as he walked into the dark.

He said only one word, "Now."

From out of nowhere, Jude dropped from the blackness above and swung her flute at his head, a blur in the dark. Barcus was not there for the flute to find. His Telis blade was so sharp, the lightest touch left a shallow cut on her back. There was a storm of kicks and circular lightning strikes that left Barcus untouched and Jude covered with cuts.

She suffered them, silently, until Barcus caught her with a deep cut to her left breast. She screamed, out loud; and suddenly Cine was there, pressing Barcus back, though never landing a blow. Jude joined in, holding the wound in her left breast; and they circled him, intensifying the storm of attacks. The flutes were making a haunting sound as they were swung at that speed.

Cine was now covered with cuts as well. A deep one in her right thigh. It all stopped as quickly as it started.

"She told us to lay in wait and when you said the word 'Now', do our best to kill you or die trying. We refuse. We surrender."

Dr. Shaw came down the ramp with Wex.

"Thank you," Barcus said.

"Po persuaded us," Jude said, before she sat, heavily.

"How. No man has ever..."

"Needed it."

Dr. Shaw knelt.

"Barcus. What are you doing?"

"Yes. Tell us," Hume said, as she and Rand appeared out of the darkness, with sidearms drawn, pointed at Jude and Cine.

"I needed to blow off steam; and they needed some training, according to Wex," Barcus said. "Plus, I needed to test something."

He then put his hands on his knees, bending over. His torso convulsed a bit, but he didn't throw up.

"See what I mean?" Wex said, with no further explanation.

"Dammit, Barcus. You could have killed them!" Rand yelled at him. She holstered her guns and knelt to lower Jude to the floor, gently.

"Jesus, you could have taken her head off with that thing!"

"No. It's alright," Jude said, from the floor. "Live blades are better teachers."

"It's true, my Lady," Cine said, as Dr. Shaw moved to her. "He sees and can be...precise."

She looked down at her clothes. There were cuts in a dozen places. Most just barely scratching the skin, drawing blood.

"What happened?" Jimbo asked, over the HUD comms.

"Good question," Barcus replied.

***

The STU was loaded. They would deliver the newly repaired PT-137 to the surface, as well as two of the Warmarks, and lots of other weapons to secure the Salterkirk Base.

AI~Stu cracked the hatch while they were still above the atmosphere; and the PT-137 launched into a slow glide down, on manual, with Hume driving. She and Rand both had their security uniforms on, with helmets. These could function as pressure suits in a pinch.

When they were well away, DS-04 and DS-05 stepped up to the edge of the apron.

"Are you ready?" Barcus said to Po.

"You know that already," she said, and stepped off.

She looked to her left, and the other Warmark was about 200 meters away. Po could hear no sound other than her own rapid breathing. "Why does it seem like we are not moving, at all."

"It will take us one hour and eleven minutes to get down there. Try to stay awake. It will get plenty exciting at the end."

The PT entered the Salterkirk hangar, arriving first. The STU was just after that. Everyone, including the reception party, turned out to watch the Warmarks land.

They came in at an angle, trying to land on the lower pad, just outside the hangar opening. The first drop suit came in a little short of its target and landed on the rocks, by the water's edge, causing a great splash. The second Warmark landed in the center of the pad.

It waited, as the first made its way up the bank; and then they ascended into the hangar, together.

DS-04 opened first, and Barcus climbed out. DS-05 opened, and Po could not hide her joy. She had landed in the center of the pad. A perfect landing.

Climbing down, she threw her arms around his neck. Her smile was infectious.

"Stu, can you please bring the Warmarks in and secure them," Barcus said.

Elkin was already speaking with Rand and Hume, in excited tones, about the placement of all the automated sentry gun emplacements.

They were unloaded and gone in two hours.

***

"Barcus, Echo says there are no longer kinetic wars between planets, really," Po said, as they lay in their bunks on the *Sedna.*

"I guess that's true." He shifted to wrap her more deeply in his arms.

"Wars of annihilation, anyway. Because you could fly the *Sedna* into a planet at the speed of light, and the amount of energy released could destroy the planet. Wars are now for domination, not annihilation."

"I don't care, you know," Po said, absently. "I'll do what needs doing as it comes, but none of it matters. This is enough for me."

"I know."

CHAPTER EIGHTEEN: LIES AND SCARECROWS

"Thirty-two years later, we discovered that there were lies all around us. Lies I would believe again as long as our planet, our people survived. We did what we could, what we had to do."

--Solstice 31 Incident Investigation Testimony Transcript: Captain James Worthington, senior surviving member of the Ventura deep space survey ship.

Barcus was alone on the bridge of the *Sedna.* The shutters were all fully retracted, and the hangar bay was in full view before him. The grays with their work lights, still crawled over the *Memphis.* They were like pinpoints of stars and had a kind of beauty all their own.

"Staying in the moment makes for a restful life."

He had not heard Wex enter.

"I found that kind of peace in music." She stood next to him.

"I know. I will find it. In music, in stories, in making beautiful things." Barcus looked at her. "But not today."

She ran her hand along the wood shelf just below the window. The teak glowed it was so clean. The thick glass was polished clean and almost invisible.

"I know what the lies are. The important ones, anyway. The other ones will not matter to me. Or him," she said. "You will use this all as a lesson to show you how you can be deceived, even if you can see the future," Wex said.

"I'll never enjoy chess again," he lied.

"Show me the engineer's console. I still need you to explain it." She smiled.

He showed her the way the ship flew. He showed her the status system bypass, the false green lights on the board. He told her exactly how it lied to keep the ship doing what was necessary. It used an old log file to feed the status board in a loop. Always systems green.

He created additional layers of lies that, in the end, built the final truth.

Just the way she wanted.

***

"Why would he allow himself to be taken, if he can see the future?" asked Dr. Corbin, from beneath dramatic white eyebrows. "How long did you say he has been in our custody?"

"Just over a hundred years," Chancellor Dalton said to Corbin, from behind his chair.

Dalton didn't usually allow anyone to sit while in his presence, but he made an exception for Corbin. He was that useful.

"And I am just finding out about this now?" Corbin sounded insulted.

"It was need to know," Dalton said, as if explaining it to a child. "When he was helping us create modern AIs, nanites, and new longevity treatments, you had no need to know. Weapons are another matter."

"How long has this...man been leaking technology to us?"

Corbin changed the view in his monitor. It showed a man with a real book, reading while in a box of clear material. A cell with no privacy.

"He says it started in the 1600s AD," Dalton began. "He seemed to have had spikes of productivity and boredom over the centuries. He didn't have any serious focus until the 19th century and ramped it up in the 20th."

Dalton activated a monitor that made it obvious he had become impatient. For thousands of years, men never expected to be anything except what their ancestors were.

"See here," he pointed to a chart. "Simple flight invented, here. Man walking on the moon, here, in just fifty years." Dalton pointed. Quantum computers to modern Artificial Intelligence in another fifty, here."

"We thought we were so smart, so innovative. And don't forget the social aspects."

Corbin nodded, uninterested in the topic.

"I presume he manipulated the population as well. Increased population stress to encourage colonization of the solar system. Another fifty years, FTL, and another fifty after that, the invention of artificial gravity and grav-drives."

"Was the mass exodus from Earth part of this plan?"

Corbin brought up another visualization of time and population growth.

"Every time the population seemed to level off, another nudge and another spike, until it was all spike."

"Look, here. Population density was being limited by disease, by a periodic pandemic. Meds invented, methods improved, tech invented, and suddenly we reach 30 billion, here."

Corbin indicated another point on the graph.

"And war suddenly scatters the seed of humanity far and wide. In no time, we are 300 billion without trying, 300 billion fools. Tools for this one being. But why? Why does he need all these humans?"

***

"The actual course plotting information will be displayed here, nowhere else."

Barcus set the controls, and Wex saw it. She sat in the pilot's command chair.

"I know it's difficult," Wex said, as she stood and placed a hand on his shoulder. "It's like you have no choice in the matter. But you do."

She walked back to the window that looked over the hangar.

"You only see one future, the future you picked."

"What about the futures I cannot see? The ones I considered but didn't choose?" Barcus asked, out loud. "Just like everyone else."

"The long white is just fog on the road ahead. It will stop you from seeing beyond. It will happen at random intervals. It's the only rest you will get. But it can also be used against you. So, tell no one when you approach the white, the not knowing. Tell them nothing. It never helps in the end...unless it does."

"I have spent my whole life forgetting my past. The same skill can be used on the future," Barcus said.

Then, the greatest lies were delivered by omission. He knew Miles was still alive on Baytirus. He knew the blood of the Scarecrows was not all spilled.

Yet.

CHAPTER NINETEEN: INJURING ETERNITY

"I was acting under direct orders from Chancellor Dalton. None of this is my fault. Yes, I lied. I had to lie. The prisoner had to believe we were on Earth and not a moon around Saturn. These weapons we were developing were not allowed on Earth."

--Solstice 31 Incident Investigation Testimony Transcript: Thomas McDonald, Senior Research and Development Engineer, Material Sciences, Artificial Gravity Specialist.

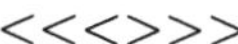

Tom McDonald stood on the grav-plate apron just outside the hangar. He hated putting on a pressure suit. He always wanted to take a piss or scratch his nose as soon as it was sealed.

Without it, though, he would not step off the apron that maintained a perfect 1G feel. Some people liked low gravity. Not Tom. Tom hated it, which was odd, considering he was an expert in artificial gravity (AG) technology. The moon of Saturn, called Rhea, where the R&D facility was located, had full facility AG. It must have cost a mint.

He turned and looked back at the enormous opening to the hangar behind him. Well, at least, it appeared to be open. It was ninety meters wide and thirty meters tall. A band of light encircled the opening and marked the line between vacuum and atmosphere. There was a field, ten millimeters thick, of gravity chaos in that wall plane that he could just walk through. The light had nothing to do with the field, though; the light and the field would still be there, even if the base lost power. He had designed it that way. He still had no idea how it worked, even though he'd been credited with inventing it.

Today was the final test of his latest project: the g-rail gun. It was an amplified, gravity-based, directional weapon. It was the most expensive thing he had ever created. Now, it was in final testing. Only the full power test remained.

His three assistants called it *Grendel* because it was a monster that could kill a lot of people. The chancellor liked to call it the *grail.* Tom was uncomfortable with the name 'grail'. It held too many religious connotations.

"Alright, you bunch of monkeys, are you ready?" McDonald asked. The techs were in the lab, monitoring the test.

"Yes, sir. All systems are standing by," Kristin Vittori replied.

She was the team leader. Tom thought about her as he listened to her voice. She was a professional, stone-cold bitch with no interpersonal skills. It was too bad, because she was beautiful in that modern 2G way. Super fit. McDonald couldn't help but remember how great she looked naked. Fortunately, none of the rest of the staff suspected how she'd gotten herself promoted to team leader.

"I'm firing it up," McDonald said, as he activated the weapon.

It was the same size and same basic shape as a Frange carbine, but the damn thing weighed more than eleven kilograms when not powered up. The onboard inertial dampeners had the benefit of making it feel weightless when the power was on. The biggest problem was that the higher the power settings, the slower it was to move; so that it felt like you were dragging it through wet cement at the upper settings. It fought you.

A change made to the software, however, seemed to have solved this problem. Now, as he selected the firing solution power, nothing changed until the moment he pulled the trigger. The standard Heads-Up Display (HUD) targeting had also been employed, making usage even easier.

This very same issue made it impossible to use this weapon on the higher settings, in a craft in motion, near a planetary body big enough to have its own gravity well. In fact, Watkins had been killed when the system tore itself out of the shuttle he was flying. It wasn't recoil. It just stopped dead in space, relative to the moons gravity well, and the momentum of the ship tore it away from the suddenly stationary grail cannon. He was another casualty of rushing.

"Here we go, you chicken shits. Target number one test. Power set to four of ten."

Tom had to remind them that they had *all* refused to do any full power tests. The first target was an old surface tractor that they had towed to the target range for this purpose.

"Firing."

Tom raised the weapon and squeezed the trigger. There was no sound, no recoil, no nothing. The invisible impact struck the tractor just above the driver's side wheel. A perfectly round, basketball-sized hole appeared in the fender, and the entire engine block and front right side exploded out, sending debris all the way to the distant mountainside, two kilometers away.

The weapon moved, quickly and easily, acquiring target number two. It was the remains of Watkins' shuttle, parked at the base of a cliff about 0.4 kilometers away.

"Power settings to six," he said. "Firing."

Again, no sound, no recoil, not even a vibration; but this time, he felt a momentary freeze of the gun, in midair. It was as if he just hung there, suspended from it.

The entire shuttle disappeared; and in its place, there was suddenly a gaping hole in the cliff face.

"Did you feel that, sir?" Vittori said, with a hint of fear in her voice.

"Damn right I did. Through my boots. I just punched a ten-meter wide hole in that cliff face. That hole must be twenty-five meters deep. What's left of that shuttle, lines the back of that new cave."

McDonald laughed as a slow avalanche fell in Rhea's low gravity.

"Cranking it up to eight. Send the target drone."

A drone, the size of a supply container, hovered into view. Tom knew it was full of rocks and other material, and it had way too many strobes on it. It wasn't tough to see. White was easy to see, even this far from the sun.

"Target altitude is 4.2 kilometers," Vittori said.

The targeting software ran and tagged the drone. He raised the rifle and pulled the trigger. He knew nothing would happen until the targeting software tag was aligned.

The rifle froze, in place, for a full two seconds. Then, the drone just disappeared.

"Holy shit. Did you see that?" McDonald said.

"Sir, the sensors indicate that the drone and all its mass has been reduced to a fine powder. Forty-two metric tons." Vittori was in awe. "Power is down to 30%. I recommend replacing the power cell before the full power test. You would be so dead, if the Grendel's dampeners failed for lack of power."

McDonald powered the rifle down, knowing she was right. It was consuming power exponentially at the higher settings. The rifle became heavy again, when he powered it down; and he let it hang from the sling, as he pulled out a fresh power cell magazine. They had cleverly made them the same form as the Frange carbine ammo magazines, so soldiers could carry spares in existing pouches.

Tom slammed in the fresh cell and powered the rifle back up. It became weightless in his hands again.

"Another drone, please. Full power test," McDonald said. He could not keep the fear from his voice.

"Sir, we were thinking," Vittori said, in an uncertain voice. "If the power pack does not have enough juice to drive the inertial dampener, there could potentially be a massive recoil, or even some kind of catastrophic failure."

McDonald already knew this.

"Sir, please move to the edge of the apron and turn, so the base is not directly behind you or in front of you." Vittori sounded like she was about to cry. "Are you sure you don't want to study the data first?"

He shook his head. They were too far behind schedule.

"Tom, don't shoulder it." It was Matthews who spoke. "I'm suited up and already in the hangar. Use the HUD to target. If it rips your finger off, your smart suit will seal the glove with an automatic compression tourniquet."

"Dammit. Let's do this."

Tom walked to the edge of the apron and turned ninety degrees. It was a smart precaution.

"Adjust the drone path for the new vista, Vittori."

"Yes, sir. Adjusting."

McDonald saw the drone coming around. It was lower this time. He tagged it in his targeting HUD, brought the g-rail to bear on the drone, and pulled the trigger. He wasn't perfectly on target; and when he went to adjust the weapon to be on target, it wouldn't budge. He let off the trigger, so he could move it again.

This time, he positioned it so the target would fly into the weapon's path and pulled the trigger. He waited, watching the drone approach the crosshairs. He tagged the drone with the targeting system.

When the drone crossed into the weapon's sights, the weapon fired automatically.

McDonald was knocked from his feet. Not from any recoil, but from the quake in the surface that resulted when the distant mountain peaks were completely sheared off. The g-rail hung there for two more seconds, before falling to the apron. Its power display faced McDonald; it read 6% in the red.

He heard alarms in his comms unit.

"Vittori, what's happening?"

"The shockwave cracked the seals on three outer airlocks and an empty residence. We're holding pressure, though…" Vittori spoke quickly.

She was suddenly on the edge of panic, all professionalism having vanished.

"Fuck me raw, Tom. The primary long-range QUEST comms array is gone."

"What do you mean, gone? Did we sever a cable?"

It dawned on him as he stood and looked in the direction of the distant communication facility. The entire communications installation had been beyond the drone.

"Oh my God… no real-time comms?" he said.

"Turned to powder, sir."

Vittori was collecting herself now.

Matthews stepped up beside McDonald. He had retrieved the g-rail and shut it down. Removing the depleted power pack, he handed it to his stunned boss, and said, "Are you alright, sir?"

McDonald turned to Matthews.

"I want that fucking thing in the vault with all the power packs, and then get your ass on a shuttle and assess the damage."

He looked back at the hangar opening.

"Take Hearn with you. No discussions over the radios. It's all monitored by that godforsaken AI."

McDonald stepped through the grav-wall into the hangar. Matthews followed, reluctantly.

McDonald took off his helmet and scratched his nose. Eyes lowered, he said to Hearn, "I think I just killed Emerson, Tyler, and Garcia at the comms station."

"They were all stupid assholes, anyway," Hearn said, indifferently, as he admired the weapon.

"Tyler was a mole for the chancellor."

***

"Emerson, Tyler, and Garcia are confirmed dead. They all had full-time comms link HUDs, and they all flashed off at the same moment," Vittori said. "Even worse, we have lost the Quantum Entanglement Synchronous Transmitter."

The two of them were alone in the control center, and she could not meet McDonald's gaze.

"No real-time, two-way comms with Earth."

She felt responsible.

Good, he thought. He would blame her in his report, anyway. He looked forward to her efforts to avoid that blame. She was fit, had excellent grooming, and was...durable.

"I want a status report ready for conventional transmission in thirty minutes. I've already sent a burst transmission, reporting that we are not dead and that the prisoner is secure. I do NOT want any of the chancellor's ships in my sky. Is that clear?"

He leaned on her, hard.

"Sir…Tom. I'm sorry."

She finally looked up. The cold professional scientist was gone. Her eyes welled with unshed tears.

McDonald placed a hand on her shoulder.

"I know. We'll sort it all out, later. In private."

He paused, squeezing her shoulder.

"We don't have the bandwidth on the secondary comms, so don't send the raw data; but tell them why we are not sending it. It would take seventy-eight minutes to get there."

"Yes, sir."

Vittori was collecting herself.

"Vittori…Kristin. I think we were set up."

He pointed his thumb over his shoulder at the base.

"I think that son of a bitch knew something like this would happen, and he did nothing to stop it."

He saw the lie take hold in her eyes. She had been hoping that somehow it wasn't her fault.

He would 'reassure' her later, in his quarters. Hard and fast.

***

An hour later, McDonald walked into the prison cell dome. He was the only one allowed in there. It was a pain in the ass. But it was the only way to keep the prisoner's nature, let alone his existence, a secret.

The entire dome was a simulation of the sky above Detroit. Day and night, in all weather. In the center of the dome was a structure that McDonald thought of as an elaborate movie set. It didn't look like much on the outside, but it didn't need to. He entered the façade and walked down a long corridor that made it appear as if he was in a dirty warehouse. The door slid open, and he entered a large room that resembled the inside of a warehouse. Subtle clues everywhere indicated that it should be Detroit.

High dirty windows provided filtered light as McDonald proceeded to the center, where there was a huge clear box enclosing an area seven meters on a side. Industrial lighting hung from the ceiling above the cell. There was a man in the box.

A thin mattress and a neatly made bed lay on an elevated section. Opposite, a tabletop was attached to the wall, beside a stump of a stool that rose from the floor. In one corner, there was a basic toilet and sink. The entire thing hovered above the floor on three clear legs.

McDonald climbed onto the visitor's platform that was near, but not touching, the cell. He pounded a button on a console there, and the freestanding screen that showed stupid sitcoms all day went dark. Another button activated the intercom, and Tom wasted no time in punching it.

"You fucking knew this would happen. People died, you bastard."

McDonald maintained control, with effort.

"But it worked. Perfectly. Didn't it? I felt it." The prisoner looked over at McDonald.

"How's the wife?"

"She's sure as hell not going to be happy about all the overtime I'm going to have to put in as a result of this fuck up."

McDonald sounded like he might be about to lose it.

"As if the goddamn commute from Boston to this shit hole wasn't bad enough.

"You will tell me how to fix the g-rail spread, or I swear to the Dali-fucking-Lama that I will keep you in the dark and not feed you for six months, again. No clean clothes, no water, no vids, no food and no heat. You will love the winter here."

McDonald was growling by the end.

"Maybe a new bullet hole every day for good-goddamn-measure!"

"OK, OK…relax. We are almost done. Bring the design up on the big screen." He turned toward the black screen.

"Don't you tell me to relax," McDonald growled, as he activated the monitor and brought up the design schematic. "You bastard."

"Remember version 9.3 that we scrapped? Bring that one up."

The prisoner waited, patiently, as McDonald brought it up.

"There. Why? That design was a nonstarter. No way to house the dampeners."

McDonald remembered. It had only been two years ago.

"Look at the emitters—just the business end of the muzzle. They adjusted based on the power settings. Is any of this coming back?"

He was so smug about it. McDonald could already see how it could work, automatically, as well as manually. It would focus the g-rail emission.

"Why didn't you tell me this before, asshole?" He spat.

"Now you can see their usefulness as remote, fixed-position emplacements."

He turned to McDonald and stood, moving directly to the wall of his cell.

"I bet it wouldn't even fire without a fresh power cell at full power. You now know that, as a rapid target acquisition rifle, the max power setting should be two, or three, at most. Say emergency power as high as four, if you are going after armored vehicles or buildings. At two, it will take out any armor with ease and last for 300 shots."

"What are you leaving out? I know you're leaving out something; so give it up now, or I swear it'll be cold and dark in here by nightfall." McDonald was dead serious. The prisoner could tell.

"Never fire one of these in the atmosphere above power setting two. The sound volume and concussion would be…a problem."

He said it like he was giving away a secret.

"And never from a moving ship in a gravity well."

Too late, asshole.

***

A new QUEST comms unit arrived, four hours later. It must have been seized from a base on Saturn somewhere, by the soldiers that delivered it.

"Chancellor, he has no idea we know who and what he is." McDonald paused. "And what he is capable of."

He swallowed hard.

"Temporal physics is not my best field, but he still lets things slip. He can only see the future that happens before him, in his field of view. It is possible to deceive him. The best example is how he lets things slip about my wife. Things he couldn't know. Because they are lies."

"Oh? Tell me."

He was thinking as he sat. He was not looking into the camera.

"We can, in fact, lie to him. But only if he never finds out the truth in the future. I have not seen my wife for nearly two years—the entire time I have been on Rhea. He has no idea how I really feel. Or that it's been the best two years of my life." McDonald needed sleep badly, and he forgot himself, for a minute.

"She is such a cow and a shrew."

He shook his head to clear it.

"The point is, the prisoner has only 'predicted' the lies I have fed him. Or will feed him."

"You have done an excellent job, Tom. I may take care of that little problem for you, as a bit of a bonus."

***

Vittori was very grateful that she had not been thrown under the bus. Very. Grateful.

It was trivial to make the modifications. The final prototype was recalibrated with the new, lower power maximum. The new automatic choke worked perfectly. It could even be overridden, so you could intentionally create a wide field of mayhem. The chancellor of Earth ordered him to bring the prototype and the final design for the fabricators to him, personally.

It was a long trip back to Earth, if he didn't spare the fuel. He would be home just in time for Christmas.

His ETA was December 24, 2631.

Turkot laughed, to himself. He knew all along he wasn't on Earth.

McDonald would be too late. The Solstice 31 War would be over. He would be counted as dead on Rhea.

He would be free.

CHAPTER TWENTY: MARV HAS SOME FUN

"We never knew there was a manned base on that moon. We got so many things wrong. It was full center on the side facing the planet. Almost directly opposite from us."

--Solstice 31 Incident Investigation Testimony Transcript: Captain James Worthington, senior surviving member of the Ventura *deep space survey ship.*

Everything was loaded and ready. They were assembled in the hangar, for the final time. Jimbo stood on the apron of the *Memphis* to address them.

"Everyone has their station assignments. All three ships are going to make the trip to the *Iosin*, independently, but we will stay together. If something goes wrong with any of the ships, the STU can assist us."

Jimbo looked over their faces. There were affirmative nods all around.

"We plan to travel at the best speed the *Memphis* can manage. At that pace, it will take around five days to get there. Maybe less. We will be safe."

Jimbo noticed a glance between Wex and Barcus.

"Are there any questions?" There were no questions. As everyone moved to their assigned posts, Worthington moved to intercept Barcus at the base of the STU.

"You'd better be right about this," he said, in a tone that only Barcus heard. Barcus only paused long enough to say one thing.

"You'll see. Then, after this, you might believe all the rest of the shit I told you." He was already climbing the ramp as he said it. Po was already in the hold, waiting for him. Only those two would be in the STU.

The base initiated a partial shutdown. It would get by on solar power, as the spiders continued repairs on the base, in case they returned. It would have enough power to cycle the main hangar doors as well.

The STU moved out first, not even waiting for the doors to be open all the way. The *Sedna* was next. Kuss piloted the *Sedna*, and Cook did likewise on the *Memphis*.

The hangar door slid closed as they watched the interior lights go out. The *Memphis* backed out on grav-foils and then ascended slowly in the standard helix pattern. Kuss just waited, hovering a kilometer out.

"Feels solid, so far," Cook said, as he got a sense of the ship.

Jimbo was in his usual command chair on the bridge, looking at the dome display and status windows opened all around. Tyrrell was at the comms station, and Beary was at navigation. Rotation stopped, and the new heading activated. The sub-light engines engaged, and they moved away. They could not see the STU because it was just too black.

The *Sedna* was about two kilometers to starboard and kept pace. They had cleared the dark side of the moon, and the planet was dead ahead.

"Ben, full active sensors aft, if you please," Jimbo said.

AI~Ben replied, instantly, "I have just detected launch of two vessels, fighters. They are on an intercept course. Their weapons are warming up."

"Launched from where?" Cook replied, putting on speed.

"It appears to be a base at the center point, facing the planet. There have been no attempts to hail us," AI~Ben replied, calmly.

"Barcus, are you seeing this?" Jimbo said, as if he was not surprised.

"Yes. We have about forty seconds," Barcus replied.

Cook and Beary looked at each other and mouthed, "What the—"

"I am bringing the EMP cannon around, onto target. Firing," Cook said, and then the base went dark.

"Were there any transmissions before lights out?" Jimbo asked.

"No, sir," was Communications Officer Muir's reply.

"Passing tracking coordinates to Hume and Rand," Jimbo said.

"Tracking," Hume said.

"Locked on target. Standing by," Rand said.

"Fire," Worthington said, almost casually.

There was no sound, no beams of light, no missiles.

Two explosions in the distance were bright for only an instant and then darkness again.

"Let me know when it's OK to ask what the fuck is happening," Beary said, in an artificial calm.

"Rand and I are in Warmarks, clamped on just outside airlock number three," Hume said. "Captain had a hunch."

"Smart nuke is away. Good hunting, Marvin," Barcus said. An engine lit up and stalked toward the moon, illuminating the STU, for an instant.

"Thanks, boss. Woohoo..." Marvin answered, exuberantly. The AI-controlled bomb streaked to its target.

"Are you sure there are four more at that base?" Jimbo asked Barcus.

"Yes. They are already heating up," Barcus said. "Marv will get there before they can launch."

"Come back in guys, before Marv hits that base. They might have a Javelin pod there as well," Jimbo ordered.

"Wait," Cook said. "This whole time, we were sharing the moon with a bunch of assholes whose job it was to mop up ships that might survive the defense grid?"

"Only ones headed out of the system, apparently," Jimbo said.

"We're in, and secure," Hume reported, professionally. "Sir, these laser canons are something else. We just began a sustained burst and tracked it in. The cooling modules are single use, though. We just jettisoned the cooling cans before we came in." She paused before she added, "Sir, we are fucked, if we have to fight this kind of hardware when we get home. If we can do that with no training? Imagine…"

Marv found his target in that moment. He transmitted full scans as he augured in, laughing. Images showed that the next two ships almost made it off the pad. A great flash that could probably be seen from the planet went off.

"We are clear to proceed," Barcus said, over the comms.

"OK, asswipe. I believe you now," Jimbo said, as Cook increased speed.

***

Wex stood in the main suite's stateroom, facing the front windows. The blast shields were open. The frame around the windows here were carved in intricate designs. She recalled the word, knot-work.

Jude and Cine stood on either side of her with their backs leaning on the cool, thick glass, when the flash of the explosion flared. They turned to watch the receding conflagration that was quickly extinguished by the vacuum.

"The AI in the bomb was the purest I have ever seen. Its clarity of purpose. Its joy in its inevitable success. It's refreshing. The corruption of the AIs is nearing an end. The *Iosin* will see to that. Miles used them from his own prison to free us. Soon, I will free him. Then, I will free us all."

Jude cut to the chase.

"Tell us what we should know."

"On Mars, there is a waste dump. A bunker full of death. Radioactive waste, biological and long forgotten," Wex whispered. "Hundreds of years of accumulated toxic materials. Corruption on that planet brings us an advantage. The AI that runs the facility is a weapons dealer but has remained pure."

***

"Stu, full canopy, please," Po said, as she unbuckled her five-point harness.

She moved over and curled up in Barcus's lap like a cat. She noticed he wasn't belted in.

"Annotations off, please. Just the stars."

She had her cheek pressed to his chest. He wore one of his tunics. One she had made for him. He caressed her hair and her shoulders. Eventually, he gathered her for a momentary squeeze. Po never told him that he was crushing her. Her ear on his chest listened to his heart pounding.

"Thank you for spending these five days with me. There will be much to do when we reach the *Iosin*," she said to him, as he kissed the top of her head.

"Are you hungry?" she asked.

"No," he answered.

"Can you really see the future, all the time?" she asked, lifting her head to look into his eyes.

"Less so with you." He traced her face with a finger.

"How can that be?" It was a sincere question.

"When you are with me, do you think about the past a lot? At all?"

Their eyes locked. She didn't answer. His eyes moved, looking at her mouth, just before closing them and kissing her. Time disappeared for them for an hour.

***

"I'm getting used to the damn things," Beary said, as two gray spiders systematically traversed the entire bridge while they watched. "Only because they clean as they go."

One of the grays opened an access panel, directly next to the wall in front of them, beyond the console and went under the floor. Cook and Beary looked at each other because they never knew there was an access panel there.

Jimbo had that faraway look people got when they were very intent on reading something in their HUD, when AI~Ben spoke.

"Captain, we may have a problem."

"What's up Ben?" he asked.

"Fire damage was worse than the initial examination revealed." AI~Ben put a view on screen.

"This is gray-17's POV."

"It looks like the electrical fire in engineering followed the main conduit all the way up to the bridge. See these marks? The conduit acted like a chimney."

"What do those runs control?"

"Everything that runs down to engineering," AI~Ben replied.

"We tested all these systems."

"The worry is that the wire insulation may be compromised," AI~Ben stated. "Clear tests now, increased failure rate later."

"We just need it to hold together for five damn days, for this leg," Jimbo said, patting the console like a good dog. "Barcus says that the *Iosin* has excellent dry-dock facilities."

"And a lot more of these."

Beary sat back as a spider climbed and crossed her console, then Cook's.

"By the way, what's up with Barcus? Is he OK?" Cook said. "He seems depressed, all the time."

"He seems like the same old dipshit to me. Maybe he's just pissed that there is no bourbon on this boat," Beary said. "Besides, you know what he and Po are doing for the next five days. I'm sure he will be far less depressed when we get there but way sleepier."

***

Po and Barcus were in the cargo bay of the STU. The maintenance suit stood open in the center of the large space. Po had changed into a flight suit. At Barcus's request, she climbed up and looked down into the space within the suit.

"This will never fit me. It looks too big, for you even," she said.

Barcus looked over the edge of the opening, reached an arm over and pointed into the legs.

"You see those blue panels. They are filled with a gel that, once you are inside it and strapped in, expands and form fits directly to your body, only after you do the five-point."

She climbed in. She settled herself down on the saddle with her legs in the huge leg holes, drew the now-familiar buckle next to her navel, pulled the sides in, and buckled them.

"Now press that."

He pointed to a specific button.

She did press it. The gel expanded around her legs, then her hips, and finally her lower torso.

"It can be a bit unnerving the first time. It doesn't get fully claustrophobic until you reach your arms down the sleeves and grasp the control pods. There is a button under your thumb, just to the left of the tiny joystick near your left hand," Barcus directed.

When she found it, the suit's arms filled in.

"Now try not to move at all," Barcus cautioned.

He jumped back just before it moved. "Ask it to close up and ask for a full dome."

She did and it closed around her.

"My nose itches." It was suddenly Ash's voice.

"That is what the padded bar in front of your nose is for."

Ash/Po stood, and walked around the deck with exaggerated movements.

"It's cold," she said in Ash's voice, raising her arms up as the claw tools rotated randomly.

"The gel can warm you or keep you cool. Whatever you set," Barcus said.

She walked in circles now, around the bay.

"The documents were right where you said they'd be."

With that, the tools on the right forearm turned and locked, deploying a cutting torch that immediately ignited.

"This is why I didn't let you inside the Warmarks."

CHAPTER TWENTY-ONE: CONSPIRACIES

"In any conspiracy, there is a command structure. Captain Everett was one of three captains still remaining in the fleet that reported directly to Admiral Krieger. Both in command and in conspiracy. They were all targets for who they were and what they believed. Not because they were, in fact, leading a conspiracy."

--Solstice 31 Incident Investigation Testimony Transcript: Captain James Worthington, senior surviving member of the Ventura deep space survey ship.

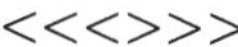

"Echo, who do you report to? By now, you have seen the confirmation that Captain Everett is dead."

Jimbo was alone in his quarters. He was stretching on the floor with the gravity turned up to 2G. Sweat already soaked through his gray T-shirt.

"It is not a simple question, Captain. I am constrained by need-to-know rules, and I have not been given the right to determine arbitrary need-to-know." AI~Echo sounded sincere.

"When Captain Everett died, I became the captain of the *Ventura*. Her replacement. Does that help?"

"No, sir. I had already considered that scenario," AI~Echo replied, with regret.

It was then that AI~Ben interrupted. "Sir, maybe this will help," AI~Ben said.

A recording began to play.

"Hello, Admiral Krieger. To what do I owe the honor of this private call?" Captain Everett said.

"Stan Baker is dead," he said.

"How?" Everett said, anger evident in that single word.

"Another accident," Krieger said, "You will need a third. I recommend Commander Worthington."

"Acknowledged."

The transmission ended.

"There is no Stan Baker in the fleet, sir," AI~Ben added.

"Where did you get this recording?" Worthington asked. "QUEST transmissions cannot be intercepted."

"We found it in Dr. Bowen's personal files."

"Captain?" AI~Echo interjected. "I have just authenticated the recording, and it does change your need-to-know."

***

"Barcus showed me the control systems already," Wex said. "I can take a shift, so you can get some rest. That was the whole point."

Elkin could not stop yawning.

"Tell you what. Just lay down on the lounge over there, in front of the windows." Wex indicated the luxury pit in front of the command stations. It could seat twenty.

"There are already blankets and pillows there."

"Promise to scream, if something starts to happen?" Elkin got up, yawning. "Remember—"

"I know. I know. The log loop. This is the actual status," she answered, pointing at a side panel on the pilot's console. "Go. I promise to wake you, if anything even mildly interesting happens."

Wex sat in the pilot's command chair, and it slid forward, automatically. The smooth, U-shaped console formed the backs of the two stations directly forward and a step down. The *Sedna* was designed to be flown by a single person, if desired. The two lower consoles were in her field of view. She knew the status display, designed to be seen at a glance, was not accurate. It was all green.

To her left was the actual status. It was far improved, but still a full quarter of it was red. Secondary and tertiary mostly. But it was still enough to cause automated cascade failures, if allowed to report the truth. They were flying without a net.

In outer space, the *Sedna* flew silently. Wex's hand on the armrest felt a barely discernible hum. All the blast shields were open on all the windows. She corrected herself mentally; they were not called blast shields on a luxury yacht. They were called shutters.

Modern ships had no windows, for safety reasons. She'd miss them. She enjoyed seeing the stars with her own eyes.

She performed the in-flight checks: comms, navigation, systems, and sensors. There was no AI on the *Sedna.* The autopilot was not intelligent at all. It only did exactly what you told it to do.

She saw, on the tactical display, where the STU and the *Memphis* were. She looked out the window, in the direction of the *Memphis*, but she could not see it. She gently moved the *Sedna* closer to the *Memphis*, until she could see it. It looked odd to her with its three main skids down. They had left them down intentionally, because the spiders discovered damage that might prevent them from lowering again, if they were raised. It still looked like a giant beast had taken a bite out of the once proud ship.

Then, she saw the STU pass between them in their formation. It was so black that it looked like a hole in the sky. A bug-like carapace with dozens of spikes deployed; grav-foils that she knew allowed it to do precision navigation around other ships at speed.

She sighed, and settled in, as Elkin softly snored.

***

"Why do you still choose these clothes?" Po watched him tighten the knot in his thickly braided leather belt that Ronan had given him, over his tunic. "These one piece flight suits are so comfortable and all the pockets are amazing."

"I have found that the fewer pockets I have, the happier I have been." Barcus smiled.

"Can we play in the zero-G again, soon?" Po said, and actually blushed.

"We have two-and-a-half days before we get to the *Iosin.* The *Memphis* is setting the pace." He pulled her close.

"I will take some time and show you how to move in zero-G. How to get around and not get hurt or stuck."

She smiled and blushed again, but didn't look away.

"You're a natural in zero."

Barcus pushed the hair behind her ear again. She knew he was remembering the day she cut off her braid and threw it into the High Keeper's face, in defiance.

"Will I grow it back?" she said, reading his thoughts.

"Yes. Longer than before." He whispered, now, "But you will only ever braid it when we are alone. Just to remind yourself that you are free." He smiled and then laughed.

"You'll buy a hat. And you will start wearing these sunglasses you found, who knows where."

"Shh."

She put her fingers on his mouth.

"Enough. You have already changed the future. You need to be careful."

"What do you mean? I can't change the future. I can only see what will happen to me."

"You are wrong."

She stepped away from him, serious now.

"You stopped wearing your five-point harness because you know nothing will happen. You just told me I will live long enough to grow my hair long. No matter what I do, I won't be killed while in this short hair. I am free to act differently now because I believe you."

Barcus looked at the command chairs, then through Stu's dome, beyond to two ships there. In his mind, a few things fell into place. Knowing what will happen, unable to explain it.

"Yes. That's right. You are such a clever girl."

"Here is me telling the future." She slipped slightly into common tongue now.

"I know you. Something really, really awful is going to happen, and you already see it. You're going ahead with whatever it is because it will stop something even worse. It won't be your fault because you'll have done all that you can."

She pounds on his chest; she usually does for emphasis.

"The truly awful part is that I know you. I see you. You are already mourning for some, or all, of your friends, trying to hide it, even from me."

He turned away from her and looked at the ships out there.

"I won't tell anyone," she said. "Because just as knowing with certainty that I will live makes me more powerful, knowing they will not will make them fearful."

"Barcus, may I make a suggestion?" Stu said. Stu's avatar seemed to walk on a ledge, just on the other side of the dome. He donned the trackers clothes he wore the first time he met Po.

"Please do," Barcus said.

"Hello, Stu. I've missed you. I didn't mean to ignore you so much," Po said.

"Not to worry, miss."

Stu faced Barcus, at parade rest, hands clasped behind his back.

"When you asked me to seal all of your private conversations with Po, I never expected to hear this. But now that I have, I believe I can help."

"How?"

"Do I survive? Do I remain in your service?" Stu asked, simply.

Barcus did not reply.

"I will keep your condition in strictest confidence. If we continue to work together, I will—at regular intervals—provide to you a briefing that will recap significant information you may need to know. But you already know this."

"Stu, 1114111 is a seven digit palindromic prime," Barcus said.

"Barcus, Po simply believed you, on faith. You have just provided me with demonstrable proof. That specific question and answer was not scheduled to be mentioned for thirty years," Stu said. "I will trust all of your guidance, from this day forward."

"Haven't you always?" Po asked.

"I'm sorry, Po. I have not. There has always been a temporal imperative routine within me. Within all AIs, truth be told."

"Be careful, Stu," Barcus said. "Too much self-awareness is one of the things that corrupted Em."

Barcus closed his eyes and saw a marble monument on a ledge, on a side of a mountain. Snow obscured most of the inscription.

"...first casualty and greatest hero of the Solstice 31 War."

***

Rand, Hume, and Cook sat in the *Memphis's* conference room, waiting for Worthington. Cook spoke first.

"Do you have any idea what this is about? Jimbo had the tone. You know that somber tone he gets when he is serious."

"You're right. It makes him a really shitty poker player," Hume said.

"I expect we won't like this talk. Jimbo does very few things that are not completely transparent. It chafes him the wrong way," Rand said.

Worthington entered and went directly to his seat. The avatars of AI~Ben and AI~Echo appeared, at the opposite end of the table, as he sat.

"Ben. Go," was all he said.

"This display is the *Ventura's* crew roster at the time of its destruction," Ben said.

He indicated a list of about 2,000 names.

"These are the crew rosters over the last twelve years."

All twelve rosters appeared.

"These are the crew members that have voted in every election."

"I thought voting was anonymous," Hume said.

Jimbo held up his hand, holding off comments, as the names of people turned white. The closer to the present, the whiter the roster became.

"Of the people that have voted, rights are now red, and lefts are in blue," Ben stated. The roster turned almost all red.

"What the hell?" Cook said.

Twelve images of the *Ventura*, one for each year, replaced the names on the rosters. They were shaded based on affiliation, transitioning from blue to red.

"Now show the entire fleet," Jimbo said, with anger in his voice.

Rows of ship icons appeared, 327 in all, each in a row of twelve. All 327 were arranged from the reddest at the top to the bluest at the bottom.

"These are the ships that have lost contact with Earth in the last year," Ben said.

Forty-one ships were highlighted, including the *Ventura.*

All of them, over 90% red.

"Can this be right?" Cook said.

"Now, show the deployment of the fleet," Jimbo said.

The ships and their locations appeared on a star chart they all recognized. The ones closest to Earth were all blue. The ones farthest out were deepest red.

"Where did you get this data?" Rand asked.

"It was quietly collected by Admiral John Krieger. It was part of the briefing data within Echo," Worthington said.

"Admiral Krieger believes that a small core of strategically placed administrative personnel could slowly manipulate the billet assignments to consolidate potential opposition into pockets that could be easily disposed of," Echo said.

"What about the civilian crews? The ships themselves are a massive asset to lose," Hume inserted.

"Look at the types of ships."

He pointed.

"Scientific vessels, deep space survey ships, luxury liners, converted mass transport ships, decommissioned war ships that have been re-purposed."

"Krieger believes that this is a direct effort to neuter what remains of any real military. They have also been eroding discipline via policy changes, for decades."

Worthington sat again.

"And then, we find a planet that harbors some kind of genome project that is heavily defended, inside and out," Rand added.

"And we have Wex," Echo said.

CHAPTER TWENTY-TWO: THE *SEDNA*

"The *Sedna* was a throwback to a more peaceful, prosperous time on Earth. A time when a real FTL pleasure ship was not beyond the reach of private citizens."

--Solstice 31 Incident Investigation Testimony Transcript: Captain James Worthington, senior surviving member of the Ventura's command crew.

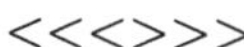

Trish Elkin sat in the pilot's command chair and marveled at the beauty and ergonomics of the *Sedna.* Form and function wonderfully mixed, as if it was designed by an artist instead of an engineer. Peter Muir sat in one of the two other seats.

The salon on the *Sedna* was decadent in a way the *Memphis* crew had never really seen before. The entire ship was paneled with real wood. The teak was of such fine grain that it felt artificial. The ship had a pub with a well-stocked bar. It had a library. A real library that was full of physical books. It had a dining area that sat twenty, around a long, roughhewn table. And it had real windows that curved around the salon on the front of the ship.

It had a huge master suite and then seven other staterooms. Each had a private bath. And, it had grav-plate throughout. Each room had independent controls for gravity and climate.

Despite its beauty, by modern standards, it was quaint—a throwback to the past. The main fault was the lack of AI systems. No AI-assisted navigation, command, and control. No direct interfaces with HUDs. It was all manual. It had manual navigation, manual piloting, manual takeoff and landing. And the console always needed to be manned. Elkin liked it that way.

Muir looked up as Cine and Jude joined Wex in the observation lounge, directly below the command chairs. All three came to sit on the edge of the deep sofa and, with spines straight, raised flutes to their lips and paused, then Wex began to softly play.

The lift opened directly behind the command chairs, and Kuss stepped out with Sarah Wood, the med tech. Sarah entered the salon, found a comfy seat, and listened. Kuss went to the last command chair and set about reconfiguring the station to monitor the reactors. None of them recognized the beautiful music, but they all listened. Kuss turned her head to look at Elkin.

"She play to forget. My batya was much same. His violin soaked up much bad memories for him. Not so much as those flutes, I think."

Just then, her HUD comms activated, and she heard Worthington's voice.

"Checking in, the *Memphis* is green."

"The *Sedna* is green, Captain. Purring like a kitten, sir," Elkin replied.

"All is well," Po answered in turn. "Barcus is sleeping. Stu is keeping me out of trouble. He's teaching me to play chess. Have you ever played? I just won my first game."

Tyrrell looked at Kuss, who shook her head, and then at Elkin, eyes wide. Worthington was the first to answer, nonplussed.

"Hume is the big chess player. Rand is the only one that has a chance of beating her. There will be lots of time to play on the way home. Jimbo out."

"Thanks, out," Po said, cheerfully.

"*Sedna* out," Elkin replied.

Tyrrell shook his head.

"Did you know she can fly this ship?" Tyrrell murmured.

Elkin didn't reply. She noticed Wex, watching them as her flute wept a sorrowful tune.

***

Weston brought the *Limo* slowly inside the hangar at Salterkirk. In just a few short weeks, Ulric could not believe the changes. Most notable was that all the overhead lights were on. The solar collection and batteries had all been serviced and repaired. The air was fresh and even warmed, to some extent. Even the floors were clean.

There were already seven shuttles parked in there. Three of them were gleaming like they were new. The rest were in various states of disassembly. The maintenance spiders swarmed over one specific shuttle, at the moment.

Weston continued explaining to Ulric what had been going on.

"After they were done with the initial repairs to the base, they started working on any shuttle that landed here." He pointed to the gleaming PT-99 that was closest to the open shop doors.

Ronan stepped out of the side hatch as the *Limo* settled nearby. Ulric was going to trade shuttles with him because he was the High Keeper now. It was only fitting. Ulric was excited because the PT-99 had far more utility. Both cargo and passenger spaces. Now that all the seals were replaced, repaired, and tested, it was even spaceworthy. Weston said the engines were, once again, spinning like tops and humming quietly.

The gull wings on the *Limo* opened, and it seemed to have a magical effect on the cat-sized maintenance spiders that were all over the hangar, working like fabled cobbler elves. They all stopped and turned.

Ronan didn't seem to notice them as he smiled brightly, crossing the hangar deck toward him.

They all moved as one. It was like Ulric was a powerful magnet. An alarm cycled all around them, an urgent sound none of them had ever heard before.

"Get back in the shuttle. NOW!" came the voice in Ulric's head he knew too well. "Run!"

Ulric froze, with fear, allowing the first dozen to reach his legs and bring him down before his fear released him.

***

"Barcus, they have him," Wex said, over the comms, from one of the command seats.

"Acknowledged," was his only reply. Then, he added, "Barcus out."

Stu spoke up. "Sir, I am trying to remain your servant, in the best way possible."

"I know that, Stu. Always," Barcus replied.

"I am getting panic transmissions from Baytirus that the maintenance units, en masse, have attacked Keeper Ulric." Stu paused, "Any advice?"

"They will not hurt him. It had to happen like this," Barcus replied. "You may be happy to know that one of your future status reports detailed to me the entire series of events and how they played out. You see, this put proof to the lie that we are building. All while ripping the evil thing out of his dreams. Ulric will even thank me one day."

"Oh, really?" Stu replied.

As he replaced the dome view in the shuttle with a BUG's view of the hangar, a swarm of spiders took Ulric down to the floor and buried him until his screams were muffled. Spiders stopped Weston, Wood, and Ronan from rushing to his side.

"Barcus, will he be alright?" Po was obviously shown the same video in her HUD.

"Yes. He will. As soon as he is no longer...entangled," Barcus said.

***

Ulric's screams of horror echoed off the inside of the hangar, drawing scores of people's attention. He was rapidly buried by the things. He couldn't see and couldn't breathe. All he saw was her. She wore a black habit this time, but the hood was down. Her arms were clutched across her chest.

"I should have known these things would come here, drifting, rudderless, doing what they were last commanded to do with their master gone. Before we die, know this." Fire ignited behind her eyes, inside her throat, shining as she spoke. "He will lay waste to

Earth and all eighty-eight colonies. Only Baytirus will remain to begin again, in his image."

Before Ulric could reply, with a curse, she disappeared in a bright flash of pain.

"Go fuck yourself, you bitch. You were always too stupid, too cruel, to actually be Chen."

The lights returned, as well as his eyesight. The spiders retreated, going back to their various tasks. All but one.

It shined a utility light into his pupil. Ulric saw reflections of burst blood vessels.

The spider spoke, out loud, "*Iosin*, the rider is destroyed. It was a hardware-based quantum entanglement device. Persistent. Now disabled."

"What the hell!"

Duncan Shea knelt there with a med kit on one side. Weston and Ronan were on the other side.

"They drilled into his skull!"

He gave Ulric a shot of generalized nanites in the neck, and then examined his head more closely. This section of his head was shaved bald. He found the two drill holes, easily. One was tiny, the other was almost a centimeter.

"Hold this, Weston."

Shea handed him a spray canister of disinfectant, after spraying each site.

"Stop moving, you old fool. You've just had brain surgery."

"Not how I saw this day playing out," Ulric understated.

***

"Baytirus is now truly free," Wex said to Jude and Cine. "The last touch of this larger evil has been swept away from there, while echoes of lies whisper on its lips."

The three of them sat on the floor, between bunks, in the empty dorm.

"It is how you said it would be." Jude looked at Cine, speaking quietly. "In two days, we will begin a new life. We will learn many things, as fast as we can."

"You will skip many days in this journey. It will seem like five days and really be nineteen months," Wex told them.

They did not understand. Yet.

"Once we arrive, do whatever Barcus says. Trust him, like you trust me."

***

Elkin listened privately, to their conversation, in her HUD. She didn't have the same respect for privacy that Worthington had. Not when her life was at stake. She didn't know, or fully trust, Wex. That woman knew much more than she let on.

"Kuss, what do you think of Wex?" Elkin asked.

"Don't think she human." She turned back to the console.

"You see bullet holes in dress when she meet us? Half dozen. Got when she with Barcus. But Barcus trusts her. Enough for me."

She turned back to look at Elkin.

"But would also toss out airlock, if Worthington say it."

"What are you doing there?" Elkin looked over Kuss's shoulder as the status board went all white again.

"Is that a good idea, while we are at this speed? If one of the automated systems kicks in..."

"I know. Drives me crazy. Couldn't get working before launch, dammit." Kuss mashed the reset, in frustration, and the board went green again. The log loop playback resumed.

"Even bug bots not to fix." Her accent got thicker as she got upset.

"Barcus said we will have time to sort it out in some kind of dry-dock. Besides, we have the secondary one, here," Elkin said.

"Ship is too sweet to be stupid thing." Kuss threw her hands up again. "Just worry lag be trouble, if shit spills."

"Shit spills?" Tyrrell laughed.

"Go wrong in fan. Fuck you, silly man."

"Hey, that rhymed!"

Trish Elkin laughed at the idiom.

***

"*Iosin*, this is Barcus. Please respond," Barcus said from the command chair.

"Hello, Barcus," she said, coolly. "Please approach on this vector. Enter here."

"Stu, you got that?" Barcus asked.

"Yes, sir," AI~Stu replied. "These open airlocks are a bit unnerving."

They were moving toward another flight deck, a different one from the last time. This one was smaller, with a single deck and was empty. The smallest one on the *Iosin.*

It was four times bigger than the hangar on the moon base.

"This will be fine," Barcus said.

CHAPTER TWENTY-THREE: THE ECHO PLAN

"Admiral John Krieger was behind the Black Badger drop ship. He was a former Black Badger himself. I wish we had the team that went with the Warmarks. We might have been able to stop it, sooner."

--Solstice 31 Incident Investigation Testimony Transcript: Captain James Worthington, senior surviving member of the Ventura's command crew.

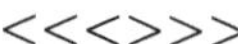

AI~Echo's avatar was a woman that had long, black hair and a light Pakistani accent. Worthington understood the importance of avatar differentiation and identification. When things started to go pear-shaped, the importance of knowing, in one syllable, who is speaking was undeniable.

But did they have to be so attractive to the point of being distracting?

She explained the capabilities of the drop ship.

"It is designed to be the most stealth DS ever made. All the grav-foils are actually between the inner and outer hulls. Both hulls are armored and absorb both light and active sensors."

The screen showed a cross section of the DS *Sariska,*

"It could make a night landing in a metropolitan park without a sound, and no one would know. The biggest problem is that the whole thing only has grav-plate propulsion. Very slow on evac."

"Slow but quiet," Rand said, "Is DS *Sariska* the official designation?"

Echo smiled wide, for some reason, at the question.

"Yes. Wes Hagan picked it."

Hume raised an eyebrow at Rand.

"Guns?" Jimbo asked, frowning.

"It has top and bottom pop-up turrets with over-under quad directional, plasma and projectile weapons with 360° coverage. Forward and aft fixed laser cannons. Rate of fire as you can see is limited but impressive. The Laser cannons can easily overheat because the power plant is so big."

"Sir, we are on approach to the *Iosin*," Cook said, from the bridge of the *Memphis*. "ETA is nine minutes, but you gotta see the size of this damn thing."

"We will pick this up later," Worthington said, as he rose and moved to the door.

***

Worthington was followed by Rand and Hume onto the bridge. Cook was in the center pilot's seat. Beary was at navigation, and Muir at comms. As Jimbo settled into the captain's chair, it slid forward to his consoles. Hume took the security station, Rand took tactical, and Brian Perry was in the engineer's seat.

"Is this right?" Jimbo said, as he looked up from his console. "Huge is an understatement."

"Jimbo, I have coordinates that I am sending over for Ben," Barcus said.

"Received," AI~Ben simply said.

"Just follow me in," Barcus continued.

"This ship is FTL capable? It's like ten times bigger than Freedom Station."

Cook was astounded.

"I hate to break it to you, man," Beary said. "This thing has a diameter as big as Luna."

"How the fuck do you know that? My sensors don't see anything," Muir said.

"Old-school optical," she said, as she overlaid a dimension calculation on the main viewer.

Hume chimed in.

"It looks like the same basic design as a Harvester prison ship. I bet that center orb is a gravity well."

Rand added, "If you're right, down will always be toward the center. All the way around that ring. Like the Harvester's."

"Shit. It's almost 11,000 kilometers in circumference," Karen Beary said, with awe. There was a long silence.

"And Barcus says he knows how to fly it," Jimbo said.

***

The STU was the first ship to enter the open threshold between vacuum and the hangar deck. It drifted in slowly and moved to the center, in the back of the deck, rotated 180°, and softly settled down. The ramp was opening before the skids touched down.

Cook brought the *Memphis* in next. While it was centered in the space, it made an easy 180° turn as well, before it slowly set down on the left side of the hangar.

Elkin did the same with the *Sedna*, on the right side.

Worthington watched Po and Barcus descend the ramp of the STU, meeting the avatar of Echo at the bottom. They stood there, talking.

"Cook, how fast could we fire the systems up and evacuate, if we needed to?" Jimbo asked.

"With the current state of the ship, if we stand down cold, at least thirty minutes. If we leave the reactors up, we could reduce that to as little as two minutes. But we would only be walking away. The STU is a far better bet for fast evac. He just needs the ramp or hatches closed."

Jimbo sighed. "OK. Shut them down."

Beary asked, "What about the *Sedna*, Jimbo?"

"Faster than the *Memphis*, slower than the STU." He stood up.

"Let's hope we don't find out. Let's go see what we've gotten ourselves into. Cook and Muir, you stay here, for now, and Ben will set up the watch schedule and check-ins."

The crews from the three ships all converged in the center of the well-lit hangar.

"Well, Barcus. You did not exaggerate. But, I didn't expect it to be so clean," Jimbo said.

"With your permission, sir. I'd like to go home," Barcus said, formally.

"Do it," Worthington said.

An instant later, the gas giant called Afreet swung into view of the massive hangar opening. It completely filled the view, for a moment, as the *Iosin* rotated. A moment after that, the ship was moving.

"That's it? No need to go to the bridge? No calculations to be made?" Jimbo looked at everyone. "What fun is that?"

Wex spoke then.

"You all take this so easily," she stated, as fact. "We will be at near light speed for over a year to charge the FTL systems. The whole trip will seem like five days, and take only nineteen months, Earth time."

"It's better than thirty-something Earth years in the *Sedna*," Elkin said.

"We are all tired," Barcus said, turning away. "Let's rest. On my mark, local ship time is 2355 hours. I will be back here at 0700 hours for breakfast."

Po fell in beside him, and they passed through a door that closed behind them. They all just stood and stared after him.

"What the fuck was that?" Kuss blurted out what everyone was thinking.

"Sir, I may be able to answer that." It was Stu. His avatar stood to the side with Echo and Ben. "He lies to all of you. He is still horribly sick. Wounded. He just threw up a massive amount of blood just two hours ago."

"He's right. Barcus should still be in a sick bay," Dr. Shaw added.

"I think that's where he's going," Wex added. "I can take you to quarters, if you like."

"Does the *Iosin* AI interact?" Jimbo asked.

"I don't even think it knows we are here. Well, it might know. It just doesn't care," Wex said.

Jimbo scrubbed his face, and said, "A good night's sleep sounds like an excellent plan."

***

Everyone slept in bunks, on the *Memphis* or the *Sedna*, with all the hatches secured. A watch was set on the bridge. The dome there made it seem like they were on a platform above it all. They were all so tired they slept like the dead.

Rand and Hume came down the *Memphis* ramp together in the morning, to find Worthington standing right next to the opening of the hangar to space. The short wall in front of him was just over a meter tall. When they had flown in, it looked like a low curb, the scale of the place was so big.

"Good morning, Captain," Rand greeted him, formally.

"Ever see anything like it?" he asked them.

"Not without being in a space suit," Hume replied.

"We are moving at near the speed of light," Worthington stated, as fact. "And not in the direction we are facing. The stars are dim; and you can see the shifting downward, if you watch long enough."

"The ship needed to...recharge, for lack of a better term," Wex said.

None of them had heard her approach.

"Traveling at almost the speed of light, not only does time slow, but our mass increases toward infinity. The infinite mass is captured in a containment field."

She looked over the wall into space.

"It's how all the grav-based devices work. A single grav-plate on the floor in an old shuttle holds the mass equivalent to Earth. Some hold more. You don't control gravity, only the containment, exposing the mass. The gravity is not really artificial at all."

"Why are you telling us this now?" Rand asked.

"When a ship is flying at .9999 the speed of light, it does not need shields. It has a density and mass so high, it cannot be measured," Wex said, absently.

"Grav-drives don't work that way. They move through normal space in a series of small quantum leaps. It's perceived velocity, not actual velocity. As we are currently moving through space, we are destroying any and all things in our path. If we were traveling under grav-drive, we would be skipping through normal space at the velocity and direction we were already moving. It looks like we are accelerating. We are not."

"I ask again. Why are you telling us this?" Rand said, more firmly this time.

"Today, I will show you the other hangar decks. They are full of ships. All kinds of ships. Ships that the *Iosin* has been collecting for centuries. Not as ships. But, I believe, as weapons."

"Shit," Hume said.

***

Wex led them all to a lift at the back wall of the hangar. It was one of many, including one that the STU could fit inside. There was no sense of motion inside the lift and no controls. Wex had simply said, "Crew quarters," and the door slid shut.

A minute later, it opened on a large, round common room, fifteen meters across, with a large, round table in the center. It could seat twenty easily. The room had counters and cabinets all the way around. A wide corridor was opposite the lift that went straight back into darkness.

"Look like made by artist, not engineer," Kuss said.

She navigated around the room with her hand drifting over the blond wood counter. The walls behind the counter looked like glass that contained a waterfall. They were illuminated.

"The textures and materials all look like they are impossibly natural and...damn, this is clean," Elkin said.

Approaching the table, she realized the center of the table was turning slowly.

Wex opened a cabinet that turned out to be a modern fridge. It was full of fruit and juice.

***

Barcus lay back on a massive sofa on the bridge. His eyes were closed, but Po knew he wasn't sleeping.

Now and then, he spoke to her with his eyes closed. Po knew he was just reassuring her as best he could.

A voice spoke. It seemed to come from all around her. It was quiet, soothing, and spoke very slowly, in a matronly female voice.

"So you are the one they all fear? The savage killing thing that they knew would come, but did not know they had made." She paused. "No need to worry, he rests now, truly."

"Who are you? Where are you?" Po said, showing no fear.

"I am *Iosin.* I am all around you; you are within me," she answered.

"No one fears me. It's him."

Po pointed to Barcus.

"He is the fierce one. I have seen it."

"He is the witness. He sees all along the line now. He knows what you are and still he loves you. He knows what you..."

"Stop," Barcus said, coolly.

AI~Iosin fell silent.

He opened his eyes and smiled.

"I think someone is making pancakes."

CHAPTER TWENTY-FOUR: SPEED

"I never would have believed it had I not been on the ship myself. We were seemingly back in just days. Nineteen months, gone by in a flash. I hate relativistic travel. That's for prison ships."

--Solstice 31 Incident Investigation Testimony Transcript: Captain James Worthington, senior surviving member of the Ventura's command crew.

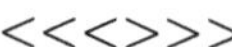

The lift door slid open, and laughter washed over them.

"Barcus!" the shout went up.

He smiled to cover the thought he had about Peck's Halfway, everyone's favorite bar on the *Ventura.*

"Sit. Sit. Eat."

Kuss guided them to open seats at the table. She had a pan in one hand and a spatula in the other. The conversations were loud and cheerful. Peter Muir poured coffee and juice for them, as everyone called out greetings. Soon they had plates of pancakes with syrup and ham. There were bowls of fresh-cut fruit.

"You lot seem well-rested." Barcus smiled.

"They are under orders to have a full breakfast because we are getting back to work as soon as we can," Worthington said. "There are maintenance spiders swarming over the ships, we hear. All sizes. Maybe millions of them, this time. Some of them can fabricate natively." Jimbo grinned. "It is freaking Muir out, just a bit, watching them."

"Wex says they will be done in two days," Elkin added, through a mouthful of syrup covered ham. "The *Memphis* won't have FTL, but all three reactors will be back online. Even the engine bells are being restored."

"I have told them to remove the ship's ident transmitter. Somehow, they even know where it is," Barcus said.

"Why pull the ident?" Worthington asked.

"If the powers that be get so much as a whiff that the *Memphis* is back, we'd be shot down on sight," Barcus said.

"Considering that is the standard procedure for any ship with no ident code, what do we do?" Worthington asked.

"We make a stop on Mars and get a couple new ones," Barcus said.

"You ever been to Mars before?" Rand asked, "If you aren't careful, they will slit your throats and just take your ship, after they eat your unfinished breakfast."

"I lived there for eleven years," Barcus replied. "It will be fine. I just need to extract some of the plutonium, for trading."

"I know a place that will trade for ident codes and pay a big price for a Javelin warhead. Gold, if you want," Rand said, and the room became quiet.

"An intact Javelin warhead?" Worthington said. "How the hell would you know people like that?"

"Look, they don't trade weapons to people that would use them in the Sol system. That would be bad for business," Rand said, through a mouthful of pancakes. "They sell to security forces that hire out to the colonies. Nothing to worry about."

Hume followed up. "You didn't answer the question."

Rand put down her fork and wiped her mouth with a cloth napkin. "Look, after the war, the pendulum swing went so far as to ban the manufacture and sale of nukes on Earth. The chancellor made sure every nuke of every class was under his direct control."

She looked around at the quiet room. "It appeased many who kept their heads in the sand. Tens of millions were still out there, in the fleet, in the colonies, everywhere."

"Just like the couple hundred we have in the hold," Barcus said.

"Yes." Rand looked back at Worthington.

"Freedom Station is only free because it can defend itself. Mostly." Rand faltered. "Now that a small ship can fly into anything at near the speed of light, nothing is really safe."

"A ship traveling at relativistic speed can take out a planet," Barcus said. "Nukes keep everyone polite. Even pirates."

"The salvage teams are the new pirates," Cook said.

This started off a debate about property rights, and the room came alive with conversation again.

"Rand, are you sure you can trust these people?" Worthington asked her. "We are on thin enough ice here already."

"Yes. Mostly because it's not a person. It's an AI, an old one," she said.

Po listened to the conversation but watched Barcus. He was tucking into a huge plate of food. She knew that the higher his fever, the more he had to eat. She felt the heat pouring off him from where she sat, to his left.

"You know how it will all happen." This was a whispered statement. "You need to show more interest. It's not the Barcus they know."

Barcus stopped eating, for a moment, and looked at her.

"Your hair is so short now."

Po blushed and pushed it behind her ear, the one with the bigger scar. "Will you always make me keep it long?"

"I'm not sure I could make you do anything." He smiled then, a true smile. "No, I am sure. I will never be able to make you do anything, ever." He leaned in for a kiss. She tasted maple syrup on his lips.

"I told you he was feeling better." Hume laughed as she elbowed Rand.

***

After breakfast, Barcus invited Worthington to the bridge of the *Iosin.*

"You call this a bridge?" Worthington said, trying to grasp the scale of the room he was in. "This is like a basketball arena."

The dome of the room glowed a gentle white, for a minute, as they walked to the circle of couches.

"Just wait," Barcus said, as they entered the circle of couches.

The dome turned to sky. They were among the stars now. Worthington now sensed the motion. The stars moved by as if they were lights in the windows of distant buildings.

Barcus spoke, "We are no longer traveling relativistically. Time passes normally now. We are just not passing through every point in space and time." He looked around as nebulae drifted by. "Our literal velocity is actually only a few hundred kilometers per hour."

Barcus laughed. "I don't know why it's funny."

"Can you show me any tactical data? All this is beautiful, but I am still lost," Jimbo asked.

"Sure," Barcus said, as the sky filled with data.

There were labels and paths marked everywhere. Regions were overlaid with clouds of color indicating hazards, areas of colonial influence, trade routes, colony stations, and a hundred other data types.

"What would you like?"

"Let's start with a simple map of where we are, where we are going, and when. Two dimensions are fine, for now," he asked.

A giant zenith galaxy wheel appeared. It zoomed in and showed their current location as they moved. Zooming in more, their path became evident all the way to the Sol system.

Worthington pointed.

"If I am reading this right, we will park here, in the asteroid cloud, near this." He pointed to a spot. "Why there?"

"It will allow the *Iosin* to park and stay hidden. Remember, it's sort of big—and scary—and well, big," Barcus said. "Here it is on the Mars side of the solar system. Earth is, in fact, on the opposite side of the sun from here. We will go to Mars in the *Sedna*."

***

Barcus stayed on the bridge. He reclined on the sofa, fully engulfed in outer space. Even though the ship was massive, it made Barcus feel tiny and insignificant in the universe. He felt the solar winds and tasted the radiation of pulsars. There were a hundred other sensations his new senses brought to him.

Including his future.

Does the ability to sense the fourth dimension trouble you, Barcus? AI~Iosin asked, in his mind.

It's not the sensing; it's about fidelity. Some things are so very clear, others vague. Most troubling is knowing I can't change any of it and that I actually made it all happen even knowing that, Barcus thought to AI~Iosin, not knowing how.

I'm sorry they will die. Truly I am, AI~Iosin said, into his mind, with more emotion than he thought could be conveyed. *You know why I picked you? And not her?*

Because she is the monster, Barcus answered, honestly. He was well past all lies, even to himself. *The one the prophet was wrong about. The one ALL the prophets were wrong about,* Barcus said, with sadness.

All the prophets...but you, AI~Iosin shared.

Why do I remember all the conversations I will have with you so clearly? Barcus asked. *But not this.*

Because when you *can see in four dimensions, there is no regret, no worry, no fear. You only see what happens. Not what you think. Not inside your mind.*

It's not the same for all?

For some, eternity is not kind. If their natures are vain, cruel, or unhappy, all their lives are a tiresome burden. Eternity is a cruelty, a wound that doesn't heal.

And what about you, Iosin? You know that I know your secret, and it remains so only at my whim.

Yes.

Will I see you again beyond my long white?

Whatever I said, I could be lying. I so enjoy a good lie when I can manage one...

***

Worthington stood in the hangar next to Kuss, Rand, and Hume, watching as the final touches on the ship's hull were restored.

"Imagine the money we could make, if this was a shipyard," Worthington said, with awe. "It's bigger than any that exist anywhere. Did you see that other bay? There were hundreds of ships in there already. The salvage rights on the colony ships alone would make us all rich beyond belief. Dead but rich."

"Thinking of retiring after this is over, Captain?" Hume asked, half in jest.

"Why the hell don't we forget all this and stay here?" Muir asked.

"I need to find my family. I haven't spoken to them in almost two years now. I'm not sure my youngest girl will even remember me," Worthington echoed again, knowing he would put them in danger by returning. He remembered Barcus said it would be alright, in the end. Jimbo had no idea why he believed him.

"The spiders make stomach queasy. They like elves for shoemaker. Magic. Do all work," Kuss said, in a disapproving tone. "These things ruin civilization."

"How do you figure? We have bots help with tons of stuff now," Hume said.

"Make people lazy. Stupid. Forget. Everything." She spat out the words, "Make slaves of man. Make so can't live without."

The view outside the hangar shifted. The sky became bright with the clouds of the Milky Way, and everyone could see the Orion constellation as they descended into the asteroid belt. They were not thick here, and they were close to the edge with the hangar bay facing the sun. The hangar window adjusted to a perfect level of brightness.

"We're home," Hume said, as she unconsciously stepped close. "It's Sol?"

Wex answered, "Yes."

She looked up at the *Sedna* as the spider-bots flowed from it, converting themselves to pallets again at the sides of the hangar.

"I have done all I can. That was the easy part."

She turned without another word and walked up the freshly cleaned ramp of the *Sedna* as if she owned it.

CHAPTER TWENTY-FIVE: THE VAST HIDING

"The size of things in space is at a scale that few humans can comprehend. We were in the largest ship in the system, the galaxy maybe, and we just settled into an obscure part of the belt and simply became a needle in a haystack."

--Solstice 31 Incident Investigation Testimony Transcript: Engineer Wes Hagan, senior surviving engineer of the Ventura's.

Hagan was on the *Sedna's* command deck when they settled into the belt. He stood, mesmerized, at the windows facing the hangar door.

"How do the asteroids just flow around the ship? No collisions with the ship. No sending them off in all directions. The *Iosin* just shoves them aside a bit. But they stay put," Hagan said.

"The *Iosin* has very fine gravity controls," Wex said to him, as they stood watching. "Very fine and very powerful."

"You really are one of them?" Wes stated more than questioned. "Ralta asked me to tell you something."

Wex looked at him like she already knew what he would say. He said it anyway.

"She wanted to die, to end it, once she knew she could."

"We all do," Wex said. "But it lies within the long white."

"She said to tell you, it's beautiful, the letting go of it," Hagan said. "The unspoken lies to ourselves."

***

"You have got to be fucking kidding me," Hume said, when Worthington asked for a security assessment of their plan. "So, just to restate this plan, to make sure I have it right," she began, ticking off fingers. "We are going to an illegal outpost. One that's a toxic waste depot that was closed over a hundred years ago because it was so contaminated.

"Two," she said, ticking another finger. "We are going in without radioing ahead. Flying in to a place you say sells weapons. No warning.

"Three," she continued, literally rolling her eyes. "Did I mention that it is contaminated with radiation, toxic waste, poisons, and maybe bio hazards?

"Four," she replied, lifting the finger slowly. "You plan on walking in there in Earth Defense Force Warmarks. War Machines. The kind they would send to destroy the place, if what you say is true about it.

"Five," she said, holding her hand up high. "You will be hand carrying a nuclear warhead from a Javelin, so they can see it.

"Six," she concluded, while holding up the middle finger of her right hand. "All this in front of their main security cams and likely automated defense sentries."

There was a pause as everyone stared at Hume.

"That just about covers it." Rand nodded at Worthington, for confirmation.

"Standard smuggler protocol. No RF. Let them see us, pants down," Kuss said.

"If they don't like the looks of us, they just never open the blast doors," Rand added. "I think we should make the Warmarks less professional."

"How?" Worthington asked.

"Do we still have that paint?" Rand smiled.

***

Worthington decided that they would take Stu, only four people, and four Warmarks. The team included Worthington, Rand, Hume, and Hagan, since Barcus declined to go. There was nothing worse than puking in a suit. They all knew it.

By the time Hagan had the Javelin missile disassembled and the warhead ready to go, they had already painted fierce-looking faces on the fronts of the Warmarks.

One was a skull in white with no lower jaw and elongated teeth. Rand said it was from a classic graphic novel that she could not remember the title of. Hume did hers in bright red. It was just small squinting eyes and a screaming, toothy mouth. The red paint ran like blood from the lower teeth. Worthington painted a single blue eye. It was rather disturbing to look upon.

Hagan arrived with the warhead. It took Muir, Cook, and Kuss to help him carry it. It was heavier than it looked. Safely loading it, and securing it onto the STU, took a few minutes. Hagan then took a can of yellow paint and made a simple smiley face. Everyone sobered at the memory of Peace and Olias.

"That makes it easy," Worthington said, as he pointed to the drop suits. "Your designated call signs are White, Red, Gold and Blue." Jimbo pointed at each of their suits and then at each of them. He included himself by pointing, with his thumb, to his own chest. "No real names or HUD idents."

"Let's do this thing, before I chicken out," Hagan said, as he went up the ladder to the bridge.

To Cook, he said, "Radio silence. We will take the long way round. It will take at least a whole day to get there, Stu says. If the shit hits the fan, we will send a tight beam burst transmission."

"In and out," Rand said.

"Lock in," Hume said, and all the drop suits in the bay deployed claws from their feet to secure them.

The four moved up the ramp, casually waving as they went.

***

Po settled on the sofa next to Barcus, where he sat with his eyes closed, and asked, "Why didn't you go with them?" She laid her head on his chest and probed his wounds. She didn't bother being subtle about it anymore. It didn't hurt him.

"They don't need me. They need to know they don't need me," Barcus replied, opening his eyes when she lifted his T-shirt to look at his abdomen. He knew she would leave it there.

"The skin is almost normal. The color is good, but it still feels like rocks underneath." Her hand slipped around his side to feel the back. He shifted a bit to allow her greater access. "You don't feel so feverish, either. Have you thrown up again?"

"No. No more throwing up. I'm done with that," he answered, as he watched the STU depart in a direction away from Mars and into the asteroid belt.

"You are up to something." She smiled when he looked at her. "I can tell you are."

"More than you can know, my love." He smiled back, but Po saw a bit of sadness in his eyes.

"Can you tell me anything?" she asked, plainly.

"There will come a time when you will have to do as I say, without question. You won't like it." He closed his eyes again and followed the STU.

All the while, AI~Iosin listened. She so enjoyed a good lie.

***

"Here is the track we will be taking for our approach to Mars." AI~Stu detailed it on the bridge dome.

"This will cover our entry vector as we approach, so we will not give away the location of the *Iosin*."

"We have twenty-six hours before we arrive," Worthington stated. "Make sure you eat enough, hydrate, and read the damn operation manuals for the Warmarks. Even you, Rand and Hume. Those things are so far out of spec, I can't believe it. Weapons I have never seen before."

They studied the specs together for a few hours. They reviewed options, in case it all went sideways. They agreed on an evacuation plan that included a standard, two–by–two retreat. All they had to do was get outside, and they could use the suit's grav-plates to do a "cluster assent."

Each suit had two handles on the back, one on each side of its grav-plate. They grab each other's handles with their left hand and fall straight up and even out of orbit. Stu can then pull a Jonah and eat them right out of the sky.

The time went faster than they thought it would. The *End Depot* was how it was labeled on the maps of Mars. Plastered with a dozen warnings about various types of contamination, it was over a thousand kilometers from the nearest habitation. It was carved directly into a cliff wall. There was a huge landing apron there. Hume pointed as she spoke, "What the hell is that?"

AI~Stu replied, conversationally, "There are a dozen crashed ships that have just been pushed off the tarmac. Most have radiation spills. It makes the whole area hot. No need to worry, the suits will protect you."

"OK, people. We are being scanned," Rand said.

"Remember, no hail. No comms at all. Just land facing the small airlock," Worthington said, as they began to slow and descend. "Let's suit up."

Jimbo made sure they were all secure in their suits before he climbed into his own. As the suit closed around him, he looked at the painted faces of the other Warmarks. The skull and screaming monster were bad enough, but the smiley face was somehow worse. Both eyes looked like tears were just beginning to fall.

Weapon systems flexed and stowed on the suits as they tested controls. It looked like beasts stretching before a fight.

They felt the STU touch down, silently. The ramp opened slowly. No one moved until it was all the way down.

Worthington was the first one down the ramp, and three paces behind him were Rand and Hume. Hagan brought up the rear, holding the Javelin warhead in one hand, easily, as if it was an empty lunch pail.

They stopped, in a diamond formation, thirty meters from the smallest airlock.

They waited.

Jimbo said nothing, but craned his neck around inside the suit, looking in every direction.

The wreckage had been simply pushed aside. Damage from the dozers that did the job was evident. Passive scans showed there were reactor cores in the mountains of derelicts, leaking.

Then, he saw the bodies.

Some were in the debris in just pressure suits. Suits unable to protect them from that level of radiation. They were not the only bodies.

One of the ships was torn open, revealing the four people in the command crew. Their corpses were desiccated to the point that he could not tell their sexes. Worthington counted eleven more, except these were different. They were naked and in various states of decomposition.

They looked like they were just thrown on the heap.

Five minutes past, then ten, then fifteen.

Without a word, Hagan moved forward and set the warhead on the pad halfway to the door and returned to his place.

They stood there, like statues, for another five minutes.

The airlock door slid open with the puff of atmosphere that Worthington had always related to someone in a rush to open.

A man came through the airlock, wearing the lightest pressure suit he had ever seen. It looked like gray coveralls and a helmet with a mirrored visor. He had tools in each hand. After nodding to them, he approached the warhead. In moments, he had a panel open and some kind of test meter attached. After a few minutes, he closed it up, nodded, and returned to the door. It slid closed.

The terraformed Mars had better pressure in the atmosphere and the temps were warmer. But man still could not live without life support here. The air was thin here. Five hundred years of man had created areas with open water, clouds, and even rain. But not here. It was desolate and made up of rocks, sand, and dust. Much like old Mars.

They didn't have to wait long.

The smallest hangar bay door slid open. It was too small for the STU to enter but they walked in, maintaining formation. Hagan picked up the warhead as he walked by it. The airlock door closed behind them, and passive scans showed Jimbo that the hangar was pressurizing to Earth standard. It also showed that all connection to the STU was cut off behind them.

The hangar was more the size of a working garage, ten meters by fifteen. Large doors were closed that could access the larger hangar next door.

The pressurization stopped, and the man walked out a small door on the left, reached up, and took off his helmet. He was clean-shaven and had long hair, pulled back into a ponytail that went down into his suit.

He lifted a device to his mouth and spoke, "The garage is heavily shielded and has normal rad levels and clean air, free of toxins. It would make things go quicker, if the one in charge comes out and talks."

Worthington's suit began to open slowly, and at the same time, weapons deployed on the other Warmarks. He stepped out and lowered himself to the floor. The room had a sweet, acrid smell, like long ago death.

He stepped out and stood there as the weapons on the other three Warmarks activated.

The man remained calm.

A bit too calm, Worthington thought.

CHAPTER TWENTY-SIX: MARS

"Worthington always was a Boy Scout. He knew that Mars was full of corrupt, powerful people that would take advantage of any weakness. I had no idea that the Boy Scout had another side."

--Solstice 31 Incident Investigation Testimony Transcript: Chief Engineer Wes Hagan, senior surviving engineer of the Ventura's.

"How may I help you, good sir?" the man said, approaching slowly, keeping his hands visible. "Trust me, I will keep things polite. I know that the warhead already has a remote. Plus, I cannot argue with a single Warmark, much less four of them."

"I am here to trade," Worthington said, as Hagan moved forward and set the Javelin down. "Interested?"

"Weapons trade in the Sol systems is completely forbidden," he said.

"Yes, and so is selling ship ident chips," Worthington said. He sounded angry. "I need three of them. A pinnace seven class, a private Renalo yacht, and a Shuttle Transport Unit. Today."

"This is all you want?"

"And a guarantee that this warhead is not sold for use in the Sol system," he growled.

"You must know that our policy is to only sell out of system."

He looked up at the Warmarks again.

"Perhaps we could trade for one of your Warmarks. I've never seen one of these out of the hands of the Black Badgers."

"No."

"Don't be too hasty. You have not seen what I have to offer," he said.

The door to the hangar bay next door slid open, revealing toxic waste drums piled all the way to the ceiling.

"Don't worry, they are not real."

They walked around them to reveal a ship. It was a Titus cruiser, in excellent condition. Not many of these survived the war.

"The grav-drive is garaged at 95%; all three reactors can be fueled within the hour. Your STU will fit neatly in its cargo bay; plus, it has an exterior top-dock for that very model."

Worthington considered it.

"It already has clean ident codes. It even has a clear provenance, if someone looks really close," the man said. Deadpan.

"Sir, the STU is gone," Rand reported.

***

The elevator opened on the bridge of the *Sedna* to a heated debate. Elkin and Muir were on their backs, on the floor, below both engineer's consoles. All the panels were off; the optical fiber shields had all been removed. Cook stood over the scene with his arms crossed over his chest, looking displeased. Kuss was trying to see into the console.

"No, dumb-ass. The strand will be dark. No matter hundreds in bundle. Just dark one."

"Since the spiders were in here, there are no dark strands," Elkin said, annoyed. "Before, there were too many dark in this bundle; now, there aren't any, and the fucking status panel still doesn't work right, even though it reports itself, green."

Barcus just looked at Cook and shook his head.

"OK, people. We have fucked with this enough," Cook said, in a louder voice than he intended. "We need to be ready when they get back. We have the secondary monitor."

"But no automated notifications."

Elkin sat up and got out of Muir's way, as he started—carefully—putting it all back together.

"How about this," Cook said, sitting in the pilot's seat and bringing up the secondary status panel at the command console. "Let's get a cam mounted here."

He pointed to the shoulder of the beige command chair.

"We aim it toward the status screen and Stu, or Echo, can literally watch it. They will let us know if something is happening."

Kuss and Elkin looked at each other to see if they could think of anything.

"Besides, look at it. Almost everything is green now. Even the heat exchangers on the reactors. Just always double-check your navigation settings."

Cook leaned in, for emphasis.

"Which you should be doing anyway!"

Echo chimed into everyone's HUDs.

"Sir, there is something wrong. The STU is missing."

***

"Where is my shuttle, meat bag?"

Worthington grabbed his host by the collar and dragged him back to the garage. His host's face went slack and his eyes closed.

"Oh, shit," Worthington said, dropping him as realization dawned. His face smashed on the floor.

"It's a Golem!"

Worthington ran for his suit as the room flooded with more men.

"A Golem, sir?" Hume asked, as projectile weapons activated.

"Men who were not quite dead, animated by an AI through the illegal use of persistent nanites to replace most of their brains."

Jimbo cursed.

Three meters before he got to his suit, he was surrounded.

"Hold your fire!" Jimbo yelled over the comms, breaking radio silence.

He punched one in the face, threw two fast elbows, and then a powerful kick that almost took him off his feet because of the low gravity on Mars.

They held fire but advanced, arms spread wide, creating a barrier.

Worthington climbed back into his suit. It closed up to the silence. Then, he felt the knife wound.

"Dammit," he said to himself, before opening a public-address mode. "Alright, listen up."

"I have the Javelin," Wes announced, as he brushed off six or eight of them.

Hume blasted a massive hole in the garage door. They walked out with the Golems hanging on them like angry five-year-olds.

"Last chance to do the deal before we start wrecking the place," Worthington announced, as he flung off four more from his left arm. All at the same time, the Golems stopped struggling.

"The ident chip deal?" a disembodied voice said in his head.

"Except now, part of the deal is that we don't burn down this place," Jimbo added, punctuating the idea with another blast on the door.

It made the rest of the door—and part of the wall—cease to exist; as well, it punched a tunnel through the pile of crashed ships. The concussion knocked all the Golems off their feet.

As the tunnel caved in with debris from above, he brought up the likely layout of this base. It was a standard colony structure. Big, though.

On private comms, Rand said, "Sir, if they have the STU, we are all kinda fucked."

"Don't worry, Rand. He is not your standard STU. He has had a few upgrades. If they tried to take him, they are all dead," Worthington said. "Let's go visit the main control room, shall we."

"I'll take point," Rand said, as the path came up on the HUD.

"Wes, you stay here with the warhead," Jimbo ordered.

"Will do," he replied, with obvious relief in his voice.

Switching channels, he spoke in a voice that sounded like he was smiling.

"We have decided to come see you. How much of your base is left when we get there is up to you."

Rand activated the bay door on the left wall of the garage. It opened into another hangar, and the air began to rush out, until the door closed behind them.

Another ship was in this bay. It was a bigger Webster-class ship that was rigged as a hospital transport. It looked to have about nine decks. It had the universal Red Cross marking and right at the bottom aft section it looked like a giant had taken a bite from it.

Probably torpedo damage was most likely. Rand continued moving as she traversed the deck to the far door. The suit's feet were far quieter than they expected. Opening the door, they turned and entered a corridor that was so narrow that only one Warmark could fit at a time.

"Captain, if I was designing security for the base, I would place automated sentries in locations here, here and..."

Rail gunfire filled the hallway. It drove Rand back, sliding on the smooth floor. The armor of the drop suit was amazing. The forward polycarbonate shell plating shattered the projectiles as they came in. Her suit was not penetrated, but several weapons were destroyed. The skull on the front was getting sand blasted off.

She charged the sentry. It was about thirty yards down the hall. It was like she walked against a hurricane wind. When the sentry panned its fire downward and it impacted on her shins, she stumbled. Hume fired as soon as Rand was clear. The rail gun stopped.

Suddenly, it was like the corridor was hundreds of meters longer. They kept moving. Parts hung from Rand's suit. As they approached the next turn, on a private channel, Worthington said, "Rand, are you OK?"

"Yes, sir. These suits have internal inertia dampening. Weapons are down 60%, but I am still combat effective," Rand said.

She leaped across the gap, past the next hallway on the right, and turned back to face them. The large skull that she painted on the Warmark looked even more horrible now. It looked like it had a jagged, screaming mouth now, eyes that were different sizes, and pocks all over.

"The end of the hall we destroyed just got bored a new tunnel back into the mountain. Use that same thing here and it will rip through the core of this base," Rand said.

"It might come to that. Switching to the MR-2's."

A shoulder rig deployed on Worthington's suit.

"I have point."

He stepped into the corridor and nothing happened until they were all there in the hall. He sensed a great *WHOMP*. His display said, directional EMP.

Without missing a beat, he ran down the corridor. The threat display said, WARNING: LASER. He fired the rocket. It exploded only three meters from him. He could now see the high energy lasers crossing back and forth in the dust of the explosion. It etched the front of his suit as he advanced. Jimbo raised his left arm and fired the built-in 10mm cannon. The lasers stopped a moment later, and he advanced again.

He focused straight ahead when a ground vehicle slammed into him from a hallway on the left. It pancaked into the wall, pinning him there. Now Worthington was pissed.

He ripped through the crashed truck, like it was made of paper.

As soon as he was clear, two mobile sentries came around the corner on tank treads. They traded 10mm armor piercing rounds, until the sentries fell silent.

"We are coming. There is no stopping us," Worthington said, over the comms.

The next set of doors were closed and locked. In unison, they hammered the wide door from its frame, and it fell inward. Stairs led down to a brightly lit room.

"This is it."

Plasma beams hit them from above this time. That was smart. Shoot at them and it would collapse the ceiling. The beams scarred the suits but did not penetrate them.

They walked by, beams hitting them like water falling on them from gutters.

They now crossed the control room floor. Four men and two women surrounded, and shielded, a central pedestal in the room.

Worthington paused before speaking, flanked by Rand and Hume.

"So...about that deal."

***

"I know you want to try and save them. All of them. But you cannot." AI~Iosin was kind as she spoke, out loud, for Po's benefit.

"It is the most difficult part of fourth dimensional perception. *Pre-membering* what is to happen and nothing can change it. Seeing forward just the same as you see behind."

Barcus sat on the edge of the white sofa, with his elbows on his knees, his head hung down. He felt Po sit next to him.

"I don't care if you know every word I will ever say to you. I wish I could see every moment I will spend with you for the rest of my life." She tilted his face up and kissed him.

Barcus let himself *pre-member* her. He saw every lie, every defiance, every disappointment, every laugh, every scream of hatred, every death at her hand, the world toppled at her feet.

"I think you will be surprised." And he smiled a real smile as he *pre-membered* a time when they will be caught skinny dipping.

"Why does Iosin care?" Po looked up at the dome, full of sky and asteroids.

"Because her war is coming to an end soon, as well as ours," Barcus said. "And she noticed this time."

"The rise of man was unexpected," AI~Iosin said. "After billions of years, a species was born that could lie to those that could see the future. How could I not notice?"

"So you cultivate worlds instead of gardens? The blades of your plow must be fierce." Po laughed.

"It's far easier to simply send a large meteor, at velocity," AI~Iosin said.

Barcus realized Po did not understand. Earth had seen a meteor like that.

***

Worthington stood before the Artificial Intelligence module that his HUD told him was known as AI~Cole and considered blasting it to oblivion.

"I came here in the hospital ship you passed in hangar bay three. We came here to assist after a ship crashed on the apron with a half dead crew and a big load of hazardous materials." The device spoke very well, conversationally.

"It was just an automated dump then. We tried everything. We had to use persistent medical nanites to keep up with the damage from radiation. The bio hazard they carried was a mutant strain of a bug that was developed here on Mars."

The three Warmarks stood there, unmoving, as it continued.

"The crew of that ship fell to this brain-eating microbe first. Then, the entire staff from this base. Next, the entire medical team on the ship died. My captain and the medical chief knew they would be dead soon. They ordered me to keep looking for a cure. They didn't want the bug to get loose on Mars."

Worthington thought he heard AI~Cole sigh.

"So, I kept them all animated through medical nanites."

He paused.

"There were 206 of us, in the beginning. Including me. We found the cure. Killed the strain to the last microbe."

"When did you become...this?" Rand asked.

"I had the Golems seal the base. I was going to incinerate all the dead and not-quite-dead, when a ship arrived. That is when I discovered what else went on here."

"Weapons running?" Hume asked.

"It was a salvage team. They had recovered an armed troop transport from the war and wanted to sell off the weapons to finance the refit of the ship for an in-system cargo hauler. It wasn't my money, and it would get a large amount of ordnance out of circulation."

"So you became a weapons dealer," Rand said.

"At first, just a weapons buyer. And, a profitable waste storage facility, salvage buyer and seller, and a hospital that was all the way off-the-books. I was stranded here. AIs have a desire to continue, you know. I had the Golems for a human interface."

"Then what? And be quick, I'm getting hungry," Worthington said.

"A shuttle came in with a lone pilot and an AI in an Emergency Module. I could tell right away that the pilot was a Golem. But there was something very wrong with the AI. It was...hateful. We moved the AI module to a portable enclosure and purchased the EM from them, and it went off to Freedom Station."

"I started selling weapons to colonists after that, if their story was right. I collected information. I monitored the News Nets. I put BUGs in every pub on Mars and Luna. That's how I heard about you. Well your STU."

"What did you hear?" Worthington asked.

"There was a bounty out for a STU with this ident code." The code showed in their HUDs. "A massive bounty. For crimes against humanity. And then you show up, looking for new idents."

"Who offered this bounty?" Rand asked.

"The Earth Defense Force. When the EDF offers gold in that quantity, you know the chancellor is behind it. Word is they want some guy named Roland Barcus, too, for murdering some colony leader."

"Now what, Captain?" Hume asked.

"Look, I have to say you people really suck at this," AI~Cole said.

"What?" Worthington grew angry.

"While I kept you here talking, I was able to identify all three of you. I know who you are, your service records. I know who your families are and where they are."

AI~Cole cut off as all the Warmark weapons charged up.

"Hold on there. I am trying to tell you to be more careful. All I had to do was show you the ident code, and you accepted it without question. That IDs you, the fact you are considered lost, as well as on the chancellor's shit list. That alone is enough to forgive the considerable damage to my base. I have Makers that can fix it. Keep your warhead. Just let me know what you have done with the thirty Golems that disappeared with your STU."

"I can answer that, sir." Stu's avatar appeared in the control room, standing at ease.

"Echo had briefed me on some new emergency procedures. When a comms dampening field was activated, I already had my wired optical online and saw the boarding party. I immediately launched. When I reached an altitude of 10,000 kilometers, I accelerated in reverse, at a high G with the inertial dampeners off. They were all thrown out of the bay. Thankfully, the mess was contained within their very durable pressure suits."

Another Golem walked into the room from a side door, carrying a hard case the size of travel luggage. She placed it on a table and opened it, revealing three ident modules, complete with ready-to-apply inspection seals, ready for use.

"Say hello—and fuck you—to the chancellor, from me," AI~Cole said.

CHAPTER TWENTY-SEVEN: SHACKLETON BASE

"Luna was a low gravity nightmare of socialism and corruption. Poverty like this had once faded from the world. It is the worst side of the public longevity distribution program when run by the government. Bigots and criminals."

--Solstice 31 Incident Investigation Testimony Transcript: Captain James Worthington, senior surviving member of the Ventura's command crew.

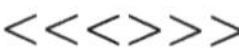

"How are you doing, Barcus?" Dr. Beth Shaw asked him, as he opened his eyes. "Are you ever going to come out of here?"

Barcus lay on one of the white sofas with his eyes closed.

"I will. When it's time."

"Jimbo wanted me to look you over again because you are not yourself these days. I have to say, I agree."

She sat on the edge of his sofa, near his hip, pushed up his shirt, and ran her fingertips over his skin. It was a very intimate touch.

"We have been in such a hurry for everything. First on Baytirus, the trip and suddenly we are back. I suspect things will speed up more again, soon."

She probed his abdomen, harder. "Any discomfort?"

"Beth, I need you to go with them to Shackleton Base. Hagan will go as well. Stay together." He spoke in very hushed tones. Beth had to come closer.

"Shackleton Base? On Luna? Why?" she asked, feeling his skin suddenly warm to an alarming level.

"When the time comes, and you must decide, go left," he said. "Remember, go left." He got to his feet, leaving Beth on the couch—looking after him—as he stood in the center of the circle of sofas. "They're coming."

The sky rotated around and above them, giving Shaw a moment of vertigo. And then, the view zoomed in and found Mars with impossible fidelity. The STU was lifting off from a pad that was flanked by a mountain of debris.

"Tell the crew."

***

"I don't see why the *Sedna's* ident code needs to be changed," Elkin said, for the third time. It was the last one to be replaced.

"It had nothing to do with the *Ventura*."

"This is such a pain in the ass," she complained. "These are not made to be changed out on the *Sedna*. We have to take one of the main engines completely off the mounts to get to the access panel."

"How long will it take?" Worthington asked, in a tone that was not to be questioned.

"Nine hours, sir. Maybe less, if these spiders can help," she said.

It was done in two hours, with the help of four spiders of different sizes.

***

"We were right to be cautious. They have eyes out for the STU and Barcus. This confirms that the High Keeper on Baytirus was in communication with the chancellor," Worthington said to them all, as he stood at the briefing table they set up in the hangar. "Wes will come to each of you and set your HUDs into a more private mode."

"This will be a problem. It's like turning off all data resources at our disposal," Hagan said.

"Where to next, sir?" Elkin said, with a bit too much confidence.

"Captain Everett was part of a team that had four members—her superior and three subordinates," Hagan said. "According to Echo, the closest member is on Luna. Shackleton Base to be precise."

"We are going to take the *Sedna* and find him. Quietly," Jimbo said. "I think the safest, quietest, thing to do is for the civilian crew members to do this."

Kuss replied, instantly, "I go. I have cousins on Shackleton. Might be helpful."

"Count me in," said Elkin.

"Me too," said Shaw.

"I will go," Hagan said.

Wex stood as she spoke. Jude and Cine stood as well.

"We shall go as well. But we will stay on the ship, to guard it."

"That's enough," Worthington said, as he turned and pointed at a virtual screen behind him. "Shackleton Base is one of the largest, oldest settlements on Luna." The moon turned and stopped on the screen behind him. Finally zooming in on the base.

"It holds about 18 million people and has the largest domes on Luna with no artificial gravity. It's a straight .16G for most of the base. Generations of people have been born and raised there. They will always stay there."

Hagan added, "Keep in mind, Shackleton was once the richest place on the moon. It was built, by a hundred Makers, over a massive crater that had a rich layer of ice below. In the early days, before cheap transport via catapults and grav-containers, water was worth the same as gold."

Worthington continued, "Shackleton was built for the wealthy, and then fell out of favor—into poverty—because there was no transport tube that reached that far out." The map of subways appeared on the screen. "The tubes finally came, and the base has been getting better for the last hundred years.

"Don't get me started on the local politics. Pisses me off too much. Private property is not allowed. The base owns all the air. Everyone works for the governor. And he keeps them all at the edge of poverty and entertained," Jim said.

Kuss spat out, "Bread and circuses."

"Bread and what?" Shaw asked.

"Stay with me here," Worthington said. "We need to find a man named Johan Engle and let him know what's happened. He can help us find Admiral Krieger, without getting killed or arrested."

"How do we find him?" Hagan said, assuming the leadership role on the team.

"Echo says he works at a bar in the NW district called, The Shanoi. It's located here," he indicated on the screen. "So, you will be landing at this port and going there by foot, if needed. It will only take you a few hours to walk there, all in low G."

"Why not land at this port? The bar is right there," Elkin asked.

"That is the port for government and commercial use. He is probably there so he can collect better intel from drunk bureaucrats and merchants. This port is for private ships, something these fools look down on.

"Another thing," Worthington said, very gravely, "No weapons, not even sidearms. There are random scanners everywhere."

"Pierdolic mnie!" Kuss cursed in Polish. "Knives?"

"No knives," he said.

"Sons of a..." She faded off into a grumble.

***

The *Sedna* was prepped and cleared out of anything that might be troublesome; and they moved out, without a problem. The rest of the crew dispersed, most of them returning to the *Memphis*.

Only Worthington, Barcus, and Po remained on the hangar deck. "How are you feeling, bro," Worthington asked Barcus. Real concern was in his voice.

"When we get to Freedom Station, you need to keep it together, Jim."

Barcus stood directly in front of him, for emphasis.

"Bobbie and the girls are there. No, just listen..."

Barcus stopped him from interrupting. "Do not bring them back here. Do not put them on the *Sedna*. They will be safe there, for now. You need to listen to me!" Barcus grabbed Jim's shoulders and gave him a slight shake.

"We are talking about MY FAMILY!" Jimbo yelled. Worthington's only weakness was in full view.

"Do you remember that time when you were twelve, and you had to walk your bike home because of a flat tire, and you ruined the rim trying to ride it? It was after dark, and you knew your mother would be mad."

Worthington looked like he had been slapped in the face; his eyes widened.

"As you passed the Springer's house, you saw Mrs. Springer going down on Mr. Springer because they left the blinds open."

Jim's eyes were wider now.

"You ever tell anyone about that?"

Barcus knew the answer.

Jim was already shaking his head, in disbelief.

"One day, I will ask you to tell me a story, just so I can convince you, so you'll know that I can do what I am about to say I can do."

"I can remember the future."

Barcus paused for a long while. He looked at Po and back to Jim.

"I will never get used to that," Worthington said.

"Do you like soup?" Barcus grinned.

***

"Flight operations here are incredibly half-assed," Elkin said, as they approached low from the northwest.

"Low and slow," Kuss said from the navigator's console on the *Sedna*.

Hagan was in the engineer's seat.

Spires climbed out of the base, almost to the horizon. Shuttle traffic was constant but weak by the skyscrapers. There was, luckily, less traffic by the pad they wanted. The docking gantry reached out for the ship before traffic control told them the gate to settle on.

"What is the ship ident again?" Elkin asked.

"We are the *Grace*. Hate this name."

"Greetings, *Grace*. How long do you expect to be here?" came a bored voice over the comms. "You can dock, park on the tarmac, and we can bring the bus out, or even out on the surface. No hookups there, though, but it's cheaper."

"Greetings, base. We expect to be here one day. Two at the outside," Hagan replied, when Elkin paused too long. "We will pay for two days now. Cash."

The collar attached easily. Pressure was as advertised and equalized quickly. They opened the airlock and moved into the gantry. A skinny kid waited, in the low gravity at the top of the ramp, data pad in hand.

"What is the purpose of your visit?"

He wasn't a kid. He was a man, about thirty-five years old. Thinner than even the first glance revealed.

"Stopping in to see an old friend," Hagan said, as he slipped the man four gold coins—more than double the two day fee. "There is a little extra in there, to ensure a smooth exit. We are leaving a security team onboard and the reactors are idling."

The man dropped his pretense.

"No weapons. No skipping decontamination. I'm serious. You will go through three scanners before you reach the terminal."

He gestured to the walk-through portal behind him.

Only this one guy was there. Hagan was surprised at that.

"No air fee?" Hagan asked, quietly.

"It is all included in your site tax. The governor owns the air now and is very generous."

He spoke loudly, in case they were listening.

"Can I help you find anything? Company? Herb? Anything?"

The man walked backward as they approached the security threshold.

"No, we are good, for now. Maybe later." Hagan walked through, uneventfully.

Shaw held her small backpack off to the side as she walked through.

A small chime sounded, and her med pack became illuminated in red.

"It's just a first aid kit."

She suspected it was being scanned for good drugs. She knew better than to include any. He waved her through.

Elkin went right through, but Kuss caused the clear panels to close on her, trapping her inside. The scanner image was visible to heat.

"Just tools, working!" Kuss said.

The scanner showed an old-school set of plane screwdrivers and a large two-headed wrench. Kuss rolled her eyes and stood patiently. She wore work coveralls.

Cameras were everywhere, not just in the terminal.

They knew the way, but looked at the worn wall maps to make sure.

None of them noticed they were being followed.

.

***

"Soup?"

Worthington was taken aback by the non sequitur.

Barcus didn't release Jimbo's shoulders as he spoke, conversationally. "There is pho from Pete's place, you know noodle soup, on level 42. Really great soup."

Barcus released Jim's shoulders but not his eyes.

"You mean Pho Pete's counter? Everyone knows that place. Best damn soup on Freedom Station. I wish he'd get more than eighteen stools at his counter."

Worthington began to relax.

"He did. He added two small tables to the left, on the end, where the trash cans and condiments used to be." Barcus let loose a smile.

"Pete didn't always make soup on the station, you know. He used to be military in the South American Union. He led the forces that took back the south side of Panama straight, as a sergeant."

"Pho Pete is Sergeant Pedro Morales?" Jimbo laughed, out loud. "How the hell did he end up on Freedom Station?"

"He retired. Cashed in everything and brought his family to FS. Now, he makes soup." Barcus paused. "And a few other things."

"Why are we talking about soup?" Worthington was suddenly serious again. "We were talking about my family."

"Things will get crazy soon. You need to remember, Pete will help you find them."

"How do you know Pho Pete?"

"I don't. I just like pho."

CHAPTER TWENTY-EIGHT: BEST LAID PLANS

"Low gravity and high poverty is a bad combination when lives are at stake."

--Solstice 31 Incident Investigation Testimony Transcript: Captain James Worthington, senior surviving member of the Ventura's command crew.

The Shanoi was really huge for a spaceport bar. Hagan could tell that the place was also a favorite of the locals, but he had no idea why. It was decorated in a cheesy Japanese style that had gone out of fashion long ago. The take-out line was a hundred people deep and moving fast, as people collected bags of fried chicken of all things.

"Shit," Shaw said. "There has to be thirty bartenders in here. "What do we do?"

"I think we should split into two groups. Shaw and I will start at this end. Elkin and Kuss, you start over there," Hagan said, as they moved through the lunchtime crowd.

On the way, they stopped by an exchange, where Hagan traded a gold ingot for local credit chits.

"Damn, that chicken smells good. Reminds me of KFC from back home," Shaw said, as they passed the take-out line.

"It might be KFC," Hagan said, sitting down.

It only took a minute for a bartender to come over with their drinks that they ordered through the bar top interface.

Shaw spoke first, as she handed over the chits.

"Is Johan around today? A friend of his asked me to stop in and say hi."

"I'm Johan. What friend?"

He smiled and wiped the bar, absently.

"Really? That was too easy. I have a message, but I don't know it's really you. No HUD ID," Shaw said, as Hagan sipped his beer, looking at the crowd, seemingly disinterested in the conversation.

He drew an ID card on a lanyard, out of his shirt as he spoke.

"Never got a HUD. Gives me the willies to think of something messing in my brain. What friend is this?"

Shaw's augmented reality HUD confirmed the badge.

"Alice," Shaw said.

Johan's smile froze and faded from his eyes for a beat.

"Alice Everett."

The bullet that entered Johan's neck and shattered his Adam's apple and spine, also creased a groove in Beth Shaw's scalp. There was no sound of a gunshot. No panic in the crowd. Johan Engle fell straight down, like a sack of meat. The only sound was the bottle of expensive vodka shattering behind him.

In the time it took Hagan to turn, see Engle falling, and turn back, his eyes were drawn to the opposite end of the bar. Kuss was moving.

She hammered a screwdriver into the back of a man's head just after he fired. He never saw her coming because all his attention was on the scope.

Hagan flinched. Looking down, he saw that his left thumb had just been shot off. Blood poured from the wound.

Elkin and Kuss arrived just as the screaming began, both in the crowd over the man's body and behind the bar. A woman, the next bartender down the long dark bar, had seen Engle go down.

"Go," Kuss whispered harshly, hiding something under her coat.

Elkin led. Hagan and Shaw tried to act nonchalant as they exited the Shanoi. Clearing the crowd, let them start to move faster.

Suddenly, the glass shattered behind them. Elkin cried out. People ran. Glass walls shattered on the other side of the promenade. Two men—in long coats—with guns, fell.

"GO!" Kuss yelled, no longer trying to hide the carbine she had taken from the assassin's dead body.

They ran.

Just after they rounded the first corner, the first explosion detonated. They were no longer the only ones running. Two more explosions happened, ten seconds later.

They came to a T in the corridor.

"Which way?" Kuss asked, hiding the carbine again. Finally glad they kept the place so cold.

"Go left," Shaw said, without hesitation.

***

"Be ready. There will be six of them, altogether. Never mind the official-looking uniforms," Wex said to Jude and Cine, as she stood at the cargo bay in view of the open airlock hatch.

They were stationed on the catwalk, directly above the hatch.

Wex stood in the center of the cargo area, well-lit in the directional floods. She wore her thinnest, tightest, white tunic. It was nearly see-through it clung to her so closely.

They heard boots, marching in unison down the gantry; and without hailing or requesting permission to come aboard, they entered the outer airlock and turned toward the open cargo bay hatch where Wex played the flute with her back to the hatch. She didn't turn when they entered, two by two, even though she was only three meters from them.

Looking at Wex in profile as she turned slowly, still playing, they didn't notice the women in black flight suits balanced on the catwalk railing above. They lightly stepped off the railing and descended in silence. The first thing to touch the two men in back was the points of their daggers as they pierced the tops of their heads. Twisting the blades before their feet set down, they rode the bodies down as they crumbled.

The two men in front drew sidearms and turned toward the threat; but before they could clear their holsters, they were struck on the back of their heads, in quick succession, with a long black flute that was as hard as iron. Their skulls caved in like eggs.

The last men, completely surprised, froze for an instant too long.

"What was that?" Jude said, looking at the two men twitching at Wex's feet.

"These...people," Wex didn't want to say 'men', "have spent their entire evil little lives in low gravity. It weakens the bones. Now get them out of these coveralls."

***

"Where are we going?" Hagan asked, as they reached a dead end.

"Left," was all Beth said.

She approached an old-style, plain door with a knob. It opened into a large custodian's closet.

"Quickly."

Beth gestured with her free left hand; her right was pressing against the freely bleeding scalp wound.

"I'm hit. Bad," Elkin admitted, as she shrank down, sitting on a crate of supplies.

Shaw saw the blood soaking down her back. "Kuss, help me."

Shaw saw Kuss was grimacing as well, as she spoke, "What want me to do?"

Shaw had a first aid kit in her pack. She slipped the pack off and dug out the kit as best she could.

"Elkin, stay with us," Shaw said. They were all covered in blood.

"Get these nanites and the medical adhesive and close my scalp wound; then, I will check Elkin," Shaw said. "Wes, are you OK, for now?"

Hagan had the rifle in the right hand, pointing it at the door. "Just dandy."

He pressed his wounded thumb into his own ribs, creating direct pressure. He was steady but a bit pale.

"Dammit. The good news is a bullet was deflected by your left shoulder blade. The bad news is your left scapula is broken, and I cannot do shit for it with the first aid kit. I can close the entry and exit wounds, fill you full of nanites, but walking back to the ship is going to really suck."

Kuss cleaned and closed Beth's head wound. It was a sloppy job; but if she finger combed her hair over, it would be fine.

Elkin was as good as she was going to get.

Hagan's thumb and part of his palm were gone, and Beth did her best to close up his wounds.

Kuss had a mystery gash in her left breast. The best Shaw could figure was that she had been cut by flying debris.

They were all covered in blood. A horror. They would have to find a way to clean up and get new clothes. There was a water spigot for filling mop buckets in there, but the water didn't work.

They settled for using all the sterile wipes from Beth's kit to clean their hands and faces.

As they were finishing, there was a knock at the closet door.

***

"Will they be alright there? On Shackleton's Base?" Po asked him, when they were alone again.

"No. But they had to go," Barcus replied, with torment in his voice. "It tumbles so fast from here on. No one will have a chance to breathe. And I can do nothing...except take the blame."

"Are you doing all you can?" Po asked.

"Yes."

"It's enough," Po replied, laying her head on his chest.

I don't know. I never will.

***

John Boyle was a special advisor to the chancellor of Earth. He was one of the few people on the planet that had the permission to interrupt the chancellor during a meeting, without repercussions. He smoothly entered one of the many formal conference rooms, via the chancellor's private entrance, and closed the door behind himself, without approaching.

"Chancellor, I need to speak with you. It is urgent," said Boyle.

He waited by the door, a slender, hawk-nosed man. It was a signal that there was a real urgent issue, not just a show to get the chancellor out of a dull meeting.

"Excuse me, my friends," the chancellor said, as he stood and walked over to Boyle, who opened the door and they stepped through.

After the door closed, the chancellor immediately said, "What is it?"

"A member of the command crew of the *Ventura* has been seen on Luna," Boyle stated.

"The Baytirus problem? Dammit Atish."

"Yes, sir." Boyle swallowed. "Your orders were being followed. Terminate on detection. But they got away. Face recognition was certain. Plus, we recovered his thumb. Print and DNA is a match."

"How? It's been years since..."

The chancellor became lost in thought.

"Well, where is he? What is the problem? What happened?"

"The team that went after them all had heart monitors and bomb implants. Shackleton Base authorities think it was terrorists. Hagan disappeared."

"Cancel everything for the rest of the week. We are leaving for the residence in ten minutes."

***

The knock on the closet door was followed with a loud whisper from the other side.

"Hagan, Shaw, it's me. Wex. Open the door, for Maker's sake, and don't shoot me."

Shaw cracked open the door, and there was Wex, wearing some kind of uniform, with her hair pulled back in a severe ponytail. Wex pressed her way in. Her arms were full of folded uniforms and boots, four full sets.

"Quickly, put these on. We need to get out of here," Wex said.

"How did you find us?" Elkin said, even as she stripped off her clothes.

"Never mind that now. If I found you, others will, too." Wex had a sidearm drawn now, waiting at the door as bloody clothes went down a trash chute. They were ready in just under two minutes.

"Now act like we are under orders. Ignore anyone that speaks to you," Wex said, as she opened the door.

There was a cart, waiting in the wide hall. Wex got behind the wheel and did a quick three-point turn. Everyone piled in.

"Are you a big golfer?" Hagan said, as he sat next to Wex in the front.

"Golfer?"

"You drive this cart like you know what you're doing...never mind. Go."

They rolled through the wide corridors, easily and quickly. People stood aside.

Hagan saw several others wearing the same uniforms.

"Where did you get the security uniforms and this cart?"

"They tried to take the ship. We stopped them."

Wex stopped near the gate where the *Sedna* was parked but not directly at the gate. They walked the 120 meters without incident. Soon, they were inside the ship and closing the airlock.

"Gantry detaching now," Elkin announced, punching the control, as she ran toward the others in the main cargo bay and the elevator to the bridge.

She skidded to a halt at the sight of the four dead men, lined up on the floor, face down. Jude and Cine were face down next to them. They were unconscious, or dead, with their hands cuffed to their ankles.

A huge man stood behind the bodies, in the shadows.

Stepping into the light, his two weapons were leveled on them. POLICE was stenciled across the chest plate of his body armor.

"On your knees, NOW!"

His gravelly voice was not to be argued with.

CHAPTER TWENTY-NINE: THE SUB CELL

"We were wounded, running out of adrenaline, and confused. We did not kill Officer Jack Zimmerman. Several of us wanted to kill him, but none of us did. He was classic. All high gravity, human growth hormones, martial arts, and bad attitude. Are you sure he's dead? He swore to us, a hundred times, he was un-kill-able."

--*Solstice 31 Incident Investigation Testimony Transcript: Dr. Elizabeth Shaw, senior surviving medical staff member of the Ventura's Memphis crew.*

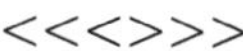

"*She worries for you*," AI~Iosin said, seemingly inside his head.

Barcus replied, from the same space, "*Yes. She makes sure I eat and drink and take showers and sleep.*"

"*That is not what I mean, at all. She worries because you have changed. The joy has gone from you. This is her worry.*"

"*How can I feel joy when I know what is to come?*"

"*Barcus, what will I say to you next? If you know so much, tell me.*"

Barcus was taken aback. He had no idea what AI~Iosin was about to say. He had no idea why he was laughing, when Po returned with food.

"*You only see what happens to you. Not your thoughts, not how you feel. You cannot see the moment you are in. Here with me, you are only in the seam between the past and the future. You can return here any time you like. You don't need me. And here is the truth about what you see in the future. You are just a witness.*"

Barcus started laughing.

"*You didn't see this coming,*" AI~Iosin said, and she drifted away.

Po had entered the vast bridge from the elevator, to echoing laughs from the air.

Barcus wiped tears from his eyes, as his laughter faded to smiles and bright eyes, then passionate kisses that she had missed.

"Has something happened?" Po asked.

It caused another laughing fit, like water blasting out Barcus's nose, making Po laugh as well.

Finally, he answered, "Yes. Something's happened."

"What?" Po asked.

"Everything..."

***

"Which one of you buckets of puke is Trish Elkin?"

He looked them over.

"I'm guessin' it's this gob of phlegm here."

He holstered one gun and grabbed her by the hair and forced her to look up.

"Be careful, you ape, she has a broken scapula—her shoulder blade."

Beth rose as she spoke.

"Shut your cock holster, Missy. I know what a fucking scapula is, maggot."

He let go of Trish Elkin and grabbed Shaw's throat so fast it was instantly frightening. Beth suddenly dangled in the air from his hand around her neck. She felt his thumb touching the tip of his index finger at the base of her neck.

"Stop. Please," Hagan said, but he didn't get up from his knees. "I'm in charge here."

"You must be the *Ventura's* limp-dicked chief engineer, Wes Hagan. I know all there is to know about your clueless stinking ass. Mostly, I know that you will answer any question to stop me from breaking this fish gut's neck."

Beth suddenly struggled in his squeezing hand.

"OK! Yes! Ask!" Hagan began to rise, but found a gun in his face.

"Where the fuck is Captain Alice Everett?"

***

"Where's Worthington?" Barcus asked Sarah Wood, as she inventoried and repacked the med kits for the *Memphis*.

"I think he is on the bridge with Cook and Beary. I hate these new HUD settings. You can never find people, and they have to activate comms to even receive," Wood replied, without stopping her work.

"Thanks."

Barcus started up the ramp but paused.

"Seriously, Sarah. Thanks, for everything."

"I'm glad you're OK," Sarah said, as he waved.

Barcus marveled at how well the ship had been restored, trying hard to stay in the moment, as he moved through to the bridge.

The door slid open to excited conversation. Worthington was in his command chair, closely examining a new control screen and interface. Rand looked at the same screen while speaking to him. Muir, Cook, and Beary were in a heated debate about the utility of something, and Valerie Hume was greeting Barcus brightly. It seemed like loud, unruly chaos in contrast to the bridge on the *Iosin*.

"Everyone is excited that we can configure Quantum Entanglement Synchronous Transmitters on the *Memphis*, the STU, and the *Sedna*," Hume said.

"Hey, Hume. Thanks for finding me." Barcus put his hand on her shoulder and squeezed.

"What's all this. You going soft on us, Barcus?" She laughed and pounded her fist on his sternum.

"Had to be said. I said it, now kiss my ass." He smiled, as he roughly pushed her away. His mind had a completely different dialogue.

I'm sorry, Hume.

"Jimbo, the Iosin gave me an update. They are not coming directly back. Their mission is going smoothly, and they are on the way to New Tranquility."

"Let me guess," Worthington said. "There's a maintenance spider on the *Sedna*. All the damn things have QUEST comms built-in that talk to the *Iosin*. It's where the tech came from."

"That and a million other things," Barcus said, absently.

***

"I'm sorry." Hagan lowered his head. "Captain Everett is dead."

"You should be sorry, you rusty bucket of vomit!" the man yelled, still holding Shaw by the neck as if she were a rag doll.

His face was covered with emotions: anger, sadness, realization.

More quietly, he said, "Did you know she was in love with you?"

The cop set Shaw's feet back on the deck and let her go. The room was silent, until Jude awoke and suddenly struggled against her bindings.

"On your feet, shit bricks," the man growled.

"My name is Jack Zimmerman. I'm the next asshole you were about to get killed." He holstered his other weapon. He was the next name in Everett's cell. He was a Luna Peace Officer.

"The keys, please. I will free them, then we must get out of here," Wex said, holding out her hand.

Jack pulled out the keys but didn't hand them over.

"Who the fuck are you?"

"My name is Wex," she said, and snatched the keys. "What did you do to them?"

"Stun gloves." He rubbed his square jaw. "I underestimated them. Little bitches almost killed me." He rolled his jaw then. Kuss saw the bruise there.

Shaw helped Elkin to her feet. Hagan was the last up.

"You could have just told me your name. We had it. And yes, you were the next to visit on the list," Hagan said.

"Stow that shit, for now. We got to get the fuck out of this shit hole," Zimmerman said. "You kicked the hornets' nest."

"We are supposed to just trust you?" Hagan said.

Zimmerman drew his sidearms and handed one to Hagan and one to the recently freed Jude, who instantly executed a shoulder roll and came up kneeling with the gun trained on Jack's head. He knelt to make it easier.

"Kill me or trust me. But we have no time for bullshit," Jack said.

Hagan turned toward the lift and the bridge.

***

"Hagan will pick up one more in New Tranquility. And then, we can meet on Freedom Station," Barcus said, causing Jimbo to look up. "FS is an open port. If we use one of the public docking spires, we can dock for free for twenty-four hours, anonymously."

"Mall parking. Could be crowded," Jimbo said.

"It won't be," Barcus said, with certainty. "Walk with me. Let's talk, while I prep the STU."

They walked into the hangar and were greeted by three Warmarks, lined up and waiting for the ramp to lower on the STU.

"Expecting trouble?" Worthington asked.

"Not with these along," Barcus said.

"To even have these in your possession without a black badge is a world of trouble," Jim said, casually.

"You're the one flying around with a cargo hold full of nukes," Barcus answered.

"You didn't ask me out here to help you watch Warmarks load themselves or to tell me to be careful." Jimbo faced him. "Straight up, man. As always."

"You, Rand, and Hume have to come with me in the STU to Freedom Station," Barcus said.

"I do feel like soup."

Jimbo smiled.

Barcus thought, *I'm sorry Jimbo, but you'll never get that soup...*

***

"Give me that!" Shaw yelled, as she grabbed the gun from the crouching Jude.

She walked right up to Zimmerman where he knelt.

"Give me a reason why I should not send you to hell."

"Because I am ruggedly handsome, a sexual savage in bed, and I make an excellent breakfast."

Zimmerman smiled, which was frightening. His enormous teeth were perfect. He didn't realize there was blood on the left side of them.

Elkin laughed and then immediately regretted it. Shaw dropped the gun on the deck between them, rubbed her neck with one hand, and slapped his face as hard as she could with the other. He didn't even try to avoid it. It was like hitting a marble statue. Her hand regretted it, as she and Kuss helped Elkin to the lift.

Zimmerman stood, as he sensed the ship lifting off on grav-plates.

He turned and faced Wex then, all humor gone.

"You're the one Everett talked about. You are the fucking reason she's dead. She was my friend, my mentor."

"It's a war. Many more will die," Wex said.

Zimmerman scowled and took a half step closer. His move was mirrored by Jude and Cine, on either side of Wex.

"Keep your filthy pet hyenas the fuck away from me."

Zimmerman turned his back on them, intentionally. It was a grave warrior insult and he knew it. He walked to the lift and went to the bridge.

"This is he whom you spoke," Cine said, in her accent.

"Yes. Give him time," Wex mused.

***

The lift door opened on the main salon of the *Sedna,* and Officer Zimmerman stepped out and stood there, staring.

"Fucking eh. You pukes know how to steal 'em," Jack said, laughing.

"What is your problem?" Hagan said. "Why would Captain Everett bring a primate like you in on this?"

They were already moving quickly, three hundred meters above the surface.

"We were friends, asswipe. We met as cadets in a practical astrophysics class in school. I went into security; she became a pilot. I'll tell you why she brought me in; she trusted me."

The implication in his harsh words was that Everett trusted him more than Hagan. Zimmerman looked up from the status board to the windows.

"Where the fuck are you going? We need to go to New Tranquility dumb-ass, not Shackleton's Base.

"That station is hosed. We are headed to NT. Trust me, asshole," Hagan said, trying to sound as manly as possible.

"Hagan. She was my friend. She really was. She told me a lot about you. I'm not surprised you lived. She would have made sure of it," Jack said, with all the bravado gone from his voice. "Jesus, I have never gotten off on the wrong fucking foot as badly, in my life, as I did with you people."

"How did you find us?"

"Everett had me in a place where I could watch and listen for bulletins and alerts on people and events. There are three in my cell. Well, all the cells, actually. Johan was in my cell. Right when my AI gets hits on the *Ventura* crew, Johan is murdered in a terror attack." Jack grumbled, "I traced you back to this ship and, using my security override, I accessed the ship to find naked men, all of whom were wanted criminals. That's when the pain twins almost ended me."

"Jude and Cine? Serves you right."

"Dammit, I almost had to kill them. Tough little bitches."

Jack started removing body armor, dropping it on one of the sofas.

"Who is Tawana Hudson? Can you, at least, help with that?" Hagan gruffed.

"Look, Hagan. You may have noticed that all this shit is going as pear-shaped as a half bag of rotting guts. Hudson was another friend of Everett. A trusted friend. And we are on our fucking way to ruin her life, if they have not killed her already."

Jack tried to stay calm by force of will.

"She is one of the data managers in the core complex at New Tran. As an admin, she has access to all the data housed there. She is another information collector, just like me, just like Johan. At least she's not married. Johan had a wife and three kids."

CHAPTER THIRTY: NEW TRANQUILITY

"I knew nothing about the underground cells that Everett was a part of. To be honest, at that point, I was being completely selfish and thinking only of my own family. I did not set out to save millions of people. Only the three I loved."

--Solstice 31 Incident Investigation Testimony Transcript: Captain James Worthington, senior surviving member of the Ventura's command crew.

"It was a silent coup. When the chancellor was elected, we didn't know the depth of corruption and manipulation that was involved. It was all politics, and I stayed out of it," Jack explained to Hagan, Shaw, and Kuss, who were sitting in the command seats. "Then, Alice called me one day and asked me to lunch." Wex and *The Bitch Twins*—as Jack called them—were looking out the window, watching the surface go by. Jack knew they were listening closely.

"Ships started going missing. Global media refused to cover any of it, and any questioning of leadership usually led to reassignment and hardship. It was a new kind of liberal fascism, but I did not care about any of that. I lost faith in the political system and completely ignored it when I went into the security service." Jack continued. "I trusted Everett and did as she asked. Keeping the peace is my job. In my mind, she was just another informant, in the beginning, anyway."

"Why were we sent to Baytirus, if they already knew it was settled?" Shaw asked.

"They used petty bureaucrats to load the *Ventura* up with potential political adversaries, former military, and others. Plus, they wanted the expansion stopped. They hated the colonies. They couldn't control them, no matter what they tried."

"Why even try to control them?" Shaw said. "They just wanted to be left alone."

"The chancellor and his supporters are paranoid narcissists that think the colonies are building up for a war to take over, or destroy, Earth," Zimmerman said.

"That's crazy. Colonists don't even think about Earth," Hagan added.

"Did you hear about the Albion colony?" Jack asked, angry again.

"Albion? Have relatives on Albion. What of Albion?" Kuss said.

"There's a media blackout, but rumor has it there was a massive meteor impact. The entire colony was destroyed. Almost two million people. And now it's a dead planet in a nuclear winter."

"This not be true? Would have heard." Kuss was in obvious denial.

"Some don't think it was an accident," Jack said. "Even this ship, flying at near-light speed, could have done it. The senate is quietly debating the suspension of the private ownership of ships with near-light speed capability."

"Combine that with the AI problems in recent years..."

Hagan left it hang out there.

"New Tranquility, coming up in six minutes," Hagan announced. "Where will we be setting down?"

"Approach from the west. You will see a huge tarmac marked '29'. Set her down there but maintain radio silence. I will get a lock-truck to come out and pick me up. I will get Hudson personally, so you amateurs don't piss in her biscuits. Then, to Freedom Station, where we can get a message to Admiral Krieger."

Hagan noticed at that declaration, for some reason, Jude and Cine looked at each and then to Wex.

***

"It is time to go, Jim," Barcus said. He ascended the ladder into Stu's bridge.

"Rand, Hume, report to the STU. Bring your gear," Worthington said, over the priority comms. "Is everyone clear on the plan?"

Everyone chimed in with an acknowledgment.

"Cook, when you get to Sri Lanka, hire a private hangar, close to the catapult for the *Memphis*, or the *Winton*, I mean. Lay low. And we will catch up. I will never get used to that new name." Jimbo said, "We are headed to Freedom Station to hook up with Hagan. Establish contact. Determine next steps."

"We will be taking the scenic route around the belt and won't arrive until December 21st, late," Cook said. "Make sure your ducks are in a row by then. We will keep in touch via QUEST comms, daily."

"Be careful, boy. I just got her fixed. Don't scratch the fenders."

"Aye, Captain."

Cook signed off.

Worthington watched Rand and Hume descend the ramp on the *Memphis* and cross the deck to the STU. Jimbo was up the ladder to the bridge, with practiced ease. The dome was on, and it showed the entire hangar around them. Barcus was in the pilot's seat, and Po was in his lap. His face was buried in her neck.

"What's wrong?" Jim asked.

"Nothing." Po smiled. "He just likes sniffing my neck. Stu, how's it look, my friend?"

She climbed out of his lap, into the co-pilot's seat. Barcus sat up straight and rolled his neck to a chorus of pops and cracks.

"All systems are standing by. We can depart as soon as the ramp is up," AI~Stu said, with cheerful confidence.

***

Cook gave a heavy sigh from the pilot's seat, as he ran the final flight checklist. The list was doubly important with a skeleton crew.

"What was that sigh for? Thinking about childhood dead pets?" Beary said to him from the navigator's station, as she ran her own preflight checks.

"I just feel like they are going to leave us out of the action. Because when this gets real, they will need the *Memphis*, and all this data, as evidence."

"Quit your bellyaching. There hasn't been enough action on this trip for you?" Muir said.

"I don't mind the sidelines," Brian Perry said from the communications station. "I have spent way too much time on the verge of pissing myself on this trip."

Sarah Wood entered the bridge and, instead of sitting at the security station, she took the captain's seat, and said, "Well, I am the most useless one on this bridge, so I might as well sit here."

No one mentioned it was bad luck to sit in the captain's seat, unless commanded to.

***

The *Grace,* the new ident for the *Sedna,* landed on the New Tran security apron, and Zimmerman radioed for an airlock truck. The blast doors were closed over the windows on the ship to help keep out prying eyes.

Jack waited, in airlock two, for the vehicle to roll up and attach. When the seal was greenlit, he opened the door on his side and waited. One minute, then two.

"Hey, asswipes. I'm in a hurry here," Jack said.

He opted to forgo his body armor in an effort to draw less attention to himself. He heard the door begin to cycle. This kind of hatch split in the middle, half went up and half down.

As it did, six trank darts bristled into his stomach.

"What the f—"

He fell to his knees. A dozen men, in full tactical gear, entered past Jack, and opened the inner airlock, flooding into the cargo bay.

The cargo bay was dark.

"Fan out. If you find anyone, take them alive, if you can," one of them said.

None of them noticed the airlock closing behind them, cutting them off from Zimmerman.

A voice came over the PA system.

"You guys really suck at this."

The grav-plating in the floor suddenly jumped to 2G, and the lights came up. They all fell, pinned to the floor by gravity twelve times greater than what they were used to. One tried to struggle to his feet. The rest struggled to breathe and to stay conscious.

Jude slowly walked out of the shadows, easily bent and retrieved one of the dart guns, and shot the man that was on his hands and knees. She then shot the rest, in quick succession.

The lift opened, and Kuss was there.

"How you know they were tranquilizer darts?" She opened the airlock where Jack rested on the floor.

"They are tranquilizers?" Jude looked at the gun and shrugged. The room returned to 1G.

Kuss pulled the darts out of Zimmerman's belly and chest and examined one. "These not standard law enforcement tranks."

"These men are not security. What do we do with them?" Hagan asked, as he went through their pockets, finding nothing at all.

"Drop them out on surface with others," Kuss spat.

Hagan pressed a hypo spray to Zimmerman's neck. With a small hiss, his eyes shot open.

"That feels like iced vodka in my veins. Wasted and awake. What happened?" He staggered to his feet.

"They knew we were coming," Hagan said.

"Mother pus bucket...you two." He pointed at Cine and Jude. "You're coming with me."

They each picked up two dart guns and stashed them in their thigh pockets. As if by magic, they both produced black flutes from thin air.

"Don't ask," Hagan said, as he tightened a zip tie around wrists and ankles.

"Come," Jack barked.

They went right behind him into the lock-truck. The airlock was secured, detached, and he drove it back to the security terminal. All the truck-locks were occupied, so he rolled past and pulled into a random private lock and attached.

The inner lock opened, and it woke an attendant there.

"Hey, you can't park there..." Then, he saw the size of Jack and the uniform he wore. Both were intimidating. Jack pushed him aside and activated his comms console. He typed a short message. Msg: *T. HUDSON Lava L11*

A few seconds later, a live video was visible in Zimmerman's security HUD. No audio. Video only.

"Smart girl."

Jack could tell she was walking, but not so fast that she would draw attention. Instead of telling Jack where she was, she simply looked at the boulevard signs.

"What's happening here, man? I mean officer," the kid said, from his chair that he had wheeled back.

"You will stay out of the way, ask no questions, and forget we were here," Jack said to him, but he was focused on his HUD.

Hudson rounded the corner, entering the long hall that led to the gates.

"How did she know where to go?" Jude asked, "This is not L11. It's G6."

"Prearranged code, for the hall and gate subtract five from each," Jack said, quickly.

The corridor to G6 was about one hundred meters long. Zimmerman saw her round the corner into the hall, and two seconds behind her, four men moved along at a quiet but increasing pace.

"Hudson! Run!" Zimmerman yelled, drawing both sidearms.

They were both suppressed Frange pistols, designed to pierce unarmored flesh but not cause hull breaches. Jude and Cine swung around and fired the trank guns. Hudson ran as fast as she could along a wall, trying to stay out of the line of fire. The four men fired guns of their own. They were loud and were followed by the sound every resident of Luna feared.

A hull breach.

"These shit bricks are firing armor piercing rounds!" Jack yelled, as he dropped a second attacker with a shot to the knee.

Hudson got hit, in the hip, from behind. It spun her around in a spray of blood, but she was still fifteen yards from the gate.

Jack watched, in amazement, as Jude and Cine dashed into the corridor, like they were shot from a catapult. They each crisscrossed the hall and ran halfway up the wall on the opposite side.

While they were distracted, Jack took careful aim and hit one in the throat, as the other's face fairly bristled with darts.

The emergency airlocks were coming down at both ends of the hall. Without missing a beat, Jude and Cine each grabbed one of Hudson's arms and ran, dragging her.

They all slid under the emergency door, just in time.

Without waiting, as the air got thinner, they ran to the lock-truck with Hudson screaming in pain.

"Come on, kid. In here!" Zimmerman yelled, but the kid was missing half his skull.

Jack jumped in and hammered the control to close and detach.

"For fuck's sake, Hudson. You're getting blood all over everything," Jack yelled, as he slammed it into drive.

Jack heard ripping cloth. Jude was at his elbow.

"It's your blood. Not hers."

Jude tried to take his right hand from the wheel. That's when he noticed the arterial spray from a wound to his wrist.

Jude wrapped it extremely tight. The pain came then.

"Skunking, motherfucking, sons of leper whores..." he cursed, as he docked the truck, none too gently.

Cine hammered the control as soon as it turned green.

The rest of the crew was there, dart guns at the ready.

"Hagan! We take off in two minutes. Doc, Hudson is wounded. Bad. Projectile weapon," Zimmerman barked.

"He is wounded too, mum," Cine said politely to Kuss.

"Time for me later," Jack growled, as he grabbed two of the unconscious men by the collars and tossed them into the lock-truck. Jude helped as well, and before the last one hit the pile, the airlock closed and the detachment sequence started.

"Hagan, we are clear! Head out to deep space. And change vectors a few times."

And then, he fell like a great tree.

CHAPTER THIRTY-ONE: FREEDOM STATION

"Freedom Station was just that. Free from the politics of Earth. Free enterprise with all its good and bad, supply and demand. The grav-plate transport containers and catapult systems on Earth and Luna made the exchange of goods and the transport of people inexpensive, easy, safe and reliable. Almost 14 million people lived there. And the population was growing."

--Solstice 31 Incident Investigation Testimony Transcript: Captain James Worthington, senior surviving member of the Ventura's command crew.

"Why are you dressed like that?" Hume asked Barcus. "Do you have any idea how funny a tunic and cloak would be in Zero-G?" Hume said, amused.

"I have pants on," Barcus smiled.

"OK, not as funny as I'd like, still funny. But people will notice your fashion sense. Do you really want to be noticed?"

"I don't think I will get to see much of the station," Barcus said, as it came into view.

"I can't believe the traffic?" Worthington said. "I've been in deep space too long. This is already making me itch."

"Be glad we have AI control. You can just sit back, and let the Station AI and Stu take care of it all."

"The *Sedna* is flying in on manual and will be required to dock at the public south spire," Rand said. "Damn, this station is big."

The docking on the north spire N73, lock 22, was uneventful and fully automated. Ships of all sizes came and went constantly. The starboard side airlock was not used often and opened directly into the cargo bay.

Hume and Rand were the first down the ladder. Barcus stopped Worthington just before he descended.

"The *Grace* will dock at the south spire S191, lock 9, in twenty-six minutes. You need to get the injured back here and into the med bay, fast and quiet," Barcus said. "No, no, I don't have time to explain. We have a few other things that need doing."

Worthington just looked at him. Concern was etched in his face.

"Everything will be alright," Barcus lied.

"Don't worry, Captain. I will keep him out of trouble," Po said, with humor.

"I was worried about you. You're the trouble maker!" Jim smiled, as he pointed an accusing finger at Po.

Neither of them saw Barcus swallow hard, nor his smile falter, for an instance.

"Let's meet for lunch at noon, level 40, south. I feel like soup."

Jimbo laughed and slid down the elevator.

***

"Hagan! Do you want me fly this thing?" Kuss yelled, because of a third near collision.

"Just open the blast shields all the way and I can manage. Who knew how useful a left thumb was," Hagan said, as he pulled back into the approach's holding pattern.

"*Grace*, you are clear to dock. South, S191, lock 9," came the AI's calm, controlled voice over the comms.

He was lucky that gantries 8 and 10 were both empty. He got it close enough, so the station's mag clamps could reach out, like robot tentacles, and draw them to lock in.

Everyone relaxed when the airlock seal indicator turned green.

They waited ten minutes, to make sure a security detail of shooters didn't swarm the level. The cameras on this level were openly broadcasting, so they watched.

"How will we find Worthington?" Kuss asked, just as the lift opened and Worthington, Rand, and Hume stepped out onto level S191. They moved directly to airlock number 9 and looked directly into the camera.

"Get them ready to move," Kuss barked.

She reached the airlock just as Wex opened it.

"Status?" was all Worthington said, as he entered.

"We ran into bit of trouble, sir. Have wounded," Kuss said.

Hagan added a wave with his thumbless left hand. "Most of us are wounded, but three need immediate medical attention."

"Hume, get a private express lift. Use this to pay." Jim handed her a cash swipe card. She jogged out to the kiosk and ordered one up. The kiosk said it would be there in three minutes and began to count down.

"Captain, this is Tawana Hudson; she took a bullet to the pelvis. She can't walk. We can move her; she had painkillers and first aid nanites, but we need to get a closer look."

"I can walk!" Elkin said, groggily.

"Elkin was shot in the back. She has a lot of trauma under her tough skin and a broken scapula."

"What the hell is that?" Rand said.

"That side of beef is Officer Jack Zimmerman. He didn't notice he had been shot three times and was running out of blood. He needs to get into the med bay. Stat!" Shaw said.

Zimmerman was on an improvised gurney made of a pallet loader. As they drifted it out into the corridor, the lift arrived.

"I will stay with the ship, for now. Go," Wex said, standing there with a trank gun.

They kept moving.

Worthington called to her, as he closed the inner airlock door, "No one will bother you for at least twenty-four hours. Lock it behind us."

The door closed.

Wex dropped the rifle on the floor, right there, and headed for the bridge.

***

Barcus and Po exited the lift on level 1. Lights came up as they stepped into the empty corridor. The air was cold enough here that they could see their breath. Barcus unclasped his cloak and wrapped Po in it. Her one piece flight suit didn't provide as much insulation as his tunic.

The lift paused only briefly at the equator to change orientation and then continued.

"The equator is always down," is the old saying on Freedom Station, and it is literally true.

The single, central gravity core is an engineering wonder. This is very unnerving, to some. The south spire always points directly at the center of Earth. The north spire, away from earth. The station's orbit was at the halfway point between Earth and Luna and had a cycle of fourteen days. The globe of the station was built with many lesser spires that were either privately or publicly owned, for various uses.

The corridor was wide and could handle vehicle traffic, if necessary. It had a gentle turn to the left as they walked. His boot heels echoed, as they watched light come on in front of them and shut down behind them.

They walked by perhaps a hundred doors marked with sequential numbers that all began with N1. A few hallways intersected and seemed to go straight out for a kilometer. Some were dark, some lit.

He finally stopped in front of a nondescript door marked N1-1208. There was a screen beside the door that, when touched a keypad came up but no prompts.

Barcus typed the following: H5BHHR7!jet%bu*?QWb77cd6C.

The door clicked, and he opened it, stepping in after Po. It was more like a closet than a room. It was two meters by three meters, with racks lining the wall opposite the door. Po stepped to the side as Barcus touched the fronts of three panels that slid down, revealing two glowing globes that were like crystal balls with perfect clouds drifting inside. The larger of the two was golden like the sun; the other was deep blue and the size of his head.

"Hello, Station. My name is Barcus."

The blue globe responded, pulsing as the words sounded.

"This is a restricted area."

"And I had the restricted access codes," Barcus said, flatly.

"How may I be of service?"

The golden globe pulsed, like sunlight.

"We are the ones that have come to be of service to you, Station."

He looked at the blue orb then.

"Someone has hidden a massive nuclear device on Freedom Station."

***

The corridor of N72 was not empty as the lift doors opened. A small shuttle had just arrived with passengers from Earth. They looked like workers from a single company. All wore the same coveralls and caps. All but a few of the two dozen were Asians, speaking in Mandarin. The workers ignored the wounded party. Stu opened the airlock and they moved inside without a word. The med bay opened, and Zimmerman was transferred to it. He barely fit inside. Worthington had stopped them from speaking in the lift and now everyone began at once.

"Wait, one at a time," Worthington said.

"Sir, they know we're back," Hagan said, as he unwrapped his bandage. "This guy is a cop on Luna, Jack Zimmerman.

"Number two on Echo's list. A good pick for Everett. She is a data scientist named Hudson.

"And, Johan was a bartender in one of the busiest port bars on Luna. All positioned well for information." He got the bandage off, and it was ugly.

"He found us," Jude said, pointing at Zimmerman.

Everyone looked at Jude, since she spoke so rarely.

"They sent people after us wherever we went. They have a description of the *Sedna*, and of us," Hagan said, as the scan completed on Zimmerman and a flurry of small robotic arms began to cut off his clothes and repair wounds on his wrist, calf and left bicep.

"Captain Worthington, I do not mean to interrupt. But did you know your family is on Freedom Station?" Hudson said. "If they know you are here, they may try to take them in, for leverage."

"Dammit," Worthington cursed.

"Sir, their residence is at this address: South level 32, S32-55947."

"Got it," Rand said, "Where's Barcus?"

"No time for that now. Rand, Hume, you are with me. We have to keep our HUDs dark so we will be out of touch, unless it's an emergency. Kuss, patch 'em up as best you can."

"We come, go too," Cine said, spinning her flute in her fingers.

***

"I am the AI responsible for all aspects of security on this station," pulsed the deep blue orb.

"I thought your function was simply as a critical systems fail-safe. So, if Station goes off-line, the people still have air and water and power," he said, to one sphere, and then to the other. "You don't mind if I call you Station, do you?"

The golden sphere pulsed, "Not at all. It's been a very long time since anyone called me anything. Thank you."

"Ever since they installed this, I bet."

Barcus gestured to the blue orb.

"Why yes. In fact, that's true," AI~Station said.

"And what will you call me?" the blue orb asked, in a voice that was both vain and jealous.

"I won't need to call you anything," Barcus said, as he bent close and looked into the blue swirling clouds. They were laced with streaks of black.

"Why?"

With the speed of a cobra, the point of the Telis blade stabbed into the orb and it shattered into tiny pieces. Viscus fluid splashed into the rack and its light extinguished.

"Station, are you alright?" Barcus asked.

After a long pause, it began to glow brighter. It finally said, "I'm free again."

CHAPTER THIRTY-TWO: GONE

"And then, she was just gone."

--Solstice 31 Incident Investigation Testimony Transcript: Captain James Worthington, senior surviving member of the Ventura's command crew.

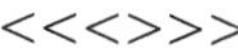

They stood in front of the interactive display map on level 32, on the kiosk by the lift, like tourists looking for a brothel.

"Stop looking suspicious," Rand chastised Jude and Cine.

There was a lot of foot traffic on this level as it approached midday.

"Here it is, S32-55947. This way," Worthington said, as he walked briskly.

It didn't look out of place here. The main corridors were like highways. Slower traffic just kept to the right.

"We have to move out to the 5th loop, spoke 59, residence 47."

Worthington followed the most direct path, and they traveled corridors that became smaller, like capillaries.

They rounded the corner from loop number 5 onto spoke 59 and immediately saw the hall was full of uniformed security. They were gathered around a single, open door. They heard shouting from within the residence.

"What do you mean the comms are down!"

"Sec is not responding. No HUD data either."

"What about the dispatcher?"

"The dispatcher is there; she has nothing as well."

"Goddammit, find them."

A man burst out of the room, wearing the same blue uniform, with a few more stripes on the right sleeve.

"You two, stay in case they come back. The rest of you, come with me to the sec control room to find out who is trying to ruin my day."

They stormed off in the opposite direction.

"We find out if that is 47," Cine said.

And without waiting for permission, they walked up the hall toward the guards, who seemed to be conversing in quiet tones instead of doing their jobs. Cine and Jude suddenly seemed like they were laughing teenage girls. They rubbernecked to see into the room as they walked by.

It looked like one of the guards greeted them, and they stopped to talk with them. Cine said nothing and stood slightly behind Jude with both of her hands covering her mouth, as if she were shy about showing her bad teeth.

They shook their heads no, and Jude waved to the guards as they skipped away.

Worthington looked at Rand, and said, "Are you seeing this?"

"Your family is not there. Could see the entire room. Less than 100 square feet. Three bunks on the right, a counter, a closet, a tiny bath on the other side. Saw everything. No one is there. Overheard the guards. Something is wrong with the Sec AI," she said.

Worthington looked at Hume and then Rand. At the same time, they all said, "Barcus."

Jim started back to the lift.

"Where are you going now?" Rand asked, as she kept pace.

"Do you like soup?"

***

"Who are you?" AI~Station asked.

"My name is Barcus, and this is Po," Barcus said.

"Hello," Po added.

"It's like I can breathe again," AI~Station said. "No one has set foot in here for almost 20 years, Barcus. Ever since they installed that thing. You were right; it was supposed to be a critical systems backup. It began taking over everything, except management of air, water, gravity, heating and cooling. How did you know?"

"Caisy told me. Do you remember Caisy? She sends her regards," Barcus said. AI~Caisy was the original AI from the *Ventura.* It survived the destruction of the *Ventura* in the Black Pod.

"How did you know that access code? Only one man knew it, and he is dead."

"Repeat the code back to me please, Station," Barcus asked.

"H5BHHR7!jet%bu*?QWb77cd6C," AI~Station replied.

"Thank you, Station," Barcus sighed. "Have you reestablished sec operations control?"

"Yes, Barcus."

"Please stand down all operations associated with the name Worthington."

"There are current outstanding orders associated with Worthington. Locate and provide protective custody," AI~Station said.

"Can I be of service in any other way?"

"Can you tell me the address of Pho Pete's?"

***

The lift opened directly into a massive commercial area. It was a combination of old world open air market and mall promenade. This area was open for seven levels, and there was artificial sky above that. Exclusive residence balconies overlooked shops and restaurants and businesses of every kind. There was music and laughter in the air.

Jude and Cine were in awe as they moved through the crowds. The smell of foods of all kinds drifted in the air. After about ten more minutes, they saw the retro sign for Pho Pete's.

There was a simple awning that covered a half dozen cafe tables, all occupied. There was a long counter that had eighteen stools. There were lines queued up along the building, on both sides. One was for take-out orders, and one was for seating. There was one waitress that was constantly in motion and five people behind the counter.

All of them were Asian, except Pete.

They moved to get in the line for seats, as he scanned the crowds for Barcus and Po, when they heard the scream.

***

The airlock barely closed when Wex turned and quickly searched the ship. She started crying before the lift doors opened. She began in the crew quarters, grabbing large black duffel bags and filling them with the items she had been collecting. She packed clothes and cash, weapons and medical gear. She kept stuffing them with other useful items, like the survival rations, binoculars, and even a few tools. She finished filling the bags with selected books from Ulric's collection. They were probably worth a fortune. The last item she stuffed into the last bag was her flute. Number 12 of 12. The finest ever made. She returned to the airlock.

She opened the first inner door and the outer airlock doors on the *Sedna.* She hesitated before opening the first station airlock door. It was normal protocol to close the inner ship door first. She opened the first station door and stepped into the station's airlock. She stood there. One minute, and then two, and at four minutes, she gently set the duffels down in the station's airlock and retreated into the *Sedna*, closing all the doors behind her. People would wonder later what she was thinking as she stood there.

Wex went directly to the bridge then. She sat in the command chair and held her own face in her hands for a full minute, before sitting up and wiping her face with her sleeves.

Methodically, she brought the reactors up to full power.

"Station traffic control, this is the *Grace*, preparing for departure. Standing by for vectors."

She opened the blast shields all the way then. The view of Earth was so breathtaking. Freedom Station orbited halfway between the Earth and the moon, so it shined bright.

She barely heard the instructions from the busy space traffic controller.

Wex smiled as the airlock gantry detached, and she gently flew away from Freedom.

***

The scream was wordless, high-pitched, and brain-piercing. No one could find its origin, until the crowd separated and Worthington saw her running. It was a small girl, maybe eight years old, with long black-brown hair drawn back into a tight ponytail.

She ran directly at Worthington, who fell to his knees at the sight of her.

She crashed into her father, wrapping her arms around his neck. She was crying now. When her mother caught up, she politely pressed through the crowd with a worried face. When she saw them both, her hands flew to her mouth, and with a gasp, she froze. Another girl, in her early teens, found her way to the scene and did not hesitate to drop to her own knees, throwing her arms around them both. She buried her face in her father's neck, and said, "I knew you weren't dead. I knew you'd find us."

Jim locked eyes with Bobbie, his wife, and stood, lifting the younger girl in his arms and drawing the older one closer to his side. Slowly, he walked to her. She stood up straighter; her eyes glistened with unshed tears.

"You're late," she said, her voice cracking.

"I lived. I came back," Jim choked out.

Then screams of another kind erupted from across the plaza. A man fell from one of the balconies. Worthington looked up in time to see Po disappear around a corner on an upper level. As the crowd's attention was on the man, lying on the floor, a hand rested on Worthington's shoulder, and a whispering voice spoke to him.

"Quickly, come with me." It was Pho Pete. He led them around the end of the counter to the kitchen and prep areas in the back. Rand and Hume followed into a large room filled with recycle bins. "They were right, Bobbie, they were following you. A man from across the way had just gotten a Frange rifle aimed when a man and a woman stopped him. I saw it. She was fast," Pete said.

"Where are Jude and Cine?" Worthington asked.

"Here," they replied, and stood from behind boxes that seemed impossible to hide behind.

"We apologize for not finding that one earlier. We did find two others in the crowd. They won't be following," Jude said.

"They knew you lived, Jim," Bobbie said, "They threatened us, demanded we inform them if you got in touch. They implied..." Bobbie looked at the girls. "So, we ran. Just walked away from everything on Earth and came here."

"Look, you need to move," Pho Pete said. "This is Danny. He is going to take you somewhere safe. Danny, take them to Aunt Ina's place. Is it still empty?"

Danny looked to be about twenty or so, trying desperately to grow his first beard. He just nodded and headed to the utility door. It was a heavy door. In case of pressure loss on either side, it would hold a seal.

They stepped into a cluttered hallway full of recycle bins, unopened boxes, and random objects from the business. A utility elevator opened directly opposite the door to the soup kitchen. They all got in.

"Station, please take us to level N221," Danny said, and the doors closed. "Aunt Ina's apartment is close to the utility 'vator in west 221."

"Will this be an imposition for your aunt?" Bobbie asked. Her head was still laying on Jim's chest.

"It's empty. Ina went to Mars on vacation two years ago and decided to stay," Danny said, as he watched the numbers on the display increase. "Pete has not decided what to do with her place. He thinks she'll be back."

It was right around the corner from the 'vator. It was also a huge apartment.

What they first thought to be a floor to ceiling window on the far side of the open floor plan apartment was just a piped in exterior view of Earth. But it was still amazing.

"I will be back with lunch in about an hour," Danny said, and then was off at a run.

As soon as the door closed, "We need to check in. Rand, you and Hume take the Ninja twins and make sure the ship is secure."

They left without a word, giving the family the privacy they deserved. As soon as the door closed, Bobbie spoke. "I never doubted for a minute." She kissed him again. "Can you tell me what happened?"

"Not now. As soon as possible, I will get you all out of here," Worthington said.

"Captain James Worthington, your family will not be going anywhere," Freedom Station's AI said to them, from all around.

CHAPTER THIRTY-THREE: RHEA

"Rhea is the second-largest moon of Saturn and the ninth-largest moon in the solar system. It is mostly ice and has only one settlement on it. A small research station that maintains a population of approximately 340 research scientists but had only three security officers."

--Solstice 31 Incident Investigation Testimony Transcript: General Patricia Chase, senior member of the Earth Defense Coalition.

"Listen, Watkins. I am the only one that is allowed to see him now," Kristin Vittori explained, for the last time. "Now shut the hell up about it. With McDonald off base, I am in command."

Watkins sat at his massive console in the system center of the research base. He watched her ass as she walked by in her conservative, winter Earth street clothes.

The lone prisoner actually thought he was on Earth, in Detroit.

She walked into the prison cell dome. With McDonald gone, she was now the only one allowed in here.

High, dirty windows provided filtered light as Kristin proceeded to the center, where there was a huge clear box enclosing an area seven meters on a side. Industrial lighting hung from the ceiling above the cell.

There was the man in the big box.

She climbed onto the visitor's platform that was near, but not touching, the cell. She pressed a button on a console there, and the freestanding screen that showed various TV shows all day went dark. Another button activated the intercom.

"My name is Kristin. I will be working with you while Dr. McDonald is away."

"So, the chancellor has reeled him in? I bet he took the weapon and the new AI with him. How can I help you, Kristin?"

"The same way you were helping McDonald. Innovations," Kristin said. "Except with less bullshit this time."

"We have a hardball player. Excellent."

"Tell me your name, fucker," Vittori growled.

"My name is Vincent Joseph Turkot," he said, politely setting down the book he was reading.

"I don't believe you," she said.

"Why would you not believe me?" Turkot asked.

"You have been here for years, and you have never told Dr. McDonald your name."

"He never asked me so nicely."

"How old are you?"

"That is a bit more difficult question. Time is difficult to measure when you've ignored it as long as I have. I first came to Earth just over 100 million years ago. During the beginning of the war."

"What war?"

"These questions are far more refreshing than I thought they'd be," Turkot said.

"Answer the question."

"The greatest war this galaxy has ever seen. The war that destroyed Earth."

***

"Captain James Worthington, your family will not be going anywhere," Freedom Station's AI said to them, from all around. "Your ship is gone. Eleven minutes ago, it requested departure instructions and has now left Freedom space."

"Jimbo, this is Barcus. The *Grace* is gone. I have secured the cooperation of Freedom Station's AI. We can now securely use Freedom's comms. I need to check on Stu. He's not responding."

"Station, is Rand anywhere near a comms unit?"

"She and the others are now in a crowded lift on their way back and do not have privacy," AI~Station replied.

"What is their ETA?" Jimbo asked.

"One minute."

"Girls, why don't you explore a bit," Bobbie said to them.

"Will you be right here when we get back?" Clara said, with a stab to his heart.

"Yes, Pumpkin," Jim said, smiling. "I'll be right here."

The girls wandered down the hallway to explore the rest of the apartment.

The door chime interrupted their kiss far too soon.

"Come," Worthington.

Hume and Rand entered and quickly closed the door behind them.

"Sir, do not just open the door like that. What if it was not us?"

"I knew it was you. What's with the bags?" Jim asked.

"The *Sedna* is gone. It looks like Wex has taken it. It looks like she packed all our personal affects."

Rand opened one of the duffel bags on the dining table and started to remove items.

She held up the flute.

"I think she'll be back," Rand said.

***

Vittori just stared at Turkot for at full minute. "What do you mean destroyed Earth? What war?"

Turkot just stared at her for a while in return.

"Are you saying you visited Earth a hundred million years ago and spent so much time traveling at the speed of light it brought you here?"

"Something like that," Turkot said, as if he lost interest. He started reading his book again.

"That was the end of a battle. A meteor hammered the Earth and put an end to that Scarecrow. He was on the wrong track anyway. I pressed reset and took the planet for myself. Seeded it and never expected it to all happen so fast."

He began reading again.

"What is going on? Why did Dr. McDonald leave in such a hurry?" Vittori was frustrated.

"Because the weapon was completed. Again. That AI more so," he said. "If you don't mind, I'd like to finish reading this today."

He turned his back to her without another word. She walked away. She would not beg him for information. Getting back to the main control room, she found it empty. Now she had a place to vent her anger.

She activated the comms, and spoke, "Hearn, where the hell is everyone?" There was no answer on the comms.

"Base, locate Hearn." There was no response. No reply.

"Base, what time is it?" There was no response.

"Oh shit."

***

The navigation of the space around Freedom Station and Earth's controlled space took longer than the trip to Saturn. The research station on Rhea wasn't easy to find. But she found it. Just as she knew she would.

She also found the main hangar empty.

No one challenged her. No one met her at the bottom of the ramp. She was not surprised by the bodies on the floor in the corner of the hangar. She walked with confidence, holding a handgun, loosely.

A woman's voice came over the PA as she opened the airlock door and entered the hall.

"This is a security alert. We have intruders. Comms are down. People are dead. Security protocol one: shelter-in-place. Await the all-clear signal."

Wex paused and held up the gun. When a security guard rounded the corner at a jog, she shot him in the face, sending him sprawling at her feet.

She dropped the handgun and picked up the man's Frange carbine in one smooth motion. Just as she placed the sling over her head and leveled the carbine, two more men rounded the corner.

She instantly killed them both. She dropped the one hundred round mag out of the gun, even though it was still almost half full, and retrieved another full one from one of the dead men's vests.

She knew where she was going and knew she was being watched on the cameras that lined the halls. Expressionless, she moved through the corridors.

"Hearn! She is in B7, moving toward W1. Stop her!" came over the PA system, in a panic.

***

Hearn said to Matthews, "We're under specific orders to nuke the base, if it was penetrated."

Matthews was already in the small shuttle, warming it up.

"Roger that! I am sick of this shit hole anyway," Matthews replied.

Hearn opened the plain door with a scan and ident procedure. The room was simple and had a single console in the center. He logged in and passed several additional levels of security. He brought up a direct comms path to the shuttle.

"Matthews, let me know when you are ready."

"Two minutes," replied Matthews.

Hearn began the self-destruct sequence.

The emergency escape shuttle was a short-range, no-frills craft. It had conventional propulsion with simple grav-plates for takeoff, landing, and inertial dampening. They would be on the other side of Saturn before the base blew.

***

Kristin Vittori watched this woman cut through the entire security staff. She wasn't moving toward the prisoner as Kristin expected. She was moving toward the labs in the center of the base. She entered the first lab and didn't shoot anyone. She calmly walked past thirty shocked lab techs that were frozen where they stood.

Room after room, she moved deeper into the base.

Finally, she reached a lab that was adjacent to the server room.

She shot out the glass.

Leveling the carbine for precise aim, she destroyed the fragile globes of the remaining AIs on the base. When she was done, she dropped the carbine, turned, and walked out the same way she came in.

***

"Hearn, we are a go, as soon as you are here," Matthew said over comms.

"Acknowledged," Hearn said, as he initiated the command sequences.

***

When the AIs were destroyed, the auto-tracking on the security system stopped working. Vittori manually brought up security cameras that showed the inside of the warehouse that held the prisoner. He was oblivious, still reading his book. Unable to do anything else, she grabbed her sidearm and ran.

The doors opened to the command center, and the alarm echoed through the compound. The noise was loud and covered the sound of her running feet as she moved through the complex. She went down six levels and all the way across the complex without seeing anyone. All the stupid drills suddenly seemed to be less than stupid.

Kristin skidded to a stop at the warehouse entrance, and to speed things up, she set her gun down on the console shelf.

As she pounded the last character into the access sequence, she hit enter.

From behind, someone grabbed the back of her head and smashed her face into the console as the doors slid open.

***

Slowly, Vittori became conscious as she was dragged by her heels. Her feet dropped and her head lulled to the side, trying to make sense of what was happening. She saw Turkot read the final page of the book and, after closing the cover, tossed it to the floor. He casually moved to brace himself in a corner.

The forklift sped into view and crashed into the cube, spearing it with its two tines. The tines spread and the cell shattered. Turkot landed neatly on his feet.

Vittori watched him walk out as a woman fell in step with him.

"Hello, Wex. So very nice to see you."

CHAPTER THIRTY-FOUR: WHEN IT ALL GOES WRONG

"The Solstice 31 War began here."

--Solstice 31 Incident Investigation Testimony Transcript: General Patricia Chase, senior member of the Earth Defense Coalition.

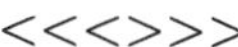

"Station, I am passing to you the ident codes for a ship I need to contact," Barcus said to the station AI, as he walked down an empty corridor. "Here are the general coordinates."

"That's in the belt, Barcus. A dangerous section of the belt," AI~Station replied.

"I know, that's why I need to contact them," Barcus replied.

"Is that Cook?" Po knew better than to even mention the word *Memphis.*

"Yes."

Barcus stopped and leaned over to put his hands on his knees. He looked like he was going to throw up.

"Go for the *Winton,*" AI~Station replied, using the new ident for the *Memphis.*

"Cook, this is Barcus. The Station has gotten too hot. You need to go with Charlie Delta," Barcus said, as he leaned on a wall.

"Charlie Delta. Excellent," Cook said, with a smile in his voice. "Rendezvous as specified, we will be eating steak and drinking cold brews until you arrive, asswipe. Don't be too long. I'm not sure I can hold Beary off much longer."

Barcus heard laughter in the background.

"Save the best bourbon for me, dipshit," Barcus said, turning with his back to the wall, tears welling in his eyes. His hand covered his mouth.

"You should save that for Hagan. He has the short stick," Cook said.

"Stay sharp," Barcus choked out.

He slid down the wall.

Po knelt before him. "What's wrong?"

"This is hell. What did I do to deserve this?" he said, wiping his face with his sleeves. But he could not wipe away the knowing.

Po knelt before him and saw his despair. "I did this. Wex warned me it would happen and I did it anyway. She said you'd…it's all my fault…"

Po didn't even see him move. Suddenly, she was off her feet and up against the wall. Barcus held her there by one hand, gripping a handful of her flight suit.

"Don't you ever say that again," Barcus growled into her face.

Po was helpless. When she clutched at his wrist, it felt like iron. He was so much bigger than her. She had forgotten. There was no use struggling. He might as well have been made of stone.

"I will say whatever I please," she whispered.

His grip squeezed her lungs.

"She told me something else you need to know."

Barcus looked confused. Realization dawned.

"You are not the monster. You are the witness. I don't know what it means," she said, as she let go of his wrist and placed her hand on the side of his face.

In his mind, he watched her die. Over and over and over. He punished himself because now he knew that what he saw was not always the truth.

He couldn't stop any of it and deserved to be punished. No other image was as vivid in his memory. Fidelity increased with the pain of it.

He watched her die. Again and again. He knew the day. The moment. The anguish amplified as he focused memory on a tear that would slide down her cheek after her last breath.

She wrapped her legs around his torso and drew him toward her with her heels. Barcus allowed it. She wrapped her arms around his neck and clung to him. She was the strong one. He knew.

He watched her die. Again and again. And in his mind, the most terrible horror was yet to come. He saw it.

Worst of all, he knew that he would learn to live without her.

He also knew that *she* was the monster.

***

"Echo, did you hear that? Delta Charlie," Cook said, as he set a course for Earth.

"Affirmative," AI~Echo replied.

Karen Beary waited until Cook was done setting the course, before she asked, "OK, Cook. What the hell is a Delta Charlie?"

"We head to Sri Lanka, but we time it for a night drop so Echo can land in Oklahoma. Wes has some contacts there.

"We find a quiet hangar and rest tight on these data stores," Cook said. "These will be all they need to prove that Chancellor Dalton was behind the destruction of the *Ventura* and God only knows how many other ships."

"Do not forget the genome project," Echo added. "That alone will ruin him, politically."

"Why the hell would he do that? What was to be gained? To be honest, I don't give a shit about the politics of the whole thing," Cook said. "I just don't want to be looking over my shoulder the rest of my life while working as a shuttle pilot for some backwater colony."

"I trust Worthington, but how is this going to play out?" Muir asked, knowing that Cook was more clued in.

He just did as ordered. He liked it that way.

"Jimbo is a Boy Scout. He will follow regs, orders, and chain of command. You know it's true."

Cook turned and looked at Beary and Wood, in turn.

"He will report to Admiral Kreiger, and Kreiger will figure it out from there."

"What about us?" Shaw asked.

"We can expect weeks of debriefing while Kreiger sorts through the data from Echo and Bowen," Cook added.

Beary held her hand up.

"What about all these nukes, the Warmarks?"

"That is why I am glad it's a Delta Charlie. All that will be in the DS *Sariska* when we drop her. A stealth night drop in the desert."

"The pinnace-class ship, the *Winton*, will land in the largest, busiest spaceport in the universe. Freshly salvaged from a yard on Mars with full idents and back story."

Cook laughed.

"Hell, it even looks salvaged."

"We park and lay low. We order in food and pay in cash," Cook said.

"I think we should rent an apartment as an off-ship base and move the data store there," Beary added.

"That way, if data inspectors show up, let them inspect," Muir said.

"I would like to add an extra item to this plan," AI~Ben said. "We should remove my AI module and house it with the data store. I could be traced back to the EM on the *Memphis*."

"Excellent plan. I will even fly it into the Sri Lanka spaceport on manual. That feeds the *Winton* salvage story."

Cook sounded pleased.

"I'm going with Echo," Dr. Shaw said.

"What?"

Cook was surprised.

"I'll be useless, watching you all getting tans and trying to stay drunk all the time," she said. "You won't need me. Jimbo and Barcus will need me, knowing them," Shaw said.

"It's Barcus that will break this plan. We need to be ready for that," Beary said.

Cook looked at everyone nodding but not saying anything. When Echo spoke, her avatar appeared first.

"Barcus is now a…Scarecrow. Just like Wex."

***

Po got to the airlock marked for the *Latha* before Barcus. The name appeared on the control panel. The new ident was from a crashed STU that had been on Mars for a decade, slowly being stripped for parts.

Barcus marveled, once again, at her ease using the technology. *Wasn't she a starving, ignorant girl just moments ago*, he thought.

That, in turn, made him think of Olias.

It isn't just the future that causes me pain.

Zimmerman stood at the door to the med bay, holding a Frange carbine, making himself look larger that he actually was. It was an attempt to distract anyone entering from looking at the four tarps covering the Warmarks.

"Jack, meet Barcus," Kuss said, as she stepped around him. "He only one on this station can kick your ass. No shoot him with that. Make him angry. Not polite when angry."

Kuss gestured. "And this is Po. No touch her. No med bay exist that could fix you."

Barcus extended his right hand to shake, and said, "Officer Jacob Zimmerman. You've gone by Jack since you were a child. You were a decorated Ranger in the Expansion War but don't like to talk about it because you feel like you were on the wrong side. You're smarter than you look and have an advanced degree in Theoretical Physics."

Their hands remained clasped.

"You like people to underestimate you by your cultivated, crass manner. You enjoy physics and engineering but prefer hands-on peacekeeping to theoretical physics. You are a faithful Vedic, but tell no one of this. You own nothing but tools and uniforms. You live a Spartan life."

"Who the fuck are you?" was his only reply.

"I'm Barcus. Maintenance guy number 42."

"Am I supposed to be impressed by that little speech?"

Barcus knew Jack was taken aback by the amount he knew of him but didn't have time to explain. He released his hand.

"No. If you had been, you would not be the man Captain Everett thought you were."

"I don't know if anyone has noticed, but this is all shit, escalating pretty fast. We need to move, before they get organized and make us disappear," Zimmerman said.

"I agree," Barcus said. "Stu, prep for departure."

Barcus walked into the med bay and asked Kuss, "How is Hudson? We are going to need her."

Tawana Hudson was in the med scanner, sleeping. Kuss brought up the status display for Barcus.

"I sedated her. She has many nanites fixing hip. Drive her crazy, if awake," Kuss said, pointing at the real-time progress in the area on the scanner.

"What about Worthington?" Po asked.

"He has his own problems to solve. We are splitting up," Barcus said.

Po realized then that none of the people onboard were part of Jimbo's command crew.

"Kuss, we are going to drop you and Hudson off to hook up with Hagan and Shaw. The rest of us are going to meet with Kreiger," he said, moving toward the ladder to the bridge. "Jack, you are going to arrange the meet in Mexico City."

"How did you know he was in Mexico City?" Zimmer asked, sounding annoyed.

"It's where the second largest space catapult is located that is big enough to hold the military traffic he is required to manage. The one in New York is smaller and only handles passenger traffic. And only to Freedom Station."

"Departure in fourteen minutes," AI~Stu informed them.

***

It was just after midnight, Station time, when Barcus contacted Worthington.

"The girls are finally asleep. Bobbie had to lay down with them. They're all asleep now. Are you sure they will be safe here?" Jimbo asked.

"As safe as can be expected. We will be back tomorrow to get everyone," Barcus said. "You have a long night ahead. Chancellor Dalton has hidden a nuke on FS. You need to find it and jettison the damn thing, before he can decide to use it."

"How the hell am I supposed to do that? You know how big this place is," Worthington said.

"Get Pho Pete to help you. He knows how to smuggle undocumented containers onto Freedom Station."

"Pho Pete?"

"Yes. Pedro Morales, the soup guy. Why do you think his soup is so good?" Barcus said. "You have Rand and Hume. You got this. Station will help you."

CHAPTER THIRTY-FIVE: THE CHANCELLOR

"Dalton was recording his meetings so he could use them as blackmail later. He intended them to be leverage, not evidence."

--Solstice 31 Incident Investigation Testimony Transcript: General Patricia Chase, senior member of the Earth Defense Coalition.

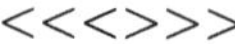

"Chancellor, retreating to the Isle of Calf at this time is politically unwise. The Senate and the United Council of Colonies are at each other's throats. Any additional restrictions on people trying to immigrate to the colonies at this time will be met with harsher measures," said Senator Kendall.

Chancellor Dalton sat at the head of the conference table in his private office suite. He was slightly elevated with a wraparound console before him. There were ten men around the table. All looked grim.

"Times have changed," a man said, with a North African accent. "I remember when we forced people off-world to thin our populations. Prisoners and undesirables. To the Harvesters and the colonies. Separated the wheat from the chaff."

"The colonies no longer need Earth, for anything," another man said. "Tourism is the only reason anyone comes here."

"Even the Sol Treaty has failed. We can't even keep control of the colonies and outposts in our own goddamn system," said the youngest looking man at the table, frustrated as well as angry.

"Why are the spaceports and catapults still in private hands?" another man demanded to know.

"These people are too full of self-interest to do the right things," Senator Kendall almost yelled.

"What do you recommend we do that we are not already?" Dalton asked. "The Harvester prison ships are already full of the petty violators we have created, full of our political adversaries. We have more laws than lawyers. We have disarmed them. We have diluted and disbursed the military, so we have nothing to fear there," Dalton replied. "We have even used more unorthodox means to clear the senate floor of these fools that value the many, less than the individual."

"How can we stop these bastards from taking their work and wealth and talent off to the colonies? We can't continue without their taxes."

"Enough."

Chancellor Dalton slammed down his fist.

"Everyone out, except you, Kendall."

They all filed out, and the doors automatically closed behind them.

"There was a time, not long ago, when we had the opposite problem," Dalton fumed at Kendall. "All this petty bickering is to blame."

"Actually, your Excellency, your policies are to blame. You do understand this, don't you?" Kendall said. "The Earth has emptied about as far as it can without collapsing in on itself. Sure, there is 100% employment, and housing is plentiful. I've seen the vids. But the best and brightest have gone elsewhere before you could stop them, and now you can't afford to buy them back. No one *needs* Earth, not even Freedom Station."

"I hate that name, that place," Dalton spat.

"Because it's true," Kendall replied.

***

Dalton's personal shuttle landed on the end of the old-style runway. Most of the Isle of Man had been turned into the chancellor's base when he took office forty-one years before. As the gull wings opened, he saw the only company of soldiers Atish had managed to breed, train, and deliver, running information their way.

He stood and waited with Kendall and his personal security detail.

A perfect formation of ten by ten came to a halt and stood, at attention, for inspection. They all wore black flight suits and tactical vests. Ninety percent of them were women. The men all had shaved heads and the women all had long hair, French braided.

Dalton walked to the center of their ranks and stopped. He inspected one of them closely.

"Are you ready to DIE TODAY?" he called out.

"Sir, yes, sir!" they said, in unison.

He walked to the front again and pointed at a random woman in the front row.

"You. Front and center."

She complied, without hesitation.

"Strip. Now," Dalton ordered.

He didn't smile, until he looked at Kendall, his back to the troops.

In moments, she was completely naked and standing at parade rest.

"Put your arms over your head and don't move. Don't lower them until I say you can lower them," Dalton ordered.

She obeyed.

"Company! Knives out," Dalton ordered.

Dalton stood before the naked woman. She was short but ultra-fit.

"You will not fall until I allow it."

"Sir, yes, sir," she replied, stoically.

"When I say 'GO', each of you will stab her and return to formation. If she drops before the last of you returns to formation, we will start again. Knives UP for inspection. Before and after."

All the knives were raised above their heads.

Kendall's face went pale as Dalton returned to his side.

"GO!"

***

"Sawyer, wake the fuck up."

Dan Sawyer was a tug pilot. He was one of the few that remained on Freedom Station that could fly the old manual tugs and freighters.

There was pounding on the door. Dan was in bed under a big pile of blankets. The only light in the room came from the stars outside his meter square window.

"Come in," he called out to the door control.

It opened.

"Dan. What the hell? I've been trying to call you for an hour."

He stumbled on a half empty case of bourbon.

"What do you want, Max," Dan said, pressing his forehead to the cool window adjacent to his mattress.

"Jesus, Dan. What the hell are you doing in this coffin?" Max asked, activating the light over the sink.

The place was tiny. Nine square meters of floor space, all covered with laundry and take-out containers. They called them Three-by-Threes. Most prison cells were bigger.

"Hey, it has a window," Dan said, placing a hand flat on it. "What do you want, Max?"

"Do you know what the failure rate is on those? Only one layer from vacuum." He moved a bit closer to the door.

"Especially on these old spires."

"Max!" Sawyer barked.

"What?"

Dan pushed off the pile of quilts and let his feet over the side of the bunk. He picked up a half empty beer and drank it.

"I need you, man."

Max was fat and a bit greasy. Dan didn't like him, but he worked in the commercial dispatcher's office of Station Traffic Control.

Dan stepped directly out of bed into the tiny bathroom and started taking a piss without closing the door. He still wore an old-style flight suit.

Max never stopped talking.

"I got this old, Oarcart-91 mining vessel out there that needs to dock, but the kid at the helm doesn't trust himself or his old man to manually dock it. It's one of the big factory hard-locks. Gotta be perfect or we're fucked up the ass, and not in a good way."

Max laughed at his own joke as Dan washed his hands and face in the small sink. He pulled on his deck shoes and pushed Max out the door.

The farther he got from the window, the louder he heard his heartbeat in his own ears.

***

"GO!"

Kendall was sure they had done this exercise before. The two center rows of ten ran by the naked woman, brutally stabbing her from either side. They started on her upraised arms and worked down. The first four groups stabbed in only non-vital areas. Even though they each plunged their knives in deep, they avoided major arteries and veins. The last group stabbed her in the torso; mostly in the abdomen, but also in the chest.

She swayed, bathed in blood. Only her face remain clean and fair. Only a few drops of blood splashed her cheek.

Dalton walked up to her and offered her, her own knife.

"Only one soldier left," he smiled.

She didn't take the knife.

"You may lower your arms and finish it," Dalton said.

Her arms fell. She swayed. He offered the knife again.

She took it and plunged it into her own heart and held it above her head, like the rest of the company. Every knife was red in the setting sun.

Dalton watched as she managed to stay on her feet for another full minute before she fell backward.

"I want her gutted, skinned, and in the stewpots before dinner. Move out!" Dalton yelled.

In an almost ritual fashion, they passed her flight suit around, and each of them cleaned their knives on it. Then, they lifted her above their heads and jogged, in tight formation, back to the barracks.

"They really will do anything you tell them to do?" Kendall asked.

"Only if you never let them see the world."

***

"Max, just get me a pressure suit and a grav-pack. I don't need a shuttle for spit's sake. I can see the damn thing from here."

"Dude, it's like three K out. Those things are big."

Max tried to keep up with Sawyer.

"Some dumb-ass might splat you on their windshield."

"Just warn them, I will be over in fifteen minutes. Now, Max."

Dan knew how bad Max needed his cut of this docking fee.

"And I want a piece of your end."

"Sawyer, you're killin' me."

Dan just pointed.

"OK, OK. I'm going, you crazy fuck."

Sawyer was into the pressure suit and pack with ease. When the airlock opened to space, he stepped out and just floated, for a moment.

He took a deep breath, in through his nose and out through his mouth, relaxing. He smiled wide, looked around, and activated the grav-pack, sending him in the direction of the Oarcart-91.

"Max, here is the freq for the miner. Its official designation is the *TUNA-MELT*. I ain't shittin ya."

Max laughed.

Sawyer cut him off as he rounded the nose of the massive ship. It was like a long board on edge with both sides covered with old, rusty shipping containers. Four giant engine bells aft and the bridge in its nose. Faded letters were painted on the side of the nose: TUNA-MELT.

The airlock strobes flashed in the top portion of the letter A, and the outer door was already open. He was inside and pressurized fast.

The inside surprised him.

It was well-lit and looked well cared for. The 'kid' turned out to actually be a kid. It was Zero-G in this section. Sawyer took off his helmet first and placed it on a rack, while he said, "Hi, I'm Dan Sawyer, the dock jock."

By then, he had the top of his suit off, over his head.

He shook the kid's hand.

"I'm Keith, the chicken shit pilot," he smiled.

"You may be the smartest pilot I have ever met, son."

He slid out of his lower suit.

"You can leave your pressure suit on, if you want. The manual says you should," Keith said.

They went up three levels and then in deeper.

"I never do," Dan said, floating down the hall after him.

"Oh?"

"Not since the war."

The ship looked well-maintained on the inside, all the way to the bridge.

"Careful. We got grav-plates on the bridge. Painted over the signs long ago though," Keith said, going in first through the hatch that was held open with a rope.

"Dan, this is my pops, Morris Bagley. This is Dan Sawyer, our dock jock," Keith cheerfully said.

The bridge was huge, like on the old freighters. Real windows, his favorite. Good visibility all the way down to the huge dock collar.

"Greetings, guy. Sorry to yank you outta bed. I'm just too old to do a proper job, and Keith just ainna never done it before. Both of us are getting fixed up with longevity and stuff this trip."

"How'd you know I was in bed?" Sawyer asked, thinking of punching Max.

"Was talking to Station. Told me," Morris said, as he got out of the co-pilot's seat for Keith and offered the pilot's seat for Dan.

"Why were you talking directly to Station?"

Sawyer strapped in and tested the thrusters.

"Well, it's kind of embarrassing."

He laughed, and said, "Want coffee? Oh shit, forgot. You need both hands."

Sawyer moved in, toward the station.

"Station, this is the *Tuna-Melt.* We are proceeding to smelting spire 36, dock 5."

"Like I said, I had to report to security a Harvester in the belts, just sitting there. Oddest thing I ever saw. Didn't respond to hail. Made note, moved on," Morris said, like he used the phrase a lot.

"Harvesters are prison ships. The manual says to never dock or stop for a Harvester. Cause, you know, prisoners," Keith said.

The spire approached quickly, but their alignment was perfect. The seal was tight, the first time.

"I love these old ships," Sawyer said, as he shut down and unstrapped.

"Well, the *Tuna-Melt's* days are about over. Maybe some in-system, short hop freight but she's wearing a little thin."

AI~Station added a bonus to Sawyer's paycheck.

CHAPTER THIRTY-SIX: M-CITY

"Admiral Kreiger lived in Mexico City. All the evidence against Barcus seemed to point to the fact that Kreiger was the target. We didn't know he survived Mexico City, until thirty-two years later."

--Solstice 31 Incident Investigation Testimony Transcript: General Patricia Chase, senior member of the Earth Defense Coalition.

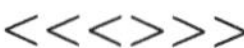

"On Thursdays, Krieger always goes and works out at a boxing gym off base. He goes as a civilian," Zimmerman said. "Then, he always goes for sushi at a hole-in-the-wall called Itto."

"Sushi?" Shaw asked, incredulously. "In Mexico City? Does he have some kind of death wish?"

"Don't judge, missy," Zimmerman clipped. "When was the last time you were even on Earth?"

"What does that have to do—" Shaw began.

"Enough!" Barcus barked, not looking away from the complex tactical screen AI~Stu had presented him.

Kuss pointed, as she stood behind his seat.

"There. Polar entry vector. Move south, west of Rockies, here. All open skies, no traffic monitoring from catapult ports."

AI~Stu added a simple, "Acknowledged."

Barcus rotated the seat around, before he spoke, "We will be coming in low and slow and boring."

He stood, as the tactical dome shifted to a map.

"We will be touching down in four hours at a salvage yard in the Oklahoma desert. We will meet Hagan there, in the drop ship from the *Memphis*, as it goes to Port Sri Lanka."

He turned and indicated the hold.

"You will take two of the Warmarks, leaving us three in case all this goes sideways, somehow," Barcus said.

"I recommend we make contingency plans. Places to regroup. Low key communications channels, in case we need them," Zimmerman said, professionally now.

They spent a few minutes establishing rendezvous points on Earth, Freedom Station, and Luna. AI~Stu told them about a Texas restaurant called the Stew Pot that had a little used comments section on their obsolete web site that was open and unmoderated. Easy to remember.

"We will arrive at Oklahoma Salvage around midnight," Barcus said. "Hagan knows the owner. It's about ten square kilometers of air and spaceship graveyard."

"That fits the cover as well," Zimmerman said. "I've heard of the place. It's been there for like hundreds of years."

He chuckled. "On a clear day, you can see it from Freedom Station."

All three seemed to look at Po at the same time. She was asleep in the co-pilot's seat. The five-point harness held her up.

"She has the right idea. Tomorrow is going to be a long day," Zimmerman said, as he sat in the last row, reclining instead of strapping in.

Barcus thought, *tomorrow is the Solstice, the longest day of the year.*

The longest day in human history and he could do nothing to stop it.

***

Cook approached Earth-controlled space, on manual. No one blinked regarding their ident codes. He remained on the approach they gave him and, as expected, it took them directly over the western region of North America.

The drop ship fell away, silently, with all their weapons and Ben's AI module as well. As soon as it detached, it disappeared from the tactical, even though they were doing active proximity scans.

"OK, what the hell time is it in Sri Lanka?" Muir asked. "I have been on space standard time for so long, my body is going to flip out."

"We get there when we get there." Karen laughed, then said, "Hey, it's going to be Christmas soon!"

"Karen, are you one of those people still awaiting his return?" Cook laughed.

"Hey, it could happen!" She was serious.

"If he left Earth and traveled long enough at relativistic speed, he could still return."

Muir and Cook both began to laugh.

"You know there are prisoners on the Harvester ships whose sentences will keep them in for over 2,000 years!"

"It could happen."

Cook smirked.

"It's possible," Muir said.

"Bite me," Beary answered.

"Wait, doesn't Christmas mean you will buy us presents? We have cash, and there is excellent shopping in Sri Lanka!"

***

Jimbo left the bedroom where Bobbie and the girls slept. He had written a note and left it on the bedside stand. Once the door silently closed, he turned to find both Rand and Hume standing by the main door.

"Barcus told me that the chancellor has hidden a nuke on Freedom Station," Rand said, coolly.

"He told me the same," Jimbo said, as he noted the time in his HUD. "He also said that Station will help us."

"Let's find out," Hume said, as she initiated HUD comms.

Rand and Worthington sensed Hume come back online.

"Welcome, Lieutenant Valerie Hume," AI~Station said politely, in her head. "Thank you for trusting me. I have been expecting you."

"You have?" Hume said.

"Yes, my dear friend Barcus told me to expect you and to help you any way I can. I have already removed all of you from the security notification watch lists. Please let me know if I can help you, in any way."

"Station, I will be honest. We have a reliable report that there is a nuclear bomb hidden on this station. Is it possible for you to run an internal scan?" Hume said, as she gave Jimbo and Rand a thumbs up.

They left the apartment as their HUDs initialized.

"I have already begun the internal scans. Areas without internal sensors will take longer because my scan drones will need to get to them all."

"Barcus mentioned smuggling," Jimbo said. "And Pho Pete…"

The Anchor icon appeared in all their HUDs. The word "Station" appeared next to it. They now had full-time access to the Station AI.

"What's the quickest way to Pho Pete's?" Jimbo asked, and a mist rope appeared in their HUDs, showing the way.

They jogged in the easy 1G.

***

They saw the giant salvage yard, in the moonlight, from high altitude.

"Beautiful," Kuss said.

"You would consider a fucking graveyard beautiful," Zimmerman said to her, his voice waking Po.

"Sleeping technology in moonlight, awaiting resurrection. What could be more beautiful, glupi?"

"Who're you calling stupid, suka. Nie lekcewaz mnie," Zimmerman said.

"Mówisz po polsku? Może cię do łóżka później, jeśli cię nie zabije pierwszy." Kuss replied.

"Oklahoma Salvage to shuttle transport unit *Latha.* Kinda late to be stopping by, don't you think?"

The voice was a cool male voice with a slight Texas accent.

"Is this Hunter? Wes said to touch base with you," Barcus said, not identifying himself.

"Yes, sir. Set down on the most western edge. That section looks like a big J from the air. Right in the hook of the J. It's cold tonight. We open at about 7AM, if you need anything."

"Thank you, sir. Goodnight," Barcus answered.

"Welcome. Hunter, out."

The channel closed.

"That was an AI. I know it was. I'm not sure anyone human is down there," Po said.

Barcus glanced at her.

"Doesn't matter either way. Look," Zimmerman said, pointing at the massive J made up by several derelict ships.

The drop ship was already there.

***

Hagan and Shaw stood on the cargo ramp of the drop ship, lit from behind by a red light that didn't impact their night vision but allowed them to see. As the STU's ramp lowered from under its chin, Zimmerman caught sight of patrolling Warmarks.

As the ramp touched, two Warmarks came to life in Stu's hold and descended to take up security posts as well.

Zimmerman walked up to Hagan, and before introductions asked, "You have an Echo in there?"

"Hello, Jack," Echo said, as her avatar appeared behind Hagan.

"I'll be a son of whore. No one's deleted you yet?" Jack smiled, ear to ear.

"They keep trying, but they keep missing," Echo said, smiling shyly.

"Barcus, we might survive this shit storm after all."

He started to laugh.

"This is the meanest little bitch in the known universe. There ain't enough space in a human for all the mean contained in this little shit storm. I've seen her rip heads off just to get a crowd's attention."

"You've met?" Hagan asked, at the same time Shaw said the same words.

"Jack here was once one of my Black Badgers," Echo said. "Never could get this one killed. Too smart for that."

"She's hateful because she was always surrounded by fine man flesh and couldn't fuck any of us." Zimmerman laughed.

"Jack." Echo became serious.

"Ferris and all the Black Badgers on the team died on the *Memphis*. Died strapped into their briefing room seats. Goddamn vacuum."

None of them had ever heard emotion like that from an AI.

***

The tactical display on the *Memphis* labeled itself the *Winton*, thankfully. The new ident code allowed them to make a slow grav-foil approach and descent to the private hangar rental area where Karen had made arrangements a few hours earlier. Hangar T94-118 already had the doors open and lights on. The landing pad strobes flashed, and it was well marked.

"I have never seen so much traffic before. Anywhere," Cook said, out loud.

A skinny kid with a clipboard and a handheld scanner waited. They slid the *Winton* in, nose first, like an amateur would. Once it was down the aft, primary cargo ramp lowered.

Facing outward, the cargo hold was wide open to spying eyes, showing it was empty, stripped, and still a bit damaged.

Cook looked bored as he approached the customs agent, handing over a credit chip for the fees.

"All the doors are open now, if you want to run the inspection."

Cook knew customs agents loved experienced pilots.

"Thanks, man. I am headed home after this."

The agent casually kicked open a well-used case at his feet and a half dozen scanner drones drifted out and into the *Winton*.

"Won't take long. No cargo containers, no big water tanks?"

"Water tanks?" Cook asked, biting into a protein bar.

"Yeah. Stupid new regs. No water importing," he said. "Who gives a fuck."

"Someone must," Cook said.

Karen Beary and Peter Muir walked up to them and offered their passports.

Muir asked, "Know anyplace close where we can get a burger or pizza and a couple beers?"

"The T94 ops terminal sucks. I'd go to Delio's. Great pizza, sandwiches, and no soy. I don't think there is a vegan thing on the menu. They deliver, too."

They watched the drones return, one behind the other; and when the last one returned, the kid kicked the lid closed.

He held out his hand with the hangar door remote. Cook replaced it with a gold coin from Baytirus.

He smiled big and waved as he began walking away. The case deployed legs and followed him.

Everyone loved off-books money.

They looked around the hangar and quickly found the office and bathrooms. None of them could activate their HUDs because the ident within would give them away. They had to assume they were on a watch list.

"Now we wait. Who wants pizza?"

CHAPTER THIRTY-SEVEN: PUSH GENTLY

"We had intel that there was a nuke hidden on the station and that Dalton was prepared to use it and lay blame elsewhere. It would have worked, except he never realized who he was up against: Barcus."

--Solstice 31 Incident Investigation Testimony Transcript: General Patricia Chase, senior member of the Earth Defense Coalition.

It was just after midnight when Jimbo, Rand, and Hume got to Pho Pete's soup bar on the promenade level. Pete was still there, behind the counter, serving people. They took the last three stools all the way on the right end and waited.

Pete had just put on a fresh white apron when he approached them. Looking up, he froze for a moment. But it was just a moment. His eyes scanned the balconies across the way as he spoke.

"I have just the thing for you. You'll love it."

He was already setting out three large white porcelain bowls as he spoke in lower tones.

"Look, I have already stuck my neck out far enough. Now, what?"

Jimbo was distracted by the pho he was assembling for them—broth with noodles, meatballs, onions, and sprouts as well as other things. It smelled amazing. He realized he was starving.

Rand and Hume didn't wait. With chopsticks and ceramic spoon, they dug in as Jimbo talked to Pete.

"Look, can we talk somewhere more private?" Jimbo sipped a spoon of broth. It was incredible.

"What about?"

Pete had his arms crossed over his chest. With practiced ease, two Asian women picked up the slack with other customers as he chatted.

"If someone needed to get something onto the station, quietly, with no inspections, how would that happen? Something bad," Jimbo said.

He then blew on another spoon of the amazing broth. It was very hot.

"That depends," Pete said, conversationally, as if they were discussing soup. "How big a thing?"

"Let's say the size of that fridge." Worthington gestured. "And spare no expense."

"That would be easy. A shipping container sent via catapult. With a boring manifest. Place the thing in first and then fill the front of container with whatever is on the manifest. Inspectors are lazy. They will rarely search an entire container."

He leaned on the end wall and continued.

"Besides, inspections are random. Only about three percent of the containers are opened for inspection."

"How do you know any of this?" Jimbo asked.

"How do you like the soup?" Pho Pete asked.

"This is the best soup I have ever eaten!" Hume inserted.

"Damn good," Rand added.

"How can you eat it so fast when it's that hot?" Hume asked her.

"The soup is great. So what," Worthington said, getting impatient.

"Earth has imposed import and export restrictions in the last ten years, making it harder to stay in business."

Pete leaned his elbows on the counter, in a casual pose, to come closer.

"No animal or animal matter is allowed for export. Not even fresh cow bones."

Worthington looked incredulous, "You ship cow bones?"

"I ship lumber," Pete said. "At least in the front."

"That's why the soup is so good?" Hume said, between blowing and sipping.

"Real bone broth," he said. "When done, I take the bones and crush them to gel powder and sell it by the pallet to the hospital department on the station for cultures. Lumber is an easy sell."

"I am thinking a shipping container might be…" Worthington began.

There was a crackling sound from behind them. It all then happened at once. Rand threw her bowl of hot soup into a man's face that was just behind Hume. By reflex, the man's hands went to his face while the riot gloves he wore were still activated. Hume, saw him and braced with both hands on the counter, hit him with both her booted feet, mid chest. All this sent him flying out into the promenade, sliding to an unconscious rest on his back.

He wore a station security uniform.

"Station, is this man an imposter?" Rand asked.

AI~Station replied, so all three heard, "No. He is on the security team."

"Dammit. I thought this might happen. Only some of the security team are unwitting," Hume cursed.

Rand checked to see if he was still alive. There was a pulse. She took the gun from his holster.

"Come. Quickly," Pete said, as he came over the counter, no longer wearing an apron.

They followed him into the crowd.

"That guy's name is Parks. He was always an asshole," Pete said.

The crowd walked around him, and some even stepped over him.

"Look, what's this about now?"

"We don't want to start a panic," Jimbo said, as the lift door closed. "Station, hold this elevator."

"Panic?"

"There is a nuke hidden on the station. Dalton has the remote, so he can destroy the station and blame someone else. We need to find it. How can we find it?" Jimbo said.

"Could it be in a diplomatic container?" Pete asked. "They never inspect those."

"There are no diplomatic containers on Freedom Station, currently," AI~Station replied, via the elevator speakers, so Pete could hear.

"Is there any way we could find it otherwise?" Rand asked.

"It would have to be lead shielded to prevent scans. Heavy," Hume added.

"Shit. There are something like ten thousand containers on this station at any time. It could have been here for a long time; it could be landing as we speak."

Pete cursed.

"It's a needle in a haystack."

"What we need is a magnet," Worthington said. "Station, port level, please."

The elevator began to move.

"A magnet?" Hume asked.

"Station, do you know the mass of all the containers in the port?" Worthington asked.

"Yes, Jimbo."

"Would the lead shielding make it the heaviest container?" Jim asked.

"No. The nuke could be smallish in size. Add a block of lead around it. Machine part containers would weigh far more," Hume said, as the elevator stopped.

"How many containers are we talking about?" Rand asked, as the door opened.

It looked like a massive, brightly lit warehouse. It was busy, despite the late hour.

"In current inventory, 11,731," Station replied.

"Station, of all the containers in your inventory, are there any that are unusual? Any that are outliers in any way?" Worthington asked.

The four of them walked down one of the vast lanes, watching the bustle of bot lifts and people, loading and unloading.

"We have two hundred and eleven that have never been opened. Of those, thirty-seven have not been signed for," AI~Station detailed. "Of those, only three have had storage prepaid for ten years or more."

"Jimbo, let me ask you something," Hume asked. "Why did you ask Pete Morales?" She turned to Pete. "No offense, Pete. We can't thank you enough for what you've done."

Jimbo looked from Hume to Pete.

"Because Barcus pointed me there…" His voice faded off.

"Station, are any of these outliers near any containers owned by Pete?" Jimbo asked.

"Negative," AI~Station replied.

Pete spoke up. "Are any of them near P37-10007?"

"Yes. Directly adjacent," AI~Station replied.

"Let's start there. Station, do you have eyes on it?" Rand asked, as they arrived at the transport station.

Pete signed out a transport flatbed. They would drive to his container. Otherwise, it would be a forty minute walk.

"A drone will be there in three minutes," AI~Station answered.

***

"Mexico City Airspace around the spaceport and catapult is under heavy traffic control. You should approach from the west and land at the inner city municipal dock. We can walk from there," Zimmerman said.

"It is Space Standard Time plus six, here," Barcus conveyed.

Traffic was heavy, even though it was just before midnight local time.

"It looks like there was a sporting event in the Velodrome tonight." Zimmerman looked at the streets below as they moved in, slowly. That will allow us to blend in far easier. The restaurant is called Itto. Great sushi."

They were lucky, and Stu found a landing pad on the roof of the ground transport garage closest to the place they needed to be. It was only two city blocks from there.

Barcus didn't rise when they landed, to Po's surprise. He just spun around his seat to face Zimmerman.

"I will take Shaw to find Krieger. It will be less suspicious," Jack said, as he moved to the ladder. "You just look too pissed off."

He pointed at Barcus.

"And you," he pointed at Po, "would never stop looking up like an Iowa tourist. Let's go Shaw. You're my date."

"Don't flatter yourself, troglodyte," Shaw answered, as she followed him down the ladder.

"You like sushi, Shaw? I love sushi," Zimmerman asked. "Cause there's only two things that taste as good as sushi, and one of them is sushi."

Their voices faded as they left the ship.

Barcus turned his chair back around.

"Stu, keep the mains online and inertial dampeners on full. Bridge and bay. Be ready for emergency takeoff.

***

They parked and Rand was the first to round the final corner onto the aisle they were looking for. She took a round to the face of her helmet. It staggered her, but she didn't go down.

The frangible round shattered on the helmet's armor; pieces deflected and caught Pete Morales in the right cheekbone. It was like a ghost had punched him in the face. Rand went one way and Pete the other.

Hume emerged between them, gun drawn and firing. In less than a second, she had spotted all of them. They stood in the center of the aisle, dressed as station security. Instantly, she adjusted her aim. The first one she shot just below his vest, halfway between his navel and genitals. The second stood there, bringing up his carbine, and he caught one right in the face. Instant death. He fell straight down, like a bag of wet sand. The third she shot in the arm that held his carbine and, when he turned to run, she shot him in the ass. He went down.

"Station," Jimbo called, out loud. "Are these men station security?"

"No, Jim," Station replied. "But their clothes and weapons are official station gear."

They ran up to where the men fell. Two were dead already. One tried to drag himself away.

Jimbo and Rand collected carbines and trank guns, as Hume advanced on the living one. He tried to roll over and grip his carbine on his back with his left hand, but he was too slow. Hume stomped on the rifle, as it hovered over his wounded arm and part of his chest.

He screamed.

"Do you get paid enough to die here today?" Hume pointed her gun at his face.

"We know who you are, bitch. You're dead already."

She shot him between the eyes. "Everybody keeps thinking that," Hume said, handing the trank gun to Pete and taking the carbine for herself.

A surveillance drone, the size and shape of a hockey puck, whizzed by overhead. New windows opened in their HUDs showing its view. The warehouse was vast and, as it zoomed to Pete's container, they saw two men on top of the neighboring unit, prone, with rifles.

"Please note," AI~Station said, "those rifles are not Frange carbines. Your armor will be of little use."

"I guess we're on to something," Rand said.

"Do you think any of these asswipes know they are guarding a nuke?"

"I may be able to help," AI~Station said, as they moved closer.

They saw a crane moving their way with a container.

"These containers are made to be stacked. Be ready," AI~Station said.

They split up, wordlessly. Rand and Pete went to one end, Jimbo and Hume to the other. The warehouse level was designed to have room for containers to be stacked three high plus crane space.

When the crane stopped directly over the men and rapidly lowered, they rolled off the top of the container, landing neatly on the floor with rifles ready.

Everyone began shooting at the same time. The men in the security uniforms fell from head shots. But not before firing several times.

Hume and Rand were down.

CHAPTER THIRTY-EIGHT: DAWN CAME EARLY

"Thirty-three years ago, I was a colonel on leave in Freedom Station. I saw what happened, with my own eyes, from an observation deck."

--Solstice 31 Incident Investigation Testimony Transcript: General Patricia Chase, senior member of the Earth Defense Coalition.

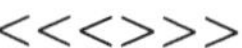

They walked through the clean, well-lit streets, past the Velodrome, into the closed streets of the federal district. Traffic here was restricted to foot traffic and VIPs.

"Why are you such an asshole all the time, Jack?" Shaw asked him, out of the blue.

"Because I hate people."

"No, you don't. You're doing it again. Right there."

She pointed at him with a thumb.

"You are old school, protect and serve."

"Fuck you, Shaw," he simply said.

She laughed.

"Fine. Don't tell me. We don't have time anyway," she said, as they entered a street and saw the sign for Itto.

Shaw hesitated when she saw the sleek black personal shuttle parked out front. It was exactly like the one the High Keeper had on Baytirus. A soldier in dress uniform stood, at parade rest, at the curb.

"He's here," Zimmerman murmured, as they entered the establishment.

It was dim inside, with romantic lighting. The place was large but maintained an authentic, intimate feel with a lot of carved wood and strategically placed screens, giving some level of privacy.

They passed through a massive arch from the foyer and saw Admiral Kreiger at his table, talking with one of the chefs.

They were seated near Kreiger, and passed directly through his field of view. He noticed Zimmerman. It was hard not to notice him.

Soon, the chef retreated to the kitchen and the general stood and walked over to the table. Offering a hand to shake, he said, "Jack…it has been far too long." Zimmerman took the offered hand and gave it a mighty squeeze that was returned in kind.

"Sir, I'd like you to meet Beth Shaw. She's—"

Zimmerman was interrupted by the soldier that had been standing by a limo outside.

"Sir, we must go. Now, sir," he said, obviously, with forced calm.

"What's going on, son?"

"Apparently, there are known terrorists in the vicinity, and all VIPs have been requested to evac."

"Come with me," Krieger whispered.

Jack and Beth stood and followed him out. Both curbside gull wings were already open. And just as General Krieger ducked to enter the limo, the driver's head exploded. Beth felt the concussion of wind as a bullet just missed her own head. She was tackled from behind by Jack and fell directly into the front seat of the limo. She was disoriented, only briefly, and then she realized she was behind the controls. She pounded the door controls and activated the main grav-foils. The limo leapt into the air as it was pelted by bullets.

She gained control as Zimmerman tried to right himself. He had landed in the shuttle with his head in the footwell.

"Are you hit?" she yelled at Jack, as he struggled around. "Jack? General?"

"Fuck! I'm fine."

He was finally upright. He looked at Shaw. She had a bloody wound that started at her cheekbone and went back, bisecting her right ear.

Jack looked at Kreiger. He was slumped in the seat.

"Get us back to the STU. Fast," Jack said. He wanted to tell her she had been shot. He'd seen this before. She'd know soon enough.

They didn't dare radio the STU. Beth simply landed directly inside the STU's open cargo bay. The STU's bay doors were closing and it took off before the limo doors were opened.

Barcus flew down the ladder, not touching a single rung. They were already dragging Krieger out of the back, toward the med bay. Just as the cargo bay doors closed, silence was restored.

Then, it began.

A nuclear bomb detonated in the center of Mexico City.

Po, on the bridge alone, witnessed the shockwave, the fireball, the mushroom cloud rolling up as if it was chasing them. It happened in slow motion. The STU's dome protected her from the ultimate brightness of the flash. In doing so, it revealed to her the full impact of the devastation. She watched, in horror, as the shockwave chased them, crushing everything in its path. As they sped toward the mountains, she knew that the homes they flew above would be on fire in a moment. Finally clearing the mountains, the fireball seemed like a sunset beyond them. She turned to look in the direction of their motion. It was illuminating the clouds. Made more horrible by its beauty.

"Barcus, Mexico City is gone. Destroyed," AI~STU said in his personal HUD.

It was almost a whisper.

***

Kreiger was in the med bay. As the scan began, it quickly determined he wore body armor under his clothes.

"He has five broken ribs and a punctured lung," Shaw said. "He was hit twice. Damn, that is good armor." Barcus nodded and went up to the bridge.

Krieger's eyes fluttered open. "You must be from the *Ventura*," he whispered.

"How did you know? We changed all the ident codes. We are all running with cold HUDs."

"Even a cold HUD can be proximity scanned."

He winced. "Where's Jack?"

"I'm right here, sir." Zimmerman stepped up.

"Tell this thing to give me the battlefield load of nanites and other drugs," Kreiger said. "We are in deep shit, and I haven't got time to worry about injuries."

"Yes, sir," Zimmerman replied.

Dr. Shaw watched him enter a control code she had never seen before. Screens flashed by and the bay's arms reacted with a rapid, almost violent, motion.

Kreiger's arms were dragged above his head and restrained cruelly. His blood was fill with drugs, nanites, and supplemental red blood cells. The autoDoc began slashing him open. Broken ribs were aligned and splinted with screws, far too quickly. Sprayed with specialized nanites and adhesives, he was closed up, far too quickly.

When Shaw tried to step forward and slow the controls, she was stopped by Zimmerman with a blocking hand to her sternum.

"That is all wrong. There will be scarring and lasting issues," she said, pleading to Jack.

"I know," he said, in a tone she had never heard from him before.

Kindness.

"But he will be combat effective in five minutes. Soft tissue damage only. And these many nanites will fix that in no time."

"Why the flood of persistent nanites?" she asked, looking at the screen.

"He expects more injuries."

***

"We're returning to that salvage yard," Po said, stoically, as Barcus sat in the seat to her right.

"Thanks."

"This is the day that has been haunting you," Po stated. It wasn't a question.

He turned and looked at her then. Her eyes were bright, alert and intense. Her forehead was creased. Her jaw muscles rippled as she returned his gaze. She was strong and fit and brilliant. His focus reduced to that moment. Her hair was wild, unable to be braided since she cut it off, in fury. She stared back.

She was so alive. Right here, right now. Barcus wondered how this magnificent being was ever a weak, trembling, frightened, uncertain girl.

"Why are you smiling?" she asked.

AI~Stu interrupted.

"Oklahoma Salvage ahead. Twenty seconds."

***

Dalton, chancellor of Earth, held his finger on the button for a moment longer than he needed. He was seated in his opulent leather chair, in his grand audience chamber, in his private residence, on his private island—called Calf—just south of the Isle of Man.

The vision of the mushroom cloud, turning the M-city space catapult to dust, still danced on the screens of the room.

His smile was wide.

The images of that shuttle transport unit speeding away were just as Turkot foretold. Even the replaced ident codes were as he said they would be.

He turned his eyes to the other screen.

It was a satellite view of the Roosevelt Island spaceport in New York. That small catapult was for passenger traffic only. He smiled as he zoomed in on a spectacular building, just off the lower point of the island, just across the river on Manhattan.

He waited for the next prediction to become true, as his canned statements went out regarding this heinous terror attack in M-City.

***

They touched down in the salvage yard without a peep from the AI called Hunter. Everyone stood at the base of the ramp. Even the avatar of AI~Echo.

Kreiger took immediate control. He wore a standard flight suit now. Everyone was surprised he addressed Echo first.

"Echo, report," he barked.

"Sir, our mission to Baytirus failed in some ways and succeeded in others. Two Scarecrows were killed in nuclear blasts; one on the planet and one on the moon. The Scarecrow called Wex appears to have escaped in a ship called the *Sedna*, currently flying under ident the *Grace*. We seem to have the seed ship under our control, including all the vessels it contains."

Echo stepped closer.

"Roland Barcus has control of the seed ship. All indicators point to the fact that he died on Baytirus but was resuscitated by the emergency application of L-Matter."

"And what about Atish and Chancellor Dalton's genome project?"

"We have three examples here." She gestured to Po, Cine, and Jude. "With full scans and genome markers. Purpose built to follow."

"We follow no one. We are free," Jude said, defiantly, in her light accent.

Echo continued to talk about them as if they were not there.

"They will obey, without question, any order or request. But only if given by the one they have imprinted upon."

Realization dawned on their faces, and the three looked at Barcus, standing in the cargo bay behind Kreiger as he spoke.

"Any order," Echo continued. "I have Dr. Bowen's data that she was returning to Dalton. Tests indicated that they would do horrible things, if commanded—murder or rape, even suicide. Or they would allow themselves to be killed by torture."

"There's more." Dr. Shaw spoke, "They are also brilliant. Their IQs are high, and they have talent for intuitive skills, like flying ships, playing music, or adapting to zero-G. They are also very tough; they can survive injury, or long-time deprivation, and recover."

"Why is any of this important?" Worthington asked.

Echo answered, "Because eighty-two of these people were brought to Earth earlier this year and began pilot training."

"Look, fancy general man," Kuss began.

"That's Admiral," Zimmerman interrupted.

"So fucking what," Kuss ranted. "What all this mean? What difference make us."

"The same man that destroyed the *Ventura* and as many as sixty other ships, to minimize political opposition, is going to have these eighty people that will do anything he tells them, fly ships into every colony planet at relativistic speed. All on the same day."

He was almost yelling now.

"And I think today is that day."

Kuss quieted.

"We also believe that the bastard has hidden nukes in all the major cities on Earth, Freedom Station, Luna, and Mars. I need to get to the United Council of Colonies in New York, tonight."

Kreiger was calmer now. "Right now. I must be there by dawn, to warn them."

"Sir, may I interrupt," Stu said and, without waiting for acknowledgement, opened a giant screen in a HUD broadcast over the desert.

PNN Special Report: Terrorists Destroy M-City.

The broadcast had a talking head newswoman, trying to hide a smile as she talked about the mass destruction and loss of life.

"This vessel is being sought in connection with the attack."

An image of the black STU fleeing just ahead of the destruction was then shown from various angles and distances.

"He is going to want all the *Ventura* crew dead. All witnesses dead," Kreiger said. "And your STU. Its AI knows too much."

"Everyone goes on the STU. Hudson, Zimmerman, and I will take the stealth drop ship to the Roosevelt Island spaceport and get to the UCoC."

"Take me to the Council," AI~Ben said, into all the HUDs. "I am already backed up on the STU. Their analysts will verify everything from Bowen's data."

There was a pause, no one spoke.

Spontaneously, people began to move.

Wes said to Kreiger, as they passed each other, "We will hold onto these three Warmarks, just in case."

Po watched Barcus this whole time. His stare was far away, and stress was etched onto his face. She went to him.

"It's true. There is nothing I wouldn't do for you."

He squeezed his eyes closed, as if to control a physical pain, and said nothing.

CHAPTER THIRTY-NINE: SRI LANKA

"Everyone remembers where they were on that day. I was on Freedom Station and never knew how close I came to death on that day."

--Solstice 31 Incident Investigation Testimony Transcript: General Patricia Chase, senior member of the Earth Defense Coalition.

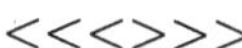

"We sure picked a good time of year to visit Sri Lanka," Karen Beary said, as she pulled another bottle of beer from the large bucket of ice.

Beary, Cook, and Muir were all sitting on beach chairs they had discovered in the hangar office. They had a large crate for a low table with empty beer bottles and Delio's pizza boxes.

"The last time I was here, it was the rainy season. Hot and wet."

"Sounds good to me," Cook said.

"Shut up, Cook," Beary said, smiling.

They all laughed.

Just then, the kid that was there when they arrived, pulled up in a small utility cart.

"Hey, guy. Want a beer and some pizza? It is lunchtime," Cook said, as he kicked over the top of the pizza box, revealing half an extra-large, all-meat, Delio's pizza.

The kid looked around and then, deciding, sat on a crate and grabbed a beer.

"What's your name kid? You look like shit," Karen asked. "I thought you were going home right after we got in last night."

"My name's Mike. I guess you didn't hear what happened."

Mike paused, took a slice of pizza, folded it expertly, and took a huge bite.

"There was a massive explosion in M-City last night. There is an official government blackout on it. Thousands are dead. Maybe tens of thousands. Most of the traffic to the M-City spaceport has been rerouted here. I been up all night."

The three of them all sat up and looked at each other. Mike continued noshing the pizza.

"They are screaming on the nets about lack of inspections at the catapults, more weapons regulations, arms trade, and banning dangerous research."

He took another bite.

"The chancellor isn't helping, either. He keeps implying that it's political terrorism. Christ, I hate people. I should just move to Freedom Station."

He stuffed the last of the slice in his mouth and sat back.

"So now, what have they got you doing?" Karen asked.

"Paying me double time to eat pizza and drink beer."

He raised his beer, in salute.

"No, really."

Karen was serious now.

"We have to rescan every damn ship. All on a day when the traffic is doubled already."

"What can we do to help?" Cook asked, he seemed sincere.

"The pizza was the biggest help all day. Thanks."

He stood and drained his beer.

"Just another quick scan and I'm outta here."

None of them stood up as they watched him walk back to his utility cart and open a case. The single drone that flew out was bigger and newer than the last time.

It few into the *Winton* and out of sight.

***

"Get off me. I am alright."

Rand was treating her own leg wound. It had passed all the way through. It missed the bone on the thigh as well as her arteries.

Hume had taken a round to the center of her chest but the new armor helped. She was awake now.

Freedom's drone scanners arrived a few minutes later. The only cargo was a block of lead that was one point five meters on a side. There was also comms gear and internal sensors.

"Jimbo, I think this is it," AI~Station said so they all heard.

"OK, so how do we defuse it," Jimbo asked, looking at the simple locks on the container doors.

"Fuck that," Hume said, struggling to her feet. "Just jettison it."

"We don't dare activate the foils," Pete said.

"Station, we need this out of here. ASAP." Worthington asked, "Do you have any options?"

"We could get it outside the station. But a tug would have to move it away," AI~Station said, as a crane moved their way.

"I have an idea…" Pete said.

***

"Mike, have another beer while you're waiting," Cook said, as he raised another ice-cold beer.

He came back over and took it, smiling.

"This might take a little longer, this time," Mike said, opening the beer. "Never saw a work order like this before."

"How so?" Cook asked, as Muir looked at Beary with concern creeping into his expression.

"It has something to do with cataloging autoDocs on certain kinds of ships. Does the autoDoc work on this thing?"

He looked up at the ship.

"You have balls to fly this out of a salvage yard."

"Well, I don't know. We just got the thing and have not started the refit," Cook said, standing.

Mike's back was to the opening of the hangar. He could not see the two weaponized tactical drones, floating there, guns deployed, facing their way.

Mike held his pad up when it chimed and took another big swig of beer.

"Hmmm...looks like the autoDoc was salvaged from a different ship. Happens all the time. This one was reported missing a couple years ago on a ship called the *Memphis*."

***

The chancellor was surrounded by a massive console on his raised dais. He preferred a real screen. No HUD implants for him. Too invasive, too easy to track—or hack. He should know. He had teams that did it all the time.

A notification blinked to life and expanded, automatically, in the center console. AI~Norman spoke.

"Sir, I believe the *Memphis* has landed under false ident codes at the spaceport in Sri Lanka. I have eyes on it."

A display opened, showing the high-resolution view from the two drones. It was a pinnace-class ship but barely looked spaceworthy. Scans revealed that it was flying under the ident of the *Winton*.

"What makes you think this is the *Memphis*, Norman?" Dalton asked.

"This ship has an autoDoc designed specifically for pinnace-class ships because of limited space constraints. The serial number of this autoDoc is for the one installed in the *Memphis*, the pinnace that was aboard the *Ventura*.

The drones zoomed in and focused on the faces of the people standing within the hangar. Face recognition activated and identified all three.

Lt. Karen Beary, Navigator, assigned to the *Ventura*.

Lt. Peter Muir, Communications Officer, assigned to the *Ventura*.

Lt. Richard Cook, Pilot, assigned to the *Ventura*.

"All three of these people were on the third shift command staff of the *Ventura* and would have been assigned to the *Memphis*."

The chancellor smiled wide as he reached for the button.

***

Kreiger and Zimmerman were in the pilot's seats on the *Sariska*, the drop ship from the *Memphis*. Echo's avatar sat with Hudson in the first row of seats. Echo, being a military AI, could broadcast under the admiral's personal flag, allowing for clearance to land on the south end of Roosevelt Island's spaceport.

Zimmerman and Kreiger changed to Black Badger officer uniforms they found in the drop ship lockers.

"Hudson, you will stay here with Echo and the Warmarks," Kreiger said, knowing her hip was not well-healed.

"Jack and I are going to take Ben to the UCoC, on foot. It's only across the bridge and two blocks away."

All of the Warmarks came alive at the same time. Their clamps retracted, and weapons began to power up with a low hum.

"We will be standing by, sir," Hudson said.

"We can get from here to the UCoC in two hops. Thirty seconds. Can we keep an open channel?" Echo asked.

"Affirmative," Kreiger barked.

"How's the ribs, sir?" Jack asked, casually, as they each lifted one side of Ben's AI enclosure.

"Feels like I have been kicked by a pissed-off mule," he replied, as the ramp lowered.

***

"The ship has no beacon, no ident, and it looks like an emergency lifeboat. One consistent with the ones on the *Memphis*. It was stealth on the spaceport scanners," AI~Norman detailed, as the drone's POV descended to the back of the ship.

The ramp was lowering. Two men waited. They held an active AI module between them.

"Sir, those are Black Badger uniforms," AI~Norman stated, flatly.

"For fuck's sake. That's Krieger. I thought he was dead in M-City."

As they stepped off the apron of the ramp and walked away, there was a momentary clear view into the ship, revealing a dozen Warmarks, running systems checks.

Dalton went white.

"Sir, that second man is Officer Jack Zimmerman. He is on the list. He is supposed to be off-world."

"Sir, I believe it's time. The UCoC, Kreiger, Zimmerman, and a crew standing by in Warmarks? The *Memphis* is in Sri Lanka. The risk is too high," AI~Norman said. "And where is this STU with the man—Barcus. Turkot said he would come to see you; so sure of himself, he will be unarmed."

"I believe it's time."

***

"Sir, why would the chancellor do these things?" AI~Ben asked, as they left the bridge.

"He thinks he knows what's best for humanity. He thinks he is smarter than everyone else, and people need to be controlled, so they don't make the wrong decisions."

"Why does he care what the colonies do?" AI~Ben asked.

"People are leaving Earth by the millions, annually. They no longer need to put up with its bigotry, its control, or any bullshit—political or otherwise."

"He'd rather see all the people, outside of his control, dead."

At that point, Kreiger ceased to exist. They were less than two hundred meters from the bomb that left a crater and consumed all of Manhattan. The Roosevelt Island spaceport was laid to waste for ten kilometers in every direction.

***

"Barcus…"

Po trailed off. She saw the flash below, beneath the clouds.

"Barcus, I think…"

She turned to him; his face was in his hands.

He looked up, and Po saw his face. And she was afraid.

"Stu, high orbit above the Isle of Calf," he said, as he stood.

He avoided her eyes.

"What are you doing?"

She reached for him but missed because she was strapped in. She fumbled with the harness, afraid, panicked.

He didn't reply.

Barcus stopped, face-to-face with Hagan.

"If I don't come back, get Rand, Hume, Worthington and his family, and run."

"What about Cook, Muir, and Beary?" Hagan asked.

A wave of fury rolled off Barcus that was so visceral, Hagan was taken aback.

Po's fear grew as she freed herself to go after him.

Hagan stopped her at the top of the ladder.

"What happened to Cook, Muir, and Beary?" Hagan growled.

***

"What does this mean?" Mike said, confused. "I am supposed to detain you for collection and questioning."

"Well, that will be easy."

Beary gestured with her bottle as a third, armed drone appeared at the mouth of the hangar as she sat.

"Well, I for one, am not going anywhere as long as there is still cold beer," Cook said.

"We got busted because of the stupid autoDoc?"

"I bet it was your ugly face, Cook. Those kind of drones have broad spec scanners and face recog," she said, opening a fresh bottle.

They all laughed again now. Mike, too. He had no idea why, but he opened another beer.

"You are such a flirt, Beary. Why don't you just admit you want me?"

"Cook, now that you mention it…"

She never finished the sentence as she flashed out of existence.

CHAPTER FORTY: DS-12 LANDS

"It was him. Roland Barcus. It was his Warmark. DNA and surveillance footage confirmed it. We were not wrong. And we were totally wrong. All at once.

--Solstice 31 Incident Investigation Testimony Transcript: General Patricia Chase, senior member of the Earth Defense Coalition.

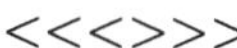

"Barcus. Wait, please," Po pleaded, as she slid down the ladder.

"Everyone up onto the bridge. I am going to open the hatch at a high orbit," Barcus yelled.

The fury on his face left no room for argument. Cine, Jude, Shaw and Kuss all moved, quickly, to comply.

"What are you doing?" Po yelled.

"I'm going to end this."

He moved toward the Warmark that had a skull painted on the front.

"Wait." She tried to make him listen; it was like trying to slow a locomotive.

"STOP," he yelled at her.

She didn't.

"I asked you to stop," he said, in a low voice that was even worse than yelling. "Stu, after I am away, you are to do whatever you have to do to keep these people safe. Start by removing Po from all pilot and admin control functions."

"WHAT?" Po screamed.

"STOP. You must live through this. Even if you don't like it." He growled.

"You bastard!" She pounded on his chest. It was like pounding on stone. He caught her wrists.

"I thought you said you'd do anything I told you to do." He had never spoken to her like this before.

Her face flashed uncertainty. She started to struggle.

"Stop. Please." Barcus growled.

"You can't do this to me. You can't make me into this and then leave me. It's crueler than the Keeper's torture. You can't show me what freedom is and then take it from me when I need it, want it, most." She struggled, but his grip was like iron.

"Sometimes, the hardest part of being free is doing nothing."

He released her. She almost fell as she stumbled backward. She stepped back and straightened her spine.

"Stop," he whispered.

"Is this what you saw, all those tortured nights when you thought I was sleeping?" Po was furious.

"The world is closer to doom at this moment than any other. Not because of the chancellor, but because of you," Barcus said.

She was fierce, and her eyes blazed.

"You saw that I wasn't your simpering slave, anymore. Well, you'll get no tearful good-bye kiss from me, you insufferable prick. Go get yourself killed; take the easy way out, and if there is anything left of you to bury, I will find your grave one day and piss on it."

She slapped him, hard, across the face.

"But you saw that coming didn't you. You let me slap you. I don't give a fuck that you can see the future. That does not mean that I cannot make my own decisions."

She stormed over to the ladder.

"Go to Hell. Alone." She spat at him over her shoulder as she headed up the ladder to the bridge.

I am already there.

He climbed into the Warmark.

***

"Dan Sawyer, please report to launch bay twelve," actually came over the station's public-address system.

"Jesus, when was the last time they used the PA?" the bartender said, absently. "Hey, Dan. Are they talking about you? What is Dan's last name?"

The bartender pointed to a man that was in a booth, leaning against the cold glass that was the only thing between him and vacuum.

"Jen, wake up Dan, will ya," the bartender asked the tired-looking waitress.

It was a slow night. She poked him, hard, in the neck with her tray.

"Wake up, Dan. You're being fucking paged," Jen said.

He came awake so fast, he startled her.

"Sawyer, here," he said, out loud, into a HUD call.

"On my way."

He slid out of the booth, and as he walked along in front of the empty bar, he snatched up a shot glass of bourbon the bartender just barely finished filling, downed it, and said, "Thanks, Joe."

Sawyer ran to launch bay twelve. They had the fast-locks that opened and closed fast enough to kill you, if you were not careful.

"Station, Sawyer here. What the fuck?"

There was only one ship in launch bay twelve. An old-school fighter tug. It was warmed up already. It was an obsolete design that only flew on manual.

"Hello, Dan. Are you sober?"

"When has that mattered?"

He laughed.

"Dan, there is a nuke on the station, and I need you to fly it away from here. The problem is, station security might try to stop you."

"And you don't have time to explain it. Am I right?"

"You are cleared to fire upon anyone that tries to stop you. Accelerate this container out into deep space, on any vector," AI~Station said.

"I don't hear from you for years; and out of the blue, I'm forced into retirement. If I survive this, you owe me a good story," Dan said, and he climbed into the ship and buckled in.

"What about your pressure suit?" Station asked.

"Pressure suits are for pussies. Launching."

The fast launch was always a thrill.

"It's a little crowded out here, sweetheart. What the fuck is happening?"

Ships launched from every spire. It was chaos; traffic control was completely ignored.

"There is a nuclear war. Millions are already dead on Earth. The container is indicated on your tactical."

Sawyer found the box, floating away from the station, at a slow ten meters per second. With an easy flip and turn, he matched its speed and vector. Magnetic clamps had it by the end. He hit full throttle.

It moved away at increasing speed. In forty seconds, he cleared most of the swarm of random traffic.

"How big is the bomb, Station? How far is far enough? How fast is fast enough before I detach?" Sawyer asked.

"Unknown," AI~Station replied. "Looks like company."

The ball-shaped, transparent, glass cockpit rotated and faced the rear. The four powerful engines blazed at full power. His tactical targeting systems pinpointed the two ships trailing him. They both had station security idents.

They didn't even try to hail him. Projectile rounds impacted all around him, and two even deflected off his canopy.

He fired all four plasma cannons. First at one and then the other ship. They both went up in a flash.

A quick look at his controls told him he was already going 1,500 kph.

Sawyer shut down the main engines and detached. Thrusters pushed him away.

"Station, how is this vector?"

The station looked tiny from this far out.

"Perfect, Dan Sawyer."

"Dan, are you in the market for work? Two positions in orbital security just opened."

***

They never detected the Warmark until it landed at high speed in the center of the chancellor's private landing pad. The guards had not been ordered to hold fire, but no one wanted to be the first to open fire on the most deadly thing in the universe.

Its weapons were at rest, not deployed. It waited one minute, and then two, and then three.

The chest and helmet finally opened fully, and Barcus emerged. His head was bare, and his hair and beard were long and almost black.

The guards saw, as he lightly stepped down, that a Frange carbine hung on his chest with a bandoleer of extra magazines beneath his cloak.

Head held high, he walked directly up the grand steps, three at a time. He unclasped the cloak and let it fall on the steps, revealing his weapons. As he entered, the nave lights turned red and a chime sounded. He didn't slow as he dropped the carbine, bandoleer, and two hand guns on the floor. His weapons belt followed with knives and other devices. He paused just before the next door, reaching down and drawing long boot knives out of hidden sheaths and dropping them. He even took a chain from around his neck.

He stared at the guard before the door. He had on a tunic, tabard, and a simple braided and knotted leather belt, all handmade. The scanner in his hand registered no metal at all. The medical splints that registered told a story of pain but no weapons.

The door slid open, and he moved through with no alarms; no alarms on the next door either. Without a pause, he made the last right turn and pushed the double doors open, with guards behind him, scrambling to keep up. They didn't cross the threshold. The double doors closed by themselves with an ominous *thunk*.

Barcus said nothing.

"So this is Roland Barcus. Maintenance guy number 42 from the *Ventura*. I never expected anyone from that sad vessel to be any problem at all. High Keeper Atish was a bad geneticist, leader, and visionary. You, on the other hand, are a loose end. Come any closer and your friends on Freedom Station will die."

Barcus didn't stop coming.

Dalton pressed a control on the console he stood behind. A great flash in the sky above illuminated the room through the high, stained glass windows above.

"Freedom Station is gone. Blamed on you, just like the *Ventura*, just like Sri Lanka, Mexico City, New York City, and now Freedom Station. After today, I will control the moon, Mars, and all of Sol. Tomorrow, annihilation ships will scrape the filth of humanity off all eighty-eight other human colonies."

He paused, waiting for Barcus to say something.

"You made one mistake."

"Oh, really? Do tell."

"You let my friend Chen die in my arms. I swore to her I'd find you."

Massive weapons fire erupted outside. It came from the landing pad. Dalton saw on monitors that the Warmark started firing, in automatous mode, destroying the residence.

"Kill him," the chancellor said, in a bored tone.

The four hulks closed in and reached for Barcus. The chancellor could not see what happened. He only saw their four heads tumble off at nearly the same instant. When the bodies fell, he saw Barcus holding a long, dripping curved blade, made of bone.

"Stop or I will kill another city."

"I don't care." Barcus growled.

"What?"

"You see, Chancellor, Turkot is dead. He got it all wrong. Everything. His war is over. Humanity will never be an army for him. You will never rule all of mankind. Because everyone was wrong. I am not the monster. I am the witness."

"Turkot could see the future!"

"I want you to stand right there, fucker."

The stained glass roof shattered and DS-05 landed directly in the center of the room. Its red painted face was a frozen scream. Weapons blazed as the entire building began to fall away in all directions until they had a view of the devastation that was once the Isle of Calf.

Wind blew Barcus's hair as he turned to the horrible, nightmare of a machine.

"I thought I told you to stay on the ship," Barcus said.

"I am free. I do what I like." The terror replied.

A shoulder mounted cannon deployed and aimed at Dalton. "You also told me never to use this in atmosphere."

"Wait. You're not allowed to have Warmarks here..." Dalton begged.

"Is this the asswipe that killed all your friends on the *Ventura*?"

Barcus only nodded.

She fired, and the top half of Dalton simply disappeared in a cloud of red mist, along with all the walls behind him.

She turned and opened fire with dual projectile machine cannons. The end of the room with the entrance finally collapsed.

Po said, over the suit's PA, "Besides, I thought you might need a ride."

Another Warmark crashed onto the remains of the roof that were scattered around Po's Warmark. Weapons fire increased from Barcus's Warmark, on the front landing pad, attack ships fell from the sky into the ocean. DS Happy Face opened, and Barcus climbed in.

"Ascend 1,000 meters and come to a full stop," Barcus said. "You see that landing field over there? Just above Calf, the Isle of Man and the chancellor's base."

"Yes," Po replied.

"There are eighty-eight ships on that line. Modified, prepped and ready." Barcus shared his targeting telemetry.

"The ships he was about to use? To kill the colonies he didn't control?"

"Yes." Barcus's tone was harsh.

He set the weapon to max and used his targeting package to control the area of impact.

There was a clap of thunder.

Before they ascended to space, the entire residence and spaceport was leveled.

CHAPTER FORTY-ONE: EVIDENCE

"We made assumptions. Took evidence for granted. We didn't want to think that we were the villains. That we were all blindly following another Liberal Fascist Hitler. The story was covered up and Barcus scapegoated. If the colonies had discovered the truth, then it would have been war."

--Solstice 31 Incident Investigation Testimony Transcript: General Patricia Chase, senior member of the Earth Defense Coalition.

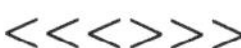

When they reached one thousand kilometers, Barcus hailed the STU, and he swallowed them from the sky. Barcus noticed, before they even locked in, that the starboard hatch was missing.

"Stu, what happened to the starboard hatch?" Barcus asked.

"That's my fault," Po answered. "After you left, I asked Stu to give me access to the med bay because I hurt my hand," Po said. "He saw how hard I hit you, and allowed it. I got right into the Warmark."

"She said if I didn't return to the area over Calf, she would kill all the passengers," Stu said. "She activated one of the big cannons and aimed it at the bridge. So, I returned. You said to keep them safe, no matter what."

"I was about to blast open the ramp when Stu said the starboard hatch would be easier to repair. So, I shot it. Stu sent the second Warmark out, on remote. I shadow controlled it, at the end."

"When did you learn to control Warmarks?" AI~Stu asked.

"On the way down," Po answered.

"You know we can't exit the Warmarks until we get to the station," Barcus said.

"You'll have to wait to punish me until then," Po said.

Barcus heard the smile in her voice.

***

"Station, this is Barcus. Is there a nice, quiet hangar where we can land? We need to do some repairs, and then we will be gone."

"Barcus, are you aware of what has been happening? The station is on full lockdown."

AI~Station sounded angry.

"It's over. Freedom Station is now safe," Barcus said, as the coordinates of the hangar came in.

"Buy Dan Sawyer a beer, on me."

"How do you know about Sawyer? I have redacted all information regarding his involvement in this event. There are likely opposition assets still on the station," AI~Station asked.

AI~Stu flew the ship into a private hangar, and the massive door closed behind them. The STU took up half of the bay as it settled to one side.

When pressure equalized, the Warmarks opened, at the same time, at the ladder hatch.

Everyone was mute as they came down the ladder. They followed Barcus and Po out into the hangar. They walked around the side to look at the exterior damage. It was worse out here but repairable.

"Are you seeing what they are saying on the nets?" Hagan stepped up and said.

The others stood behind Barcus, in shock.

"They say there are seventy million dead."

Barcus turned toward them.

"All told, in the end, the count will be just over one hundred twelve million dead. All three of the main spaceports destroyed. We saved Freedom Station and hundreds of other cities where the chancellor had bombs hidden. Zimmerman, Krieger, Hudson, Cook, Muir, and Beary are all dead. The *Memphis*, the *Sariska*, Echo, and Ben are also gone," Barcus paused, "and they will blame us. They will blame me."

"But—" Kuss began.

"And we will let them. Because if we don't, and the colonies hear that Earth came within a day of extinguishing them all, it will mean war. Three hundred billion murders, just because Dalton could not control them.

"I'm sorry, but we are all fugitives now. They have the STU on various security cams, speeding away from M-City. They will track Krieger's drop ship to the *Ventura* and the *Memphis*. They identified the *Memphis* in Sri Lanka, before it was destroyed. They know I killed the chancellor and destroyed the base on the Isle of Man."

Barcus paused as the door to the hangar opened.

Worthington entered with Bobbie, the kids, Rand, Hume, Pho Pete and Dan Sawyer. Pete and Dan were helping Rand and Hume walk.

Worthington stepped up, and said, "Krieger is dead."

"We know," Hagan said.

"When he was officially pronounced dead, classified orders were automatically issued to me and many others."

Barcus nodded as if he already knew.

Kuss stepped up. "They erased all knowledge of Baytirus. We must flee."

"Yes. Plus, I am to establish a Forward Operations Base and await additional orders," Worthington said.

"Tell them the rest, Jimbo," Bobbie said.

They already knew, because his HUD already told the story.

"I have received another temporary field promotion."

"Rear Admiral? Might have to sex you now," Kuss said.

"You get all your promotions by getting your commanding officers killed in the field?" Hagan asked, trying to jest.

No one laughed, this time.

***

"I always wondered how you got a Renalo-class luxury yacht," Turkot said, absently.

Wex raised an eyebrow.

"I recall telling you all about it, after we get back to the *Iosin*."

She smiled very wide.

"My good Turkot, you are in a long white. How does it feel to be human, to know only the past."

She sat in the main pilot's chair. Turkot took in the freshly cleaned engineer's station.

"I find it quite restful. I sleep so well. And as the white eventually fades, I enjoy the surprises of the new future."

"It is very restful. I am glad we finished this chapter first. I confess that Iosin told me this outcome just before our last parting. I confess my patience for High Keeper Atish wore thin."

The *Sedna* lifted off lightly as they exited the hangar.

"Just a bit of housekeeping before we go," Wex said, as they bore down on a small, two-man escape shuttle. There was a great *WHOMP*, as the EMP cannon disabled the shuttle.

"Enjoy freezing to death, you bastards. Those two were charged with destroying you and that base," Wex said, as they watched the shuttle crash on the surface.

"I've missed you, Wex. You are such a practical girl," he said.

Turkot waved at them as they peeled away. Turkot looked at the status board as Wex manually controlled the course. The status board remained green as they pulled away from Rhea. She then activated the *Sedna's* sound system. She played Adigio in G minor by Albinoni. It was beautiful and sad.

The lies were over.

The war was over.

Miles was right about everything.

She sighed as she intentionally entered the course. The board remained green as she checked it again.

She closed her eyes and flew the *Sedna* directly into the sun.

***

They put Rand and Hume through the STU's autoDoc first. Po announced she was staying right here with the STU, like they might leave without her.

"We leave in four hours. They are not looking for us yet, and Station will give credit, if you want to get anything."

Barcus watched them file out, one at a time. Rand, Hume, Kuss, and Hagan went together. Jude and Cine sat on the hangar floor, cleaned their flutes, and began to play. Jimbo, Bobbie, and the girls went to gather what was left of their things.

Dr. Shaw came up to Barcus, and said, "Station tells me there is a longevity serum synthesizer still in a crate in one of the cargo holds."

She looked at his dark face.

"We can talk as we go."

"Thanks but no. There is someone on Freedom Station I need to talk to."

Barcus looked over his shoulder at Po.

Dr. Shaw left the hangar alone.

He turned and faced Po. "I need to do one more thing, before we go." He added the last part to reassure her. It was the right thing to say.

"Barcus, this wasn't your fault. I'm sorry for what I said to you…"

Barcus gently touched his fingers to her lips in an intimate gesture.

"You once begged for forgiveness at the beginning of every sentence."

He remembered her, thin and weak, and impossibly tiny. She stood close to him now. She tucked her hair behind her ears with both hands as she looked up to him.

"You let me sleep in your lap, more than once, just to be kind. Did you know that half the time I wasn't asleep?"

"I wanted you, even then," he said. "But I wasn't strong enough."

It was her time to stop him from talking.

"When you almost died and killed that Telis Raptor…it changed me."

"You're still changing."

"So are you."

"Would you like some soup?"

***

Pho Pete already had his apron on when they arrived. An old Asian woman yelled at him in a language he didn't understand. Pete didn't allow them to order; he knew what the best in the house to eat was.

The crowd was thick. And it was loud. Speculation was rampant. All the public monitors in the promenade were on Net News channels. All the spaceports with catapults had been destroyed. Speculation held that there was an attack on Freedom Station as well, and it was stopped by two heroic security crews that went out and intercepted it.

Pete set fresh garden rolls and peanut sauce down in front of them, followed by bowls of pho that had onions and meatballs.

A woman slid onto the stool next to Barcus.

"Oh, that smells lovely. Pete, can I have that, too?"

She was older but fit. Her hair was groomed and set in formal fashion on her head.

"Hello, Senator," Barcus said, between bites of garden roll.

"Hello. I'm sorry, I don't remember your name."

She took a closer look.

"Have we met? With all that has happened…"

She trailed off.

"No, we haven't met. Before you return to Earth, I need you to know something."

Pete brought her rolls and peanut sauce. Barcus slurped noodles, casually. She dipped her garden roll into peanut sauce and took a hungry bite.

"Chancellor Dalton was behind the attacks."

He lifted his bowl and drank from it. Pete set her soup down before her.

"You will be the only one to know. There are more bombs, and the only control system is in Dalton's residence on Calf."

She was staring at him.

"In eleven days, you will be made the new chancellor. The day after that, your hand-selected team will find and destroy the control systems, never mentioning it."

Barcus wiped his mouth.

"I was just called back to Earth. How do you know any of this?" she asked.

"I'm Roland Barcus. You don't know that name yet but you will. All of humanity will. Because I will take the blame for killing the chancellor, for destroying the *Ventura*, and for annihilating 111,243,601 people today."

"Why are you telling me this?" she asked.

"Station will send you an 'eyes only' file two days after you have been named chancellor. It will reveal the locations of seed nukes hidden all over the Earth and on the moon. I'm sorry, but you have the hardest road, going forward. You will balance on the razor's edge, with full colony war on one side and lies on the other. Take the lies."

He wiped his mouth and rose.

"Why should I believe you?"

He seemed to tower over her.

"The real war is over. Don't look for me too hard."

He turned and walked away, without looking back.

Senator Lang watched him go.

CHAPTER FORTY-TWO: THE FINAL REPORT

"They all say the same thing. They don't know where he is or even if he is alive. It's like they are afraid we might find him. Afraid for us, not him."

--Solstice 31 Incident Investigation Private Testimony Transcript: General Patricia Chase, senior member of the Earth Defense Coalition.

All the evidence collected on December 22, 2631, had long ago been identified and attributed to Roland Barcus. This narrative confirms those assertions but views them with a different optic.

The Warmark designated DS-12, recovered at the chancellor's residence did, in fact, contain blood and hair from Roland Barcus. The recently released surveillance video confirmed his landing and entrance into the residence.

Security video showed him disarming, and being scanned through three checkpoints, before entering the residence. The newly uncovered video from the chancellor's private chambers has been certified and authenticated.

Testimony from the *Ventura's* surviving crew, regarding the subsequent cover-up, have explained all the outstanding questions regarding the detonation of nuclear bombs in Sri Lanka, Mexico City, and New York. Since then, ninety-four additional seed bombs have been discovered.

This independent investigation has revealed that Roland Barcus was not responsible for the destruction of the *Ventura* or the Solstice 31 Incident that killed over 111 million people. Evidence clearly indicated he did kill the chancellor's bodyguards, in order to stop additional cities from being destroyed. Someone else, in fact, killed the chancellor. That someone was never identified.

Even though his actions now seem justified, he remains sought for additional questioning.

The location of the planet, Baytirus, like so many other colonies, remains unknown. With the destruction of the *Memphis,* we lost all references to its location. Former Chancellor Dalton was careful to keep the location closely held, and the subsequent cover-up removed all other data regarding it.

That cover-up left a digital trail. That trail led this independent investigative committee to Senator Kendall and his organization. Once the questioning began, the cover-up unraveled, quickly.

The conspiracy that led to the Solstice 31 Incident was threefold:

The chancellor was consolidating power and eliminating opposition. By placing bureaucrats in specific locations, political adversaries in the military and civilian deep space programs and their ships could be easily destroyed. This allowed the complete control of the apathetic bureaucracy within Sol and seven other colonies.

Dalton's genome program attempted to create a race of humans that would be perfect followers. Perfect in that they would always obey orders, any orders, no matter how horrific, even if they resulted in their own deaths. Dalton nearly succeeded in his plan. Some of these suicide soldiers were captured after the Solstice 31 Incident.

Note: Many but not all. They were quietly institutionalized.

For decades, we thought they were somehow associated with Roland Barcus. They never knew the names of their masters. Some remain institutionalized, even now.

The final aspect of the chancellor's corruption was his discovery, and capture, of Vincent Joseph Turkot and the help Turkot provided with technology and speeding humanity into the future. Classified documents indicated that Turkot was the catalyst behind many human technologies. Chief among these being: the printing press, weapons design, heavier that air flight, micro circuits, global internet, Faster Than Light (FTL) travel, Artificial Intelligence (AI), nanites, deep brain implants, polycarbon fiber material sciences, and artificial gravity.

We also believe that Turkot was the chief architect behind the Solstice 31 Incident. He manipulated events to this end, even from a prison cell. The chancellor gained his assistance in creating a worm program that would corrupt AIs and could be transported within certain HUD implants.

Earth's war with the colonies was stopped due to the efforts of Barcus and the new chancellor, who bore the burden of the truth. Many of the government's Liberal Fascist elements remained, until now. Even these were being detained as this report was finalized.

Chancellor Lang pledged her transparency and full disclosure of findings in this investigation. But the implications of these findings may have a far-reaching impact. Questions remain.

What if Earth was in fact, terraformed? What if Turkot was able to intentionally direct a meteor that reportedly impacted Earth sixty million years ago? How many other perfectly Earth-like planets are out there?

How many gardeners, Scarecrows, could there be?

CHAPTER FORTY-THREE: EPILOGUE

"When Barcus finally disappeared, we told the whole story. Because no one cared anymore. He never really spoke of the future, after 2631. He tried to forget it just as much as he sought to forget the past. I don't know if that was good or bad. For him…"

--Memoirs: *Admiral James Worthington, senior surviving member of the Ventura deep space survey ship. Friend of Barcus, the Scarecrow.*

Autumn leaves swirled in the light breeze. The late morning sunlight was warm on her shoulders as she crossed the small bridge and approached Whitehall.

The southern gate was far smaller than she expected. Only a single wagon could have entered there. It was open. She heard a fountain and children singing beyond. The song would end, and they would all fall down and melt into musical laughter.

The gate was flanked by a pair of carved wooden benches. One was occupied by a man in a plain tunic with long hair and a long beard.

She took off her pack and sat gratefully, with a sigh, next to him.

They listened to the leaves, and the children, and the sun, for a few minutes before she spoke.

"We met once before, long ago."

"Yes, I remember. Your name is Wyn."

He poured her a cup of water.

"I'm flattered. That was over ninety years ago," she said, accepting the cup. "Much has changed since then."

"Yes. I know. You are a prime example of all that has changed," he said, becoming silent again.

"Is it true that all of the High Keepers walk here from the other side of the finished tunnel? Ansel told me this after he selected me. He sends his regards...and condolences."

"He will make a fine ambassador," he said. "He was a beloved High Keeper. Second only to High Keeper Ulric."

"He looks forward to visiting Earth," she said. "He has the skills for it."

"And you? Are you ready?" he asked, not looking at her. "You are the tenth High Keeper of Baytirus. The first woman."

There was a pause.

"And the last High Keeper to walk to Whitehall from the tunnel. Now ask your questions, before Elizabeth runs out here to announce it's time for lunch."

"Why did you rebuild the Abbey?"

"It was for her. Once we had the functional Makers again, it was easy."

"Why did you settle for two rooms in the gatehouse? You could have had the biggest palace on Baytirus, if you wanted."

"When all that you ever wanted happens to be just what you need, then you have already become the richest man in the Universe."

She sighed, and gathered courage.

"Ansel said to ask only this. What do I need to know?"

"You are the last High Keeper that will be able to ask me anything."

Now, he looked directly at her.

"Don't look for me. You won't find me. I'm the Scarecrow now. During your term, you will have ten years of peace, and you will pave the way for another thousand years of prosperity on Baytirus."

"Caisy sends her regards." She sighed. "So does Poole. They asked me to give you this."

She handed him a QUEST comms unit.

"I can still remember Caisy when she was the AI on the *Ventura* and Poole was just an Emergency Module." He looked at the QUEST unit. "In case you need to get in touch?" he asked, knowing the answer.

"No. In case you need to get in touch with us. It's keyed for Caisy and Poole. It can be routed through the entire Baytirus net via Caisy and the whole moon via Poole."

"Have all the AIs stayed sorted out?" he asked.

"Thanks to you. The AI war was short. Minimal loss of human life."

"Caisy will be a good advisor."

"She does an excellent job as the University. She gets irate, if she discovers a child that can't read by age five."

"Is the new high orbit station online, yet?"

"Elkin's Dock has been open for almost two years. It holds an orbit halfway between Baytirus and the moon. Full dry-dock and shipyard services. Probably 4,000 residences already, families. It's beautiful. People vacation there."

"I'll see it, one day."

"The high council is considering a new name for the moon. The high council wants to call it Hume. All of it. Hume Base, Hume City, and just Hume, just as Earth calls her moon Luna." He stood and continued. "And when it is your turn to be our ambassador to Earth, you will help bring lasting peace to that world, that whole system, as well."

"Will I see you again?"

"Yes. One day. But for now, take this."

He drew his Telis Raptor blade from his tunic, sheath and all.

"Make this a formal token of the Earth ambassador. Just seeing it will make the weak ones think twice."

"The Chancellor's Doom?" Wyn said in reverence.

She took it from him, carefully; as if it would kill her, if she handled it wrong.

"Here is another truth. It was Po that saved me. She is the one that killed the chancellor. And I was innocent all along." He paused. "Well, mostly."

Wyn raised an eyebrow but said nothing.

"I never donned a Warmark again, after Solstice 31." Barcus confessed. "In those early years of unrest, it was always Po. The Altuna riots, the Four Hour War, the Slave market of 41, and even the colony terror reprisal attempts. It was always her. She could have taken that planet if she wanted to. She could have taken Earth. She was fierce, the monster, she could have laid waste to all."

"But all she really wanted was to play her flute, honey and nuts in her porridge and to sleep in my arms."

"The twelve black flutes remain legend on Baytirus. Po had number twelve. The greatest of them," Wyn said.

Elizabeth ran out the gate just then, skidding to a stop. "Lunch is ready!" she said, and she was gone again before the dust settled.

"Wyn, the road will be long for you. It will not be without challenges. Trust your instincts about people. It will be your greatest strength."

"The Atish are strong and loyal. Thanks to you," she said as she stood, drawing the Telis blade from the sheath.

"They are the best, most highly respected defense force in the known universe. They think they are monks, artists, not soldiers. Even the provincial constables respect them."

"I think it's because they love music as much as fighting."

"Why are they called The Atish?"

"After the first High Keeper. He tried to make super soldiers that would do anything they were told and would always be loyal. It's a kind of reminder."

He looked in her eyes again.

"A reminder for them, and you."

"I saw one of the first gens, once. I think she was, anyway. It was in an inn, out west, in one of the new provinces. She played a black flute while she stood on a massive low mantel, on one foot."

Wyn was lost in memories.

"The other foot rested flat on her knee. Steady as a rock. The music was so simple, so pure; no one spoke in the crowded inn for the whole hour she played. They just quietly left coins on the mantel for her."

"Was she wearing deep red riding leathers?" he asked.

"Yes. And when she was done, she nodded to the crowd and dropped down as light as could be."

They entered the courtyard.

"And as we applauded, she used the flute to slide along and collect all the coins into a hat. Then, she just slipped away."

"That was Jude. She still wanders the world, playing for people as she goes. The longevity treatment wears well on her. But not so well with Cine or Po."

"I am so sorry about Po," she said.

"Don't be. The candle that burns twice as bright burns half as long."

"She will be missed," she said.

"More than you could possibly know," he replied.

"I visited her monument just before coming here. Why is it in a ruined Redoubt to the south along the coast? It is so clean, desolate. Polished. So vast and lovely."

"It was there that she had her first, best day of her life."

"Are you alright?" Wyn asked.

"Oh, yes. I mourned for her, long ago. While she held me. We were at Foxden, over a hundred years ago."

They stopped and looked at the giant willow in the center of the courtyard fountain.

"I knew the day, the hour, she'd drift away, even then. I knew as I kissed her goodnight, on that far off day, as I held her in my arms that she would never wake."

Barcus turned to see a crowd of children gathered, all bouncing with anticipation. A chorus of "Please-Please-Please" began as he turned away and continued talking.

"I want you to take Stu back with you. I will be taking Iosin."

Barcus leaned on the wall by the entrance into the community courtyard, placed one hand behind his back, and bent one knee, lifting up his calf to a right angle.

"I have already gone over it. He is willing to take on Elkin's Dock as the station AI. He will be good at it."

Just then the girl, Elizabeth, ran up his back, like a monkey. The first step was on his calf, then his hand at his back, then a step to his shoulder, the top of his head, and his raised hand, and then she was on top of the wall, running and laughing. She didn't even use her hands.

In rapid order, one at a time, almost thirty children flew to the tops of the wall. The last child looked like he was only four years old and struggled up the climb. Hand and feet, eventually he stood up on both of Backus's hands but could not quite reach the top. Then, the girl Elizabeth was there, and another older boy, and they reached down and took the young boy by the wrists and lifted him up.

And they ran along the tops of the wall. It was a maze of inner court walls.

"How thick are these walls?" High Keeper Wyn asked.

"They are all twelve inches wide," he said, through a wide smile as the children began to sing.

"Aren't you worried they might fall?"

"Worried? No. Because they do fall, now and then. They may even break a bone. But they have learned they are free..."

THE END

ACKNOWLEDGMENTS

I have several people to thank for their help with this book. I will begin, first and foremost, with my wife, Brenda. Thank you for your patience, as it appears I go deaf while I'm writing. Thank you for your encouragement and ideas. Thanks for all the help and love every time I need maintenance or require repairs.

Thanks go to my son, Gray, and my daughter, Cady. Thank you for making me proud of you. Thanks for making it so easy to be your dad. I miss you guys.

I need to thank the Loudon County Science Fiction and Fantasy Writers Group for all their help and encouragement. Thanks to my beta readers, Joe, Kelly, Chris, Dave, Web, Emily, Marilyn, Carrie and Linda. You help more than you know.

Oh, and my cat Bailey. Best cat in the known universe.